"Urgent, intimate narratives, framed as confessions and quests and edged with quickening threat. Everything that is good can be ruptured with as little as a single accidental touch … not only heralds the arrival of a fully formed, entirely distinctive new voice but reinvigorates the short story itself. In the end, there's no doubt who the lucky ones are: we, the readers."   —*Observer*

"In these nine memorable stories Brinkley shakes each of his main characters in turn, and we, as we read, are shaken too … both subtle and striking."
—**Chris Power, *The White Review***

"Set mostly in Brooklyn, the nine stories in this debut collection are full of subtle poignancy … Each story is a trenchant exploration of race and class, vividly conveying the tension between social codes of masculinity and the vulnerable, volatile self."   —*The New Yorker*

"Sure-footed and elegant … Brinkley writes like a dream, mixing intoxicating, rhythmic street talk with high poetry, his beautiful seductive sentences rich with insight. The toughened, fragile, good-hearted men in Brinkley's stories will burrow into your heart. Lovers of musical language, fill your boots."
—*Big Issue*

"Seductively enigmatic … Brinkley's portrait of New York and its edges are full of people who feel contained pushing at the boundaries of their lives … through pages of peerless prose and startlingly sharp sentences, what emerges is a constantly reframed argument about the role and power of masculinity."
—*L.A. Times*

"Among *A Lucky Man*'s many wonderful accomplishments—the way the length of each story affords its characters room to move; the use of linear, progressive time to knit the individual stories into a social fabric, à la Alice Munro or John Edgar Wideman—one in particular is genuinely path-clearing. Brinkley offers visions of manhood and masculinity that demonstrate candor without false intensity, desire without ownership. His male characters have fictional experiences that, in the hands of the right reader, can become equipment for living."
—*Los Angeles Review of Books*

"One of the many striking qualities in Brinkley's stories is how precarious his male characters tend to be, so uncertain, deep down, of their cocky masculinity. He observes his characters from a small distance, watching patiently as their swagger, their anger, their love and lust deflate like a leaky balloon. It's an extraordinary ⬚⬚⬚⬚⬚⬚⬚⬚⬚⬚⬚⬚⬚⬚⬚⬚⬚⬚⬚⬚⬚ ⬚e a series of small trage⬚⬚⬚⬚⬚⬚⬚⬚⬚⬚⬚⬚⬚⬚⬚⬚⬚⬚⬚⬚ *s Review*

"Brinkley's depictions of love's many varieties are subtle and deeply observant … In the space of 25 pages, he's capable of creating complex and memorable emotional worlds." —*Minneapolis Star Tribune*

"In Brinkley's work, no character is left untended, no aspect of identity is overlooked, and the results are well-inhabited worlds that feel infinite. A lot of short stories exist in a snow globe, but the nine stories presented here are each a big bang. They burst forth through space and time. They are larger than the sum of their components … *A Lucky Man* is not only a standout debut for the year, but also a testament to what can be achieved in a short story."

—*Chicago Review of Books*

"With equal parts precision and poetry, these nine audacious stories step into the minefields awaiting boys of color as they approach manhood in Brooklyn and the Bronx—testing the limits of relationships, social norms, and their own definitions of masculinity." —*O: The Oprah Magazine*

"There's something magical about a great story collection … In *A Lucky Man*, Jamel Brinkley's stunning debut collection, the stories are not formally linked, and yet they are, implicitly, by their beautiful prose, by their intimate gaze at character, by their focus on black men, by their setting in New York City. A collection as fine as this, of fiction that is reflecting our world and searching for the truth, is one to be treasured, read and reread, admired, and loved."

—*Ploughshares*

"An assured and important collection that could not be more timely."

—*Kenyon Review*

"A stunning debut imbued with pathos, sexuality, and moments of violence and tenderness. With this memorable collection, Brinkley emerges as a gifted and empathetic new writer." —*Booklist* (**starred review**)

"An assured debut collection of stories about men and women, young and old, living and loving along the margins in Brooklyn and the Bronx … It's difficult to single out any story as most outstanding since they are each distinguished by Brinkley's lyrical invention, precise descriptions of both emotional and physical terrain and a prevailing compassion toward people as bemused by travail as they are taken aback by whatever epiphanies blossom before them. A major talent."

—*Kirkus* (**starred review**)

"Sensuous, sensual, sharply observed stories. A really striking debut."

—**Adam O'Riordan**

"*A Lucky Man* is just one of those collections that takes your breath away: the voices we hear, the people we meet, they scratch and pull and ache and rage, revealing secrets we usually keep hidden. Every line is pitch perfect. Jamel Brinkley is a writer of extraordinary talent."

—**Daniel Alarcón, author of** *The King Is Always Above the People*

"Jamel Brinkley writes the kind of fiction that reads like the whole truth. As his characters—from estranged siblings in Virginia to surrogate families in Brooklyn—love, hurt, challenge, and sometimes save each other, their stories vividly expose our ideas of masculinity and the fumes of racism and injustice in the American air we breathe. *A Lucky Man* is full of insight and music—a bold, urgent debut." —**Mia Alvar, author of** *In the Country*

"I loved this book. From sentence to sentence, these stories are beautifully written, and they are wonderfully moving and smart about the connections—firm, broken, or mended—between siblings, and parents and their children, and couples who profess to love each other. Jamel Brinkley writes like an angel, but he also knows how low human beings can sometimes go, despite their own best intentions. How does luck, or its absence, visit our lives? Read these stories and find out." —**Charles Baxter, author of** *There's Something I Want You to Do*

"There's just no way to overstate this: *A Lucky Man* is a stunning debut. Richer than most novels, this collection calls a whole world into being, and the names and fates of these people will follow you into your life and never leave. Ambitious themes arc across the entire book—troubled masculinity, family in all its broken forms—but on a lower frequency these are love stories, intimately told. And they could come from no other than Jamel Brinkley, so there's the pleasure of that encounter too, of hearing a new voice for the first time, and taking a deep plunge into the allegory of an artist's soul."

—**Charles D'Ambrosio, author of** *Loitering*

"The stories in *A Lucky Man* have a necessary urgency—their characters need to confess or seek comfort, to tell the reader how they've been wounded or whose hurt they carry. These stories do not shy away from heartbreak and brutal consequences, but they always remember how much of the way to despair was beautiful and full of tenderness and joy. An unforgettable collection by an important new voice."

—**Danielle Evans, author of** *Before You Suffocate Your Own Fool Self*

"This is the rare debut that introduces not a promising talent but a major writer, fully formed. The psychological penetration of these stories astonishes me, as do the grace and emotional scope of their sentences. Jamel Brinkley is brilliant, the real thing, a revelation."   —Garth Greenwell, author of *What Belongs to You*

"*A Lucky Man* is subtle yet loud, heartbreaking yet utterly unsentimental, uncompromising yet a damn good read. These breathtaking stories find energy in the friction of humanity's contradictions. In this masterfully written debut, Jamel Brinkley proves he's got next."   —Mat Johnson, author of *Loving Day*

"Jamel Brinkley's stories tell of absence and abandonment, sometimes confronted and sometimes met with resignation, but always edged with pain and beauty. In vibrant yet restrained prose, Brinkley illuminates the longing for home, which lurks in all of us. A magnificent debut."
—Laila Lalami, author of *The Moor's Account*

"There's true magic in Jamel Brinkley's stories. He finds the subtle and humane lurking within the drama of our lives. Brinkley writes with great insight and honesty about people you'll recognize, flawed but still worthwhile. By using all his formidable talents, he's shown us a vision of ourselves."
—Victor LaValle, author of *The Changeling*

"*A Lucky Man* is filled with characters who long to become better sons, better fathers, better friends, better lovers. Often they have no words for their complicated feelings. Happily they are the creations of an author who has all the words. Jamel Brinkley is a wonderful writer and these richly imagined stories will stay with the lucky reader long after the last page."
—Margot Livesey, author of *Mercury*

"The lucky men of Brinkley's debut are haunted: by the past, by family, by love and ultimately by masculinity itself. These sober and elegant stories delve deep. A debut of subtlety and power."
—Ayana Mathis, author of *The Twelve Tribes of Hattie*

"An extraordinary short story collection."
—George Pelecanos, author of *The Man Who Came Uptown*

"Jamel Brinkley's *A Lucky Man* captures so perfectly the myriad ways in which we struggle daily not only for connection but to be heard and understood. At once covert and exuberant, ferocious and tender, heartbreaking and hilarious, these are the stories we always needed. A marvellous debut, glowing with life, and a major new voice in American fiction."
—Paul Yoon, author of *The Mountain*

A Lucky Man

A Lucky Man

Stories

Jamel Brinkley

This paperback edition published in 2020

First published in Great Britain in 2019 by
Serpent's Tail,
an imprint of Profile Books Ltd
29 Cloth Fair
London EC1A 7JQ
www.serpentstail.com

First published in the USA in 2018 by Graywolf Press, Minneapolis

Designed by Rachel Holscher

10 9 8 7 6 5 4 3 2 1

Printed and bound in Great Britain by CPI Group (UK) Ltd, Croydon CR0 4YY

A CIP catalogue record for this book is available from the British Library.

ISBN 978 1 78816 322 4
eISBN 978 1 78283 588 2

For my mother and my brother,

Marilyn and Christopher

The difference between
God and luck is that luck, when it leaves,
does not go far: the idea is to believe
you could almost touch it. . . .

—Carl Phillips, from "If a Wilderness"

Contents

No More Than a Bubble

It was back in those days. Claudius Van Clyde and I stood on the edge of the dancing crowd, each of us already three bottles into one brand of miracle brew, blasted by the music throbbing from the speakers. But we weren't listening to the songs. I'd been talking into the open shell of his ear since we'd gotten to the house party, shouting a bunch of mopey stuff about my father. At one point, sometime around the witching hour, he stopped his perfunctory nodding and jerked his chin toward the staircase. "Check out *these* biddies," he said. Past the shifting heads of dancers and would-be seducers I saw the two girls he meant. They kept reaching for each other's waists and drawing their hands quickly away, as if testing the heat of a fire. After a minute of this game the girls laughed and walked off. We weaved through the crowd and followed them, away from the deejay's setup in front of the night-slicked bay windows, and into the kitchen, where we took stock of the situation. One of the girls was lanky and thin-armed, but notably rounded at the hips. She wore a white tank top, which gave her face and painted fingernails a sheen in the dimmed light. A neat, lady-like afro bloomed from her head, and she was a lighter shade of brown than her friend with the buzz cut, a thick snack of a girl whose shape made you work your jaws.

The party, thrown by a couple of Harvard grads, happened just weeks before the Day of Atonement, in late September of 1995. Claudius had overheard some seniors talking about it earlier that Saturday after the football game, as they all smoked next to the pale blue lion statue up at Baker Field. Later he dragged me from my dorm room. We slipped out of the university's gates and took the subway down to Brooklyn, determined to crash. The party had been described as an affair for singles, so when you arrived you had to write your name on a sticker and affix it to your body. The taller girl with the afro, Iris, wore her sticker on her upper arm like a service stripe. The friend had placed hers cleverly, as both a convenience and a joke meant to shame. "Hello," her ass told us, "my name is Sybil."

"Dizzy chicks," Claudius said to me, and we gave each other these goofy, knowing grins. The main difference between a house party in Brooklyn and a college party uptown was that on campus you were just practicing. You could half-ass it or go extra hard, either play the wall or go balls-out booty hound, and there would be no actual stakes, no real edge to the consequences. Nothing sharp to press your chest against, no precipice to leap from, nothing to brave. You might get dissed, or you might get some play. You would almost certainly get cheaply looped. But at the end of the night, no matter what, you would drift off to sleep in the narrows of a dorm bed, surrounded by cinder block walls, swaddled in twin extra-long sheets purchased by someone's mom.

We approached the girls and pointed to our stickers to introduce ourselves. The tall one with the afro said her name was Iris and did so with her nose, putting unusually strong emphasis on the *I*. True to this utterance, she seemed the more insistent and lunatic of the two. She vibrated. We asked where they were from. Most of Iris's family came from Belize. Sybil was Dominican. Claudius and I liked to know these kinds of things.

"You enjoying the party?" I asked. Iris didn't respond. Her attention flew all over the place. The party house was old—you felt its floorboards giving, perceived its aches being drowned out by the music and conversations that swelled with everyone's full-bellied bloats of laughter. In hushed moments, you heard the creaking of wood, followed by the tinkle of glass, the crunch of plastic, or the throaty rise of the hum. Iris seemed attuned to all of it, to every detail of the house and its subtle geographies. She stared now through the glass doors that led to the backyard, where lit torches revealed little groups of smokers breathing vividly into the air.

I tapped her on the shoulder and she turned to me.

"Oh, it's you again." Then she gave her friend a bemused look.

"Yep, they're still here," Sybil said.

"Enjoying the party?" I repeated.

Iris waited a long time to reply: "We're bubbling." From the living room the deejay began to play a new song. "What is this?" she said. "I've heard it before."

"You don't know about this?" said a guy standing near us. He had a patchy beard and double-fisted red cups of foamy beer. Maybe he was a Harvard man. "Man, y'all are late," he said. "This is 'Brooklyn Zoo.' Ol' Dirty Bastard."

Claudius and the girls nodded in recognition but to me it all sounded like code.

"Why's he called that?" I asked.

The guy laughed at my ignorance. "Because," he said, "there's no father to his style."

The girls turned to each other and began a kind of stomping dance. "Damn damn damn," Iris said, "this song is so bubble!"

They understood the good life according to the image and logic of this word—simultaneously noun, verb, and adjective—its glistening surface wet with potential meaning. Their faces became masks of anger, nostrils and mouths flexed open as they danced. Iris kept her arms pinned to her sides while Sybil jabbed the air with her elbows. Claudius nodded at Sybil and told me, "I call dibs."

"Nah, man."

"Already called it," he said.

We both preferred girls of a certain plumpness, with curves—in part, I think, because that's what black guys are supposed to like. Liking them felt like a confirmation of possessing black blood, a way to stamp ourselves with authenticity. But Claudius had made his claim. I was left to deal with Iris, the prophet of the bubble. Fine, no big deal. He could have his pick. This was all his idea anyway. We wouldn't even be here if it weren't for him. He knew I needed a good distraction.

A few weeks earlier, late one August morning in Philadelphia, shortly before the start of sophomore year, I sat with my father, Leo, at the kitchen table and got drunk with him for the first time. He told me to beware of crazy women, angry women, passionate women. He told me they would ruin me. "But they are also the best women," he said, "the best lovers, with a jungle between their legs and such wildness in bed that every man should experience." I felt I knew the kinds of women he meant, and I knew for sure he was talking about my mother, Doreen, but I didn't give a damn. She had left us, left him, a few years earlier, and recently she'd announced she was getting remarried. I saw how this news affected my father. He had stalked around our house all summer and appeared smaller and more frantic by the week. He searched as though the answer to the question of how his life had gone so wrong were hidden in one of the rooms. All but undone by this effort, my father regarded me that morning through his heavy eyelids and long Mediterranean lashes. He'd inherited bad teeth from his own father, and before he turned sixty he'd had a bunch of them yanked right out of his mouth. He wore a partial denture but didn't have it in as we drank. The bottom of his face was collapsed like a rotten piece of fruit. "The best," he repeated. "And so . . ." His Italian accent deepened the more he drank. His tongue peeked out of his broken grin. "And so every man should experience this, Ben," he said. "Once." He held a chewed fingernail up by his high nose and then reached into his pocket for something. It was a condom, wrapped in silver foil. "Use this with the most delicious woman you can find, *una pazza*. Let her screw your brains out, once and never again. Then marry a nice, boring, fat girl with hands and thighs like old milk. Make a dull life. It's the only way to be happy." He gave me the condom. It was an ill-timed ritual—I'd already gone out into the world. Still, he believed in it, just as he believed there was a guaranteed way to be happy. Since I was his disciple, and quite drunk myself that morning, I believed in it too.

Claudius and I slid in behind the girls and danced with them right there in the kitchen. Iris moved well but with aggression. She spun around, hooked her fingers into my belt loops, and slammed her pelvis into mine. She ground herself against me for a while and then backed away to show her perfect teeth and claw the air between us. She was a kitten on its hind legs, fiercely swiping at a ball on a string.

I leaned in and asked if she'd gone to Harvard too. I tried to sound older, like I'd already graduated and was fully a man.

"We're Hawks," Iris said in her nasal voice. Then she spread her arms like wings and slowly flapped them. Claudius had a theory that I liked about girls with nasal voices. He said girls who spoke this way, cutting their voices off from their lungs and guts, did so as a kind of defense, a noisy insistence meant to distract men from the flesh.

"Hawks?" I asked.

"Hunter College, ninety-four. Hey, why don't you get me and my girl some whiskey bubbles?"

"That would be whiskey and . . . ?"

"Magic."

"Where do I get that?"

She gave a disappointed shake of her head. "It's just whiskey," she whined. "Be a good boy."

Passing Claudius and Sybil as they danced, I winked to let him know we were in. The sensation of Iris's moving hips ghosted against me. There in the face of the kitchen cabinet floated her pretty smile and dark eyes, flecked with a color close to gold.

After making four healthy pours of Jack, I carried the cups back over. Sybil sniffed the whiskey and let her eyes cross with pleasure. Iris lifted her cup and with a dignified tone and expression said she was thankful for the universe and all of its moments. "And for whiskey and music and madness and justice and love," she added.

"And for the sky," Sybil said. "Have you seen the fucking sky tonight?"

Their words were completely meaningless. It was a toast to nonsense.

"And for your tits," Iris said. She reached out and squeezed Sybil's right breast. "Doesn't she have great tits?"

Claudius stared brazenly at them. "She does," he said. "She really does."

He had come to New York from West Oakland with certain notions regarding life out here, that the city's summer heat and dust, and its soot-encrusted winter ice, were those of the cultural comet, which he ached to witness if not ride. Because of these notions, he manipulated gestures and disguises, pushed the very core of himself outward so that you could see in his face and in the flare of his broad nostrils the hard radiance of the soul-stuff that some people chatter on about. Though the features of his face didn't quite agree, he could convince you he was handsome. For this trickery his implements included a collection of Eastern-style conical hats and retro four-finger rings. His choice for tonight: a fez, tilted forward on his head so that we, both of us, felt emboldened by the obscene probing swing of the tassel.

Claudius and I knew what *we* were toasting: the next phase of life. At parties like this the crowd was older, college seniors who already had New York apartments, graduates who were starting to make their way, and folks who were already far enough into their youth to start questioning it. The booze was better and the weed was sticky good. The girls were incredible, of course, especially here. You could taste a prevalent Caribbean flavor in the air, as if the parade through Brooklyn's thoroughfares on Labor Day had never stopped and this had been its destination all along. If not Caribbean like Sybil, the girls were something else distinct and of the globe. Each girl had her own atmosphere. We were convinced they wore better, tinier underwear than the girls we knew, convinced they were mad geniuses of their bodies.

"So where'd you two escape from?" Iris asked, though her gaze drifted out to the backyard again.

"Uptown," Claudius said. "Columbia."

"*Roar, Lion, Roar,*" Sybil said.

"We graduated in May," I lied.

"Mazel tov," Iris said.

Sybil shook her head.

Iris's attention snapped all the way back now. "What? I can totally say that."

Sybil made a popping sound with her mouth, and the two of them laughed.

Claudius and I laughed too, though neither of us really knew what was funny. Before we could pick up the thread of the conversation, the girls left without saying a word.

We slid up the stairs after them and wound past the partygoers perched there gossiping or flirting or losing themselves in mazelike privacies of thought. On the second floor, a group of people stood shoulder to shoulder in the doorway of one room, as though to block something illicit from view. Claudius and I pushed past them and found ourselves in an immense bathroom, where voices echoed off the tiles. Two girls stood fully clothed in a tacky, powder blue Jacuzzi, their heads framed by a backlit square of stained glass over the tub, but they weren't our girls. We returned to the hallway and caught Iris and Sybil coming out of a bedroom, trailed by the skunky-sweet odor of marijuana. We pursued them downstairs and out into the backyard.

Claudius jumped into their line of vision and said, "So let's play a game."

For a moment the girls acted as though they had never seen us before, then Sybil's eyes widened. "Wow," she said.

Claudius announced that we should all trade confessions. "Shameful stories," he said. "Secrets. The worse they are, the better." This idea seemed to have been inspired by the refrain of "Brooklyn Zoo"—*Shame on you! Shame on you!* The girls seemed amused but unconvinced by his suggestion; Claudius went on anyway. "Who wants to go first?" he said, and waited. But this waiting was just a sham. Of course he would be the one to begin.

What we aimed to achieve in these moments required patience and a strategic silence. Then, when we did speak, there was a distinct lowering of our voices—even in loud places, so that we'd have to lean in close. We made eye contact that was both firm and soft, not quite a stare, and we broke it occasionally to let our gazes trickle down the full lengths of their bodies. This had to be less wolfish than a leer, more a sly undressing. The total effect would be a kind of hypnosis, inducing a gradual surrender of the self. As we'd developed it, this method had worked plenty of times with the girls on campus, but we knew that this was nothing to be proud of. College is nothing if not four years of people throwing themselves recklessly at one other.

In his affected murmur, Claudius told us a story I had heard before. The story may or may not have been true, but it shocked people, or aroused them, or made them feel vulnerable and sad. Claudius wasn't what you would call a patient guy. He needed to know as soon as possible where people stood, especially girls. Here is the story: When he was in high school, he discovered that the old lady who lived alone next door was watching him from her window. Every morning and evening, with the door locked against his alcoholic mother, he would exercise in his room wearing only his briefs. Furiously blinking, Claudius told them: "Calf-raises, push-ups, chin-ups, and crunches till I dropped. And there she was, this old biddy, looking dead at me with her old biddy glasses on like it was the most natural thing in the world, like I was putting on a show. So that's just what I did. At first I stood at the window and stared right back at her, rubbing my chest and abs. Then, after a week or so of this, I started rubbing baby oil on myself. Took it up a notch by walking around butt-ass naked, and when that didn't faze her, I tried to get my girlfriend to help me put on a sex show. Well, she wasn't having it. Too innocent, I guess, so get this: I masturbated instead, stroking it right in front of the window. The old biddy watched this too, but the next night she wasn't there. Poof, gone. Wasn't there the next night either. That was the last night she watched me. I guess she got to see what she'd been waiting for all along."

In unison the girls let out a shriek, which spilled into rapid chatter that was like another language. Even in the dim party lights, their darting eyes stood out, fine russet and amber stones. Their bodies shook with laughter as they slapped their thighs and rocked their heads back. The flurry of motion seemed to release scent from them: ripe sweat and vanilla oil with traces of almond. Iris's perfect afro eclipsed broad sections of the room in its orbit. Other girls had been either repulsed or aroused by the story, unambiguously so. None had ever reacted like this. And something else was off. Iris's wild mouth and eyes appeared to move independently of the rest of her face. She looked like a defective plastic doll.

"What the fuck?" Sybil said finally. In her accent, the word *fuck* became for us a powerful sexual clue. "This one thinks he's a freak," she said and then sent Claudius's tassel spinning with a flick of her finger.

"Shame is the name of the game," he replied, with a flare of his nostrils. "It was the nonsense of that age." He was speaking a little too grandly now, even for him. "Let's get on with the nonsense of *this* age."

The girls whispered to each other, blew soft gibberish onto each other's necks.

"Well," Claudius said, "who's next?"

"Him," Iris said. We had their attention now. "What's he got to say?"

All three of them stared at me, waiting. There were a million ways I could go, but every corridor of my mind led to the same place.

"My dad," I began, saying the first and only words that came to me. I explained that he was a white man, born and raised in Italy. He would always call my mother his *cioccolata*. Whenever she was angry with him, yelling for one reason or another, he would laugh and pet her cheek. In those moments he would tell her she was *agrodulce*, always retaining some of her sweetness.

Claudius smiled when I said this. He liked when I used my Italian on girls.

I told them how much my father loved my mother and her family. He especially liked when her younger sisters would visit us. This was when I was a boy. Before they arrived I would sit on the rim of the tub and run my finger along the edge of the shower curtain, watching as he beautified himself. He'd put on cologne and decide whether to leave one or two buttons open at the neck of his finest shirts. He'd make sure his cheeks were perfectly stubbled. During the visits he charmed as he mixed drinks, kissed the backs of hands, and admired new hairstyles. He ladled praise over my pretty aunts in easy pours. I had always adored him.

Claudius had stopped smiling. I wasn't telling a shameful story. My story wasn't helping our cause at all. I wasn't sure what I was doing, but I kept on.

Things like this would frustrate my mother, I told them; she accused him of flirting and loudly complained about his lack of respect for her. One day, when I was twelve, something else really brought out her fury. She came home from work hours before I was expecting her, and found me at the kitchen table looking through my father's collection of dirty magazines. I had seen his nudies before, and had previously avoided detection by taking only quick peeks, but this time I discovered, or could no longer ignore, the fact that my father had specific preferences. I was riveted by the curves of the women's buttocks, their dark nipples, and the dense blackness displayed between their thighs. My mother picked through the pile—I hadn't realized until then how many there were—and from time to time, between glances at me, she would touch a finger to the mute faces of the women in the pictures, strained into expressions of pleasure. Her deeply brown skin pressed against the images of theirs. My mother's silence unnerved me. I desperately wanted her to say something, anything at all, but she didn't. She simply took the entire stack from the table and gestured for me to go to my room.

When my father got home, he and my mother argued in the living room. I crept out and watched from the hallway.

"He's *twelve*," she kept saying to him. It was as if my father had sat me down to show me the magazines himself, or, worse, as if he had taken me to a whorehouse. Why would she blame him for what I did? I couldn't understand.

"Benito's curious, Doreen, almost a grown boy," my father replied. He thought it was no big deal, nothing to fuss about, and I agreed. "And isn't it good that he learns such women are beautiful? That his *mamma* is beautiful?"

"That's not what he's learning!" my mother screamed, and in that moment she looked hideous to me. "Don't you realize what you're teaching him? Don't you *see* what you're doing?"

At this, he took her into his arms and kissed her on the neck, a generous response to her wild nagging. She struggled against him for a little while, infuriated more by his actions than his words. But he kept kissing her neck, and biting it. He snuffed out her anger with his embrace, and between laughs he murmured his pet names for her: *cioccolata, agrodulce*. I raised myself a little, still observing them from the hallway, filled with a distinct feeling of pride.

I stopped the story there, unable to go on, unsure how to continue. For a while no one said anything. Iris took a sip of her Jack. Sybil looked around, as though she'd left something in another room. The music blared on. Finally Claudius grabbed the back of my head and laughed.

"This dude's a psychopathic thinker," he said. "A sensitive soul, a killjoy. He wears his heart *and* his mind on his sleeve."

The girls remained unconvinced.

"Okay, ladies," Claudius said. "Your turn now."

"Oh, we haven't had nearly enough to drink for all that, boys," Iris said. "Not really feeling your game."

Sybil nodded. "Plus, you know what they say. Women and their secrets."

"And bubbles," Iris added with a wink.

Then they turned away, and just like that sealed us off from them. I marveled for a moment at this female power. Claudius stared at Sybil's ass, continuing to make a claim on her, the only one he could still make in this moment of rejection. "*That's* a goddamn bubble," he whispered to me. It was held up for scrutiny by the tightness of her jeans and the heels of her boots. Her sticker was beginning to peel off. Claudius glanced at me and began to ramble on about the miracle of tight jeans—he recognized these as *Brazilian*, he said, nodding slowly as he uttered the word with reverence. Then he fell silent. Looking again at Sybil, the long and deep curve of her that communicated with something primal in him, he moved his lips as if trying to remember a forgotten language. But she and Iris were lost to us, for good this time, it seemed. Though Claudius didn't say anything about it, I couldn't help weighing our two stories in my mind. I was clearly the one to blame.

He and I spent the next two hours or so chatting, smoking, and drinking out in the backyard, where the torches flattened everyone's faces and made them gleam. Eventually we returned to the house. In the kitchen, I munched on cookies and a sopping leftover square of rum cake. I was intent on some sweetness, despite my own troublesome teeth, as we approached the end of the night. Claudius, having gathered himself again, began to scramble around the emptying party, in search of other girls worth our attention.

Not long after the incident with the magazine, my mother left us, and later she divorced my father. She claimed he loved her with his eyes but no longer with his heart. She said a woman couldn't spend her whole life with a man like that. But she was wrong about my father's feelings. Sure of this, arrogant in my knowledge, I ranted it to myself. My father worshipped my mother, every fact and feature of her. All he'd ever done was lavish her with affection. After she left, he became bitter. One day he complained to me that she wasn't really gone at all, that she was much too wicked for such a mercy. She was still there, he said, stuck in him: a froth in the veins, a disease of the blood. That's how I began to think of her, as a sickness, a betrayal on the cellular level. My decision to stay with him became a badge of loyalty, and I brandished it in her face as often as I could, until she stopped trying to talk sense to me. She did write on my seventeenth birthday though, asking me to come to Newark to see her, to meet her new man and his kids. She also called my dorm room at the end of freshman year, right before final exams, to tell me about her engagement and to let me know how much it would mean to her to have me attend the wedding.

"What makes you think I would *ever* do that?" I asked.

She was quiet for a moment, and even this interval of thought enraged me, primed me to pounce on anything she said. I stared at the shadeless lamp on my desk and forced my gaze into the bulb's hot center.

"What makes you think you wouldn't?" she said. "At some point, son, you'll have to give up whatever idea you went and got fixed in your head."

I cursed and hung up the phone, shaking, purblind with anger, completely closed to her. She was a coward, unable to withstand the force of my father's affection, as if there were such a thing as too much love.

My father. The old version of him would have enjoyed this party. I walked into the living room smiling at this thought. There was a time when he would have hosted such an event, casting invitations far and wide to young, magnificent, colorful people, people he referred to as "the essence of the earth." For these parties, he'd let me stay up, all night if I could manage it. So I could imagine him kissing the cheeks of the four girls who were now heading toward the door, whose brown feet were tantalizing in their heels and sandals, wearing jeans smoothed on like blue oil, and summer dresses like saintly robes. My father would hold their hands and beg them not to go yet. He'd tell them about a special bottle, some vintage he'd been saving for the right moment, and offer the promise of a home-cooked breakfast at the first hint of sunrise. He'd say almost anything he could think of to get a smile to flash across one of their faces, to make them stay, to keep the party going as close as possible to forever.

But my father was wasting away in Philly, not here, the man he used to be long gone, and so the four girls were allowed to pass out of the house without ceremony. Noticeably more guys than girls were left now, and most of them had these hangdog looks made more pathetic by the dreary music the deejay played at a lowered volume.

Iris and Sybil were standing by a makeshift bookcase, giving these three lames the same treatment they had given me and Claudius. Now, drunk or high, maybe both, they lifted their feet and flailed their arms, swimming in a thick sea of hilarity. Then one of the lames clung to Sybil's arm as he begged her to stay, to give him her phone number, to go home with him. The guy looked older—old, frankly—and he and his buddies had probably crashed the party too, though not the way we had. They seemed to have come from someplace else en-

tirely, another time, another dimension, and the stink of it emanated
from them. That was it: something I couldn't name festered in their
horniness, and it made their solicitations coarse, mean, and frightening. I could have interfered, played the gallant hero as my father
would have, but Iris was able to pull her friend away from the lames
and out of the house.

Claudius came into the room holding his fez upside down like a
bucket without a handle. His hair was matted and kinked, and he resembled certain homeless folks you'd see begging on the subway,
crackling with foul energy, offended and beseeching. He stormed ahead
and almost walked through me.

"No luck?"

"Fucking sausage fest," he called back.

I followed him outside. He put the fez back on and its tassel
flapped in the breeze. I had seen him this way before, in this state
of extreme agitation. He was terrible at idleness, much worse than I
was, and could quickly lose his way. Without an exact destination,
the map of his life had no significance or shape. We stood together
at the gate of the house, surrounded by the high-pitched barking of
a neighbor's dog, the buzz of a faulty streetlight, a faint clinking of
metal. I clapped him on the shoulder and said we should head back
up to campus. He took out his pager. The greenish glow of its dis-
play told us it was nearly four in the morning. Subway service would
be awful.

Just then, on the sidewalk, Iris and Sybil teetered by on bicycles,
their front wheels doing a spastic dance. They rode a little past us before Sybil swerved and crashed into the side of Iris's bike. She caught
herself, but Iris fell. We rushed through the gate, over to them, and
I helped Iris up. There were tears in her eyes, but she was making a
noise that eventually revealed itself as a laugh. Sybil was laughing too.

"We're messed up," Iris admitted. Without apology she belched into her fist and then examined her arm. A fresh cut rimmed with dirt ran from her elbow halfway to her wrist. She gently poked at the wound and then stared at the reddened tip of her finger.

When I asked if she was okay, she responded by trying to mark me with the spot of blood. I jumped back and she laughed. I exchanged glances with Claudius and then suggested we walk the girls home.

Iris hummed as she peeled the sticker with her name from her upper arm. "A couple of goddamned gentlemen," she said. "Chivalry is undead."

We walked with their bikes while the girls, holding hands, staggered ahead of us. Their very movements, synced in drunken exaggeration, suggested a new rhythm to prolong the night. It was like the records my father would play in the wee hours of his parties, after the more delicate guests had gone home and those who remained sat and considered the hands of the clock. He had a selection of special vinyl, mostly bop, that made things jump into life again, nothing like the bleak music the deejay played back at the house. My father's music persuaded you that nothing ever had to end.

Claudius and I, feeling good again, stared at the girls. Iris's calves and thighs were shapely for such a thin girl, but Sybil's ass was still the prize.

Eyeing it, I said, "That's a goddamn onion."

"Make a grown man cry," Claudius said in response to my call. But then he looked doubtfully at me. "You wouldn't even know what to do with that though. I called dibs, remember?" He jutted his chin at Iris and said, "That's more your speed, B. Two sticks make fire."

With a wink he picked up his pace and ripped off the sticker dangling from the seat of Sybil's jeans. They had a good laugh about that and began to walk together, and eventually, trailing after them, I was back with Iris. Another cut split the skin near her wrist. Whenever the wound grew rich with blood she sucked at it like an injured child.

Despite her strange behavior, I pictured sleeping with her, maneuvering her thighs and hips as easily as I did the handlebars of her bike.

We walked for a long time, deeper into Brooklyn. It felt as though we were actually sinking. Wooden boards slanted across the windows of the apartments above a corner store and lines of stiff weeds punched through cracks in the sidewalk. We passed a bar called Salt, which looked as though it hadn't been open for business in years, and around the corner, a series of names tagged on a brick wall. Each of the names had three letters—SER, EVE, RON, REL, MED—and the drips of paint made murky icicles of color. The ground became more densely littered with crushed paper bags, empty bottles of malt liquor, and other shapeless hunks of trash. I guided Iris's bike around inexplicable puddles layered with scum. It hadn't rained in weeks, and it wouldn't tonight. Men sat on the edges of ramshackle stoops or stood in front of shuttered bodegas. They leered at us, but their looks were less threatening than mysterious. Receptive to whatever the men were bombarding us with, I felt irradiated, all the way down to my bones.

Iris talked incessantly, invoking the bubble, picking her words with drunken deliberation. "It's not about being all profound and shit," she said. "It's not even about that. It's like, can you tiptoe over every surface? Can you go anywhere and be open to every little thing?"

I tried to appear interested in what she had to say. There was no way I would screw up our chances a second time. I softened my tone and asked, "What's all this bubble stuff about anyway?"

Sybil's laugh drifted ahead of us. The sound of another dog barking shot through the air. Iris said something I didn't understand, and I asked her to clarify.

"It's Japanese: *mono no aware*," she said. "A sensitivity to things. An awareness. Everything lacks permanence. A way of understanding beauty. I studied world philosophies, in college, and did a year abroad." To illustrate the idea, she started talking about *sakura*, the cherry blossom tree.

At first this all sounded like more pothead gibberish. Then the notion of *abroad*, and the mysterious worldliness it suggested, began to excite me as much as her hips did. Iris was black, Central American, maybe Jewish somehow, and who knew what else. She was even more exotic than I had thought.

She talked about a dream she'd had about the cherry blossoms, a vision like a time-lapse video: the pink buds flowering, paling, and drifting down in bunches, left like soft skirts on the grass. "I asked my mom about it," she said. "She can read dreams. She told me life is exactly like that."

Iris was holding something out to me, something real, but I couldn't quite grasp whatever it was. "Here's what I want to know," I said, and then blurted, "Have you ever made love in the grass?"

She frowned and opened her mouth to reply. But then a thin, straw-colored dog appeared from between two parked cars. Claudius, startled, let Sybil's bike fall to the ground. When the dog began to growl and bark, we tried to get around it. It didn't move well but was able to stay in front of us. It may have been rabid. Some of its pink skin showed through its patches of fur, and in the glow of the streetlight it looked like a mix of hyena and pig. Its rheumy eyes gleamed, the sound of its growling nearly subliminal. I kept my eyes fixed on it. Though the night air had cooled, waves of heat pounded my head. My teeth clenched, and my chest tightened.

The dog edged closer, ready, at any moment, to spring at us as we backed away. Claudius cradled the fez against his chest and cursed under his breath. He slipped behind the rest of us and used us as his shield. I lifted Iris's bike, ready to throw it, but then Sybil rushed at the dog and kicked its snout. The dog listed for a moment, whined in a way that seemed almost grateful, and then fell over. Iris joined her and before it was over they gave several more solid kicks, aimed at the dog's head and shriveled belly. Then the animal wasn't moving or breathing. All of its wildness had been extinguished. I turned my back even though the violence was done, but odd little murmurs from the girls, disturbing sounds, still reached my ears. Someone's arms wrapped tightly around me—my own arms, I realized. Not far from where I stood, Claudius's mouth gaped wider and wider.

The girls got quiet. Sybil walked her bike to us. She breathed heavily through her nostrils, skin shining from her brief exertions. She went right up to Claudius, grabbed the back of his head, and pulled him down to her for a rough, hungry kiss. His fez crumpled in their embrace.

Unsteadily, I made my way to Iris. As she stood over the unmoving dog, her shoulders rose and fell. She turned to me and ran the palm of her hand down my forehead, smoothing it. "Stop being so . . . *astonished* all the time," she said. "It makes you look old."

Just then, a man across the street shouted from behind the bars of an apartment window. "Goddamn!" he said. "Y'all bitches fucked that motherfucker *up!*"

We laughed, first the girls and then me along with them. Claudius, holding his ruined hat, didn't join in. I laughed with the girls and felt a sense of relief. All of a sudden everything seemed okay—what the two of them had done and how they had done it, that they had been the ones who were brave. It wasn't just okay; it was exciting, and more.

As we walked on, Iris stared ahead, in a dream state. "What was the dog offering us?" she asked. "What did its choice of death release into the world?"

I couldn't reply. It wasn't even clear that her question was meant for me.

We approached a station for a subway line I'd never taken before, and Claudius looked back at me. A question formed on his tired, wary face, and I knew what he meant. I shook my head, and he knew what I meant. When I nodded, that was understood too. We weren't going back to campus. Wherever this night led, we would follow it all the way.

The girls' building was set far back from the street and constructed in two moods, with clean brick on the first floor and gray vinyl siding on the second. A single window peeked out from the siding like a jaundiced eye. The girls skipped through the gate, up to the door, and stood on the threshold, waiting for us.

"Where *are* we?" Claudius muttered.

"Doesn't matter."

"I think I'm done, man," he said. "We got them home safe. Like they even fucking needed it."

"And now they want to thank us," I said. "A couple of goddamned gentlemen."

"Man, I don't even know where the hell we are."

I placed a hand on his shoulder. "Who cares? The whole world is ours tonight, baby."

Iris asked if we were coming up or what, said to hurry up, she had to pee. I gave Claudius our habitual goofy grin. He stared at me. Finally, in a low voice, he said okay, but he didn't grin back. We carried their bikes inside.

Other than two Elizabeth Catlett prints on the walls, the living room was barely decorated, as if the girls didn't actually live here. Did anyone live here? The suggestion thrilled me, that the place was available to anyone in the know, who wanted or was fated for a crazy night.

The girls dropped some tablets into our palms—"love drugs," they said—and I swallowed mine down with a swig of their overproof rum. Claudius followed my lead. The girls told us to sit tight and went together to take a bath. We sank into the softness of their couch. I let their voices caress me through the slightly opened door. The girls talked solemnly, like two sages, in the tub.

"Does it hurt?" Sybil was saying.

"It does," Iris said, "but I'm not afraid of the pain."

"Good. No avoidance."

"No diminished capacities."

I joked, knowing it was lame, that the girls must be taking a bubble bath. Claudius didn't say a word. Sweat ran from under his warped hat into his eyes. As the girls' voices floated on and time got fat and lazy, my heart pummeled my rib cage. Drunk and high and nervous, I was ready nevertheless.

They emerged at what felt like the edge of forever, at first wearing only the thinning steam from the bathroom, and then essentially nothing, just some stray suds. Iris had strips of bandage on her arm. They stood in front of us and began to pose, slowly turning their bodies so we could admire them from every angle. Their wet feet stained the hardwood floor. I'd never seen such blatant female nudity in person before. Whenever I reached for them, eager to move things along from this drawn-out moment, the girls took a step back. They wouldn't let me touch them. "Just watch," Iris said, and I did, we did, until Sybil went into one of the bedrooms and gestured for Claudius to follow.

In the other room, Iris lit some candles and told me to sit on the bed. As she approached, the door opened and Sybil scurried inside. Claudius, still fully clothed, shuffled along behind her. "I got lonely," Sybil said. "I missed you." Iris said she missed her too. The girls kissed in the skittish candlelight. Then Sybil asked if we wanted in on the action. I said yes and they laughed at how quickly I said it. Sybil told us to take off our clothes. Quickly again, I began to undress but Claudius just stood there, gazing around the room. It seemed like he was trying to remember everything there—the large bed, the flickering candles, the heavy curtains—as the setting he might use for an entirely different story. He was remembering everything, it appeared, except the people in it, ignoring and therefore omitting us. Maybe he was even omitting himself.

While Sybil urged us on, saying she wanted to see what we were working with, Claudius forced his attention through the opening in the curtains, into the darkness outside, in denial of her voice. But then I called his name, scolding in my tone, and pulled his attention back into the room. What was it? The amount of booze we'd had, the drugs, the crazy talk, the vision of that animal dead in the street, or simply the girls themselves? All of it, in combination, made glorious sense to me. We had reached the proper destination of this night. Obviously Claudius and I had never been undressed in each other's presence—but so what? The girls we'd wanted from the start were finally offering their fragrant brown flesh to us, and all we had to do was get naked too, together. Why should shyness, if that's what it was, or fear, or a bit of further strangeness, a little kink in the first blush of day, stop us now? Why shouldn't this, all of us collected in one room, be our path? I stared at Claudius until he understood I wanted him to do it. He could have said no, to the girls, to me, to that part of himself that also wanted to keep going, and for a second, when he opened his mouth, I expected him to say just that, to shout his refusal. All he did was stand there and tamely nod in assent.

Then he took off his clothes, as I did, watching the girls as they watched us. When Claudius and I were naked, they didn't do anything. They weren't satisfied yet.

"Well," Sybil said, "look at him."

I was confused for a second, but it was a command meant for both of us.

"You have to be fully present," Iris said, her first words in a long time.

"Look at him."

"He's your friend."

"Don't pretend he's not there."

"There's always more to what you want than what you wanted." It was Iris again. "You have to take that too."

I turned to Claudius, standing there with his hands clasped in front of his genitals. Sybil went to him and moved his hands aside. His calves were thin in comparison to his muscular thighs. He had a well-developed chest but a bulging stomach, bisected by a vertical stripe of fuzzy hair. His penis was half-erect. Sybil placed the crushed fez back on his head to complete the description of his nudity.

The girls told us to keep looking at one another, through the fear and embarrassment, all the way through the entire exposure. They wouldn't let us proceed otherwise. Four naked bodies on the verge of sex together in one room had to be exactly that.

We managed to arrive at sex—Iris with me, and Sybil with Claudius—as light began to slip into the room through gaps in the curtains. I didn't get to enjoy Iris's body, not really. I was too concerned with keeping matters organized, under some semblance of control, fending off the orgiastic. I was much too aware of the other bodies on the bed, much too aware of my own. I did, however, get to use my father's condom. I'd intended to use it, had become fanatical about doing so, and finally did, just as Claudius—perhaps another true son of another confused father—got to use the condom he carried around in *his* pocket. We had found our so-called wild and crazy women, and they slept with us. But first they made us look, for a very long time.

My father died, or completed his long process of dying, a year ago. On the day of his funeral, watching his rigid, almost smiling face in the casket, I was flanked by my mother and her new family. I had kept my distance over the past decade or so, estranging myself, and therefore hadn't seen her in what felt like ages. At one point, she squeezed my arm and then she nodded. She didn't force me to speak to her. Everything she had to say was expressed in those gestures. In her black blazer and dress, with her gray-streaked hair pinned under a slanted hat, she remained a striking woman. Perhaps my father still would have thought so. What struck me even more than the elegance and dignity with which she was growing older was the presence of her husband and his, *their*, adult children. They didn't have to be there. Later, unable to settle my stomach or my mind, I stood alone, just as I had arrived, and my mother and her family talked together on the other side of the room. Other than me, I realized, they were the only black people in attendance. Together the four of them formed a portrait of serenity and grace that made me feel even more sick. I thought about the last public event my father and I attended together, a celebration of his long and successful career. There was desperation in the way he led me by the arm from guest to guest. To anyone I didn't already know, and to some I already did, he said, "This is my boy. This is my boy." He showed me off like a prize, as if to eliminate any doubt that I belonged to him. He'd done this kind of thing ever since I was a child. That day was the very first time it didn't make me proud.

What did he mean back on that August morning in Philadelphia before I returned to college? Did he believe what he had told me about happiness? Could he have meant it? Or was he just heartbroken, bitter, drunk? Maybe he knew he was talking to a young fool. Or maybe observing what I did with my life would be his way of figuring everything out. I don't know. I don't know, but I keep imagining what it would be like, to be a father to a boy who loves and believes in me and, despite all our differences, wants nothing more than to be a man in my image. I see that spectral boy, my son, vividly, and feel frightened when he is near. I want to speak to him, but I have no idea what to say.

Sometimes I feel all I'd have to offer, other than questions, are my memories of that time in Brooklyn and that terrible apartment I had driven us to, obsessed. It sounds ridiculous, even to me, yet it's true. Among the strangest touches I felt there was my friend's hand gripping my shoulder, long after Iris and Sybil had left us alone in the bedroom. I gasped when Claudius first touched me. I didn't look back at him and I didn't move his hand. I just lay there on my side with my eyes closed and tried not to be awake anymore. When I finally rose it was past noon. My head throbbed, and the faraway sound of the girls' voices rang in my ears. Claudius was sitting up in the bed, staring at me. All at once an acute ugliness shuddered into being, a face revealed within his face, and he must have seen it within mine too. It has been that way with people in my life, with people I have loved: a fine dispersal, a rupture as quiet as two lips parting, a change so sudden one morning, so slight, you wonder if they had ever been beautiful at all.

J'ouvert, 1996

All I wanted was fifteen bucks to go to the barbershop, but the thought of asking for it made me feel like punching a wall. It stressed me the hell out to ask Ma for anything, especially that summer, when I'd decided to leave my boyhood behind. Pop would have known just what to say to calm me down or make me laugh. He wasn't around anymore though, and he had stopped responding to my letters. So I went to our room to gather myself and practice my appeal, but of course my little brother was there, too bizarre to ignore. Omari still had on his stupid rubber mask, a caricature of a great horned owl. A candy cigarette poked out at an angle from under its mottled beak. He was sitting at our desk, his butt swallowing the chair, and the clock radio played that boring white-people music he liked. The oscillating fan rattled as it blew his newspaper clippings across the floor. Our room was strewn with these sheets of taped-together headlines. As he paged through a neighbor's discarded *Daily News*, a few caught my eye: HOMELESS YOUTH UNDER HOUSE ARREST, DEATH NAMED COUNTRY'S TOP KILLER, ONE-ARMED BOY APPLAUDS KINDNESS OF STRANGERS. Together they formed a patchwork calendar of the world's absurdity.

A pathetic cloud of chalky smoke, made of powdered sugar, fell from the tip of Omari's cigarette. He'd found something he liked, a small but representative peculiarity. After testing his scissors on the air, he slowly snipped out a headline, making a show of it.

"September's the weirdest month," he said. The cigarette bobbed up and down under the beak as he spoke.

"September just started, dummy."

"I can already tell." He rose and stretched. At eleven he was nearly as tall as I was, and broad like Pop, his body an unchiseled slab. The ear tufts of his mask were sharp enough to scratch you. He squeezed between the fan and our bunk bed and went to the window. Though the kitchen was on the other side of the apartment, we could hear sink water speeding through the pipes.

We lived on the second floor of our building, not even high enough to see the top of the tree outside. Leaves from a bough pressed against the window. In a month the view would be pretty, the panes tessellated in autumn shades, but it wasn't so nice now. When I was younger, right when Pop stopped coming around, I had nightmares about that tree breaking through the glass and reaching inside to grab me with its branches.

"I invited somebody over today," Omari sang. He gestured toward the window frame. Apparently his newest imaginary friend was there. "Her name's Angela."

"Who cares?" I said.

Omari turned his face toward me, twisting his neck as far as it would go. He unwrapped the paper from the cigarette and bent the hard gum until it broke. Reaching under the beak, which curved from the bridge of his nose, he slipped the pieces into his mouth. The black-and-amber eyes of his mask were large and round. But the freaky thing was Omari's eyes within those eyes. They stared directly at me now, two pennies sunk in a bucket.

Where we lived, it didn't matter what a room was called. Ma would wash her hair in the kitchen, careful when she was done rinsing not to hit her head on the bottom of the cabinet. Sometimes she'd take phone calls in the bathroom or go in there to listen to the radio. When she was sick of me fighting with Omari, she'd take her dinner plate into her bedroom and go out to eat in peace on the fire escape.

Now she was in the kitchen washing dishes. She used scalding hot water and never wore rubber gloves. Her hands were tough, long and deeply lined. *She* was tough, with wiry, muscular arms. But this afternoon, as she cleaned, she also concealed the woman I knew by making herself look soft. Pink plastic rollers filled her hair. The smell of dabbed-on Florida Water rose from her skin. Mike, her new boyfriend, was coming over.

Our dish rack rested on top of the refrigerator—there was no other place for it—and she handed me clean plates to stack there as I made my case. She leaned against the wall, seemingly exhausted, her long slip spotted with spray from the faucet.

"Money's tight," she said. "You know that, Ty. I told you to get a job this summer, but you hardheaded. A lazy boy does things twice."

She shoved a fistful of wet utensils at my chest, but I just looked at them. I wanted to get my haircut at the place Pop used to go. I was seventeen and had never been to a barbershop, homegrown afros and cornrows all my life. Maybe I wouldn't know what to say once I got there. Maybe I'd ask for the wrong thing or laugh at the wrong time, surrounded by all those clever men, grooming each other's masculinity. Still, even if I embarrassed myself, I felt ready. I was almost a grown-up, not a boy. Plus tomorrow was the West Indian Day Parade. This was the first time she was letting me go by myself.

"If you not gonna help," she said, "get out the way and quit breathing all over me."

Now we both stared at the forks and knives clutched in her hand.

"Ma, I need to look good."

She shut off the water, jammed the utensils in the rack, and side-stepped by me. "Been doing this boy's hair all his life," she muttered.

"I'll just cut it my damn self." She started banging around in the closet where we kept photo albums, boxes of discount toilet paper, and Pop's old winter coats. Next thing I knew, I was sitting in the living room with my shoulders draped in a towel. Here was the woman I knew—a force of nature—and I was totally helpless against her.

Maybe, just maybe, some invisible force would steady Ma's hand, but who was I kidding? I had probably just stumbled again into that stagnant puddle of mud: belief. It was silly to think good things could possibly happen, but I had no choice. I described the style I wanted, picturing it as I spoke: a skin fade like Pop's, with the taper smooth and balanced, perfectly even all the way around. A timeless look.

Ma wasn't even listening. She fumbled with the box, which had a white person cheesing on the front, proud of his bowl cut. "You sure you don't want one of those high-tops?" She hovered a hand several inches above her head. "Looks easy enough to do."

I began to fidget in the chair and made one more attempt. "All the guys from school go to the barbershop," I told her. "Trip's been going since before he could walk."

"Like I give a damn about some fool calls himself Trip," Ma said. "*Trip*. Trip ain't in this family. Trip ain't got to make the sacrifices we do."

"Sacrifices . . ."

"That's right. For your brother, and for you too."

"Don't you mean Mike?"

The heat rose quickly on my ear after she hit me, my cheek stinging from her still-moist hand. Though she yelled plenty at me, almost never at Omari, Ma rarely hit. Before she could scold me or hit me again, the intercom buzzed.

Ma made her voice all sweet to call Omari and tell him to buzz Mike up. Then she started on my hair. Soon Mike walked in with a bottle of bright pink wine and his dopey grin. Ma got dopey in response and apologized for her appearance.

"Always look good to me, babe," Mike said.

He kissed her on the cheek and plopped down on the couch, the coffee table sandwiched tightly between us. Omari sat too, exactly where Pop used to relax with a beer and watch TV.

"You keep nicking me," I said. Ma was being rough with the clippers.

"Well, stop talking. Your whole head moves when you talk."

"I'm not the retard here."

"What I tell you about saying *retard*?"

Mike grinned extra big as he took in the show. "Ruth," he said, "you truly a woman of many talents."

Ma nicked me again when she laughed, and the clippers barked at every botched contact with my scalp. When she stood apart to take in her progress, they hummed in her hand.

Mike said, "Boy look like he could be on TV—right, Birdman?"

Omari's eyes shifted within the owl's; he was smiling. Though shy around Mike, he didn't seem to mind him. This pissed me off, even though he was too young to remember when there had been a real man around.

When Mike offered to add some finishing touches, I hopped up and hair rained from my shoulders. I rushed to the mirror by the front door. I couldn't believe what I saw. On top, a tall crumbling brick of hair. Edged by a jagged line, a sharp wandering border. There was no fade, no taper at all. My mouth got tight, ready to curse loud and long, but Ma gave me a look that stopped me in my tracks. She said she wanted me to take Omari out for a while.

"For what?" I said. "Because of *him*?"

Mike spread his arms, a gesture that meant *Don't you dare talk to your mother that way* at the same time that it said *Hey kid, just leave me the hell out of it*.

"You got a problem with that, Ty?" Ma said.

"I'm not the one bringing in problems."

"Do you pay the rent here? You pay any of the bills? I'm a grown woman, and I work my ass off. I'll be damned if I can't have a friend over."

Omari sang, "*Everybody needs to have a friend*," but I told him to shut up.

"I need to take another shower," Ma said wearily. "By the time I'm done, I want you boys out enjoying the day."

"Can we at least get some money?" I asked.

Ma went to the window and switched on the hulking air conditioner we rarely used. "Be back in time to set the dinner table. Six o'clock sharp. You'll be all right till then."

When she shut herself in the bathroom, Mike flipped something at me. A quarter.

"Case you think about coming back early," he said, eyeing his bottle of wine, "go on and give us a call first."

It was a hot breezeless day, the air gauzy and wet. Though the sun was high in the sky, a lone and distant object, its energy came from everywhere at once. I wandered around the neighborhood tugging down the bill of my Knicks cap. Omari trailed behind. Families walked from afternoon church service, sweating in their dress clothes. Fathers unbuttoned dark jackets from their paunches and slid down the knots of ties. One man, with a bushy soul patch under his lip, shouted for his little girl to stop running as she neared a corner.

The weather was similar when I'd gone to the West Indian Day Parade with Pop. This was before he went away, when I was seven and Omari was a baby. I heard Pop come in early Labor Day morning and get ambushed. Ma was yelling because he had stayed out all night. They argued like crazy and woke Omari, then Pop came into my room, bleary-eyed, and told me to get ready. When we left, Ma was still screaming and Omari was crying in her arms.

The parade was heat and laughter, flags and floats, music so loud

I felt it was shaking me more and more awake. I had my first taste of jerked pork there. I even got to pick the exact pieces I wanted from the vendor's smoking grill. After we ate, Pop lifted me to see over the crowd on Eastern Parkway. The women dancing in the procession were nearly naked, but plumed, with sprays of brilliant multicolored feathers. When I shifted my eyes away from their bodies, Pop laughed and told me it was okay to look.

Mike's quarter felt warm and dirty in my shorts pocket. I was tempted to pitch it into a gutter. Omari muttered as he lagged behind me, walking with one foot on the sidewalk and the other in the street. I was melting in my cap, and here he was with that mask. He'd been wearing it since Mike began coming around. All of a sudden Ma had started acting girlish, humiliating herself. She even smiled in a ridiculous way, like she did in her pictures from high school. You could see all her teeth and, held like a tiny bud between them, the bright red tip of her tongue. She crossed and uncrossed her legs with extreme awareness of herself, awareness that Mike enjoyed looking at her, delighted that he did, as if she were some other woman and not our mother.

The first time she sent us away from the apartment, in June, Mike wasn't gone at the time she had told us to come back. They were in her room. We could hear the muffled sounds of an old corny love song, plus other sounds. I knew what they were doing. I rushed Omari into our room and slammed the door, not that it did much good. We could still hear them. I went on a rampage. I yanked the sheets from our beds, knocked toys from Omari's shelves, tore his drawings and posters from the walls, and even ripped up some of his headlines. When I came out of it, he was curled up in a corner, rubbing the sides of his face. He stared at me like he didn't know who I was. After Mike finally left, sneaking out like a thief, Ma seemed embarrassed. She apologized, but only for dinner being late. She made us something extra nice but it didn't matter. Before the end of that night he was already hiding his face in the mask.

Omari still lagged behind me. "But even the moon wants to get away from the earth . . . ," he was saying. On the street, crawling along beside us, a jeep blasted music so loudly its metal frame shook: *"Ready or not, here I come, you can't hide. Gonna find you and make you want me . . ."*

Once the jeep passed by, I called to Omari: "Hey dummy! Aren't you hot with that thing on?"

He laughed in reply, strange and birdlike, a deliberately false squawk.

The park I liked wasn't far, just past Myrtle Avenue. On the way, we passed some rowdy corner boys and, in front of a Chinese take-out joint, a man in a mesh marina sitting on a milk crate. As we went by, he glared at us. He took the dead cigarette from his lips and then, real slow, mouthed, "Fuck you." He shut his eyes and angled his head back. His laughter was nearly silent too, all breath. As though we weren't even worthy of his voice.

After Ma kicked him out of the apartment, Pop used to come see me at our local library. In the reading room, he would lick his flaking lips and airily chuckle at things that weren't funny. He slouched in his chair, distracted by everything happening around us, books being shelved, words whispered, children shushed. The final time I saw him, before he got into that bad business, he paged through my stack of fantasy novels. The disapproval on his face said, *You shouldn't read shit like this*, but he didn't say the words, or couldn't manage to.

We were near the little park now. I was careful not to step on dog shit or pats of old gum or the dark stains of mulberries dropped months ago by trees. Omari hopped around behind me, holding out his hand as though Angela, in distress, were grasping it. It was fun for him to imagine that the world teemed with obstacles.

Out of nowhere, someone slapped me on the back of the neck. Then my cap was snatched off.

"Shit, somebody jump you? They fucked your head up real good."

It was Trip. Though younger than I was, only a rising sophomore, he stood over six feet tall. He held the cap high so I couldn't reach it. Eventually, after he'd had enough fun, he gave it back. "Why you so pressed about that raggedy-ass lid anyway?" he said.

I shrugged and put the cap on tilted to the right, the way Trip wore his. He said he was heading home to get out of the heat. As he talked, Omari made circles around him, doing a little war dance. "No, like this. Do it like this," he was saying. Trip smacked him on the back of his neck too, and I laughed. He made a grab for the mask, but Omari slipped out of reach.

"Yo," I said, "you going to the parade tomorrow?"

Trip sucked his teeth. "Damn the parade. J'ouvert's what's up."

"J'ouvert?"

"That's where *all* the shit happens."

I'd heard of it before, but didn't really know what it was. "When is it?"

He stroked his jaw and looked around, as though there might be someone way more interesting to talk to. "Tonight. Way past your bedtime, kid. When the freaks come out."

"Where?"

"You don't know a damn thing, do you?"

"I know some stuff about it."

"Yeah right."

"I *do*. My pops used to go." The words leaped from my mouth, but I didn't regret saying them at all. I liked that they were out in the world. They sounded true.

Trip laughed. He craned his neck from side to side, squinting past me. "Maybe your pops will take you then."

"Come on, man."

"If he ever gets around to it."

"Hey, fuck you."

Suddenly Trip's fist was in my face and I flinched, but it stopped short. He plucked the brim of my cap so that it came off again. Before I could, he grabbed it from the ground.

"Trip, stop playing."

He fended me off easily and then stuffed the cap down the front of his baggy basketball shorts. "You want it so bad? Take it, fag. Go ahead, it's right there."

I stared at it bulging from his crotch. The cap had belonged to my father. He used to wear it whenever we listened to Knicks games on the radio. I kept staring at it until Trip shoved my chest and sent me stumbling backward onto my butt. He stood over me, face contorted. "So fucking gay." Then, my cap still in his shorts, he walked off cowboy-style. From some distance away he shouted, "See you, bitch. You, your retarded brother, and your busted-ass fade!"

I sat right where I was on the ground, wishing for somewhere to hide. Every eye in the city seemed to be turning in my direction. Omari stood in front of me, stroking the air. "It's okay," he kept saying. "It's okay." I finally realized he was talking to Angela, not to me. I scrambled to my feet, hands crushed into fists and blindly flailing, my mouth stretched wide by everything I yelled at him. By the time I ran out of words it was Omari on the ground, as if he were the one Trip had shoved there. He was as small as he had been that day earlier in the summer, curled up in that corner of our room.

The laughter of the men comforted me a little. It rose from the park like a thrown net of sound and I wanted to be caught in it. Before setting foot inside though, I stopped and felt my sun-pricked scalp. This stupid haircut. I pulled off my T-shirt and began to fold and tie it around my head. Soon I had made it into what felt like a turban. Omari stared at me.

"What are you looking at, fag?" I said, and then walked away in case he was stupid enough to answer.

The park was a narrow triangle of grass that stretched along

Willoughby Avenue. The men, most in their fifties or sixties, would arrange themselves in a small group on benches surrounding chess tables made of concrete. They ate packaged oatmeal cookies or wax-coated cups of *coco helado*, and drank from cans of beer kept hidden in little brown paper bags between their thighs. Sometimes they actually played chess, but usually they just talked a world of shit about how everything was getting terrible.

From other adults I resisted this kind of talk, but these men were so adept at it, as verbally skilled as the boys who freestyled over by Marcy. I loved the slang they peppered into their speech, archaic and strange and wonderful to my ear. And there was an underlying gentleness they had with one another. They reminded me a little of Pop. I sometimes imagined that I would find him one day, sitting here among them.

I walked to the playground area and rested my forearms on top of the four-foot-high chain-link fence that ran directly along the men's benches. Omari began to play behind me, pushing Angela higher and higher, the empty swing faintly squeaking. I tried not to cry about the Knicks cap. On the other side of the fence Mr. Boone, the ringleader, held forth. The sun leaned west—it was past four already—so his perspiring face appeared blue in the shadow of a large tree.

"Nah, I ain't imagining it and you ain't either. It's real, and there's a reason you got little girls out here looking like Pam Grier. It's the *chicken*." He paused dramatically and wiped points of sweat from his nose. "They injecting those birds with so many damn chemicals, got our girls all thicksome while their breath still smelling like milk."

"What you mean, Boone? What they do that for?" said a younger, unfamiliar man. He wore a straw trilby pushed back on his head.

"What you mean what I mean? They do it to drive the black man out his mind. So he don't know up from down or right from wrong when he see these girls. All buxom but still got doll babies in their hands. Then you got babies making babies. *Then* you got black families good and fucked-up. That's why they do it."

"*Experiments*," said a third man, Sidney, as though he hated everything about science. He sat closest to me. A rum-scent of cologne rose to me from the back of his neck.

"Yeah, but I heard it was from those perms they get in their hair. The chemicals."

"You heard that?" said the man in the trilby. "Who told you, Boris or Natasha?" He pronounced each burst of his laughter like a word, his voice a little destroyed around the edges. "Y'all sound like some jive motherfuckers is what you sound like. Paranoid."

"And you just sound plain stupid," Boone said. "Tuskegee. Ever heard of it? Holmesburg. And shit like that's still happening. What you know about it, you ignorant son of a bitch?"

At this, all the men, including the one in the trilby, broke out in raucous laughter. I laughed too, and Boone's gaze fell on me. "You calling me a lie, Cuffy," he said. "Let's ask Ali Baba over here what's what." They all turned to me. Omari came up and claimed a place just to my right, leaning heavily on the fence, but I ignored him. Boone said, "You notice anything different about the girls in your class last year, little man?"

"Why you asking me?"

"Don't be shy about it," Sidney said. "You know what we talking about." His hands made exaggerated curves in the air.

I looked each of them in the face. They were being serious. "Mister, I'm almost eighteen years old."

The men broke into hysterics. Hands slapped the tables, and a can that fell from a bench filled cracks in the ground with rivulets of foam.

"Goddamn, boy, you need to order ten buckets of that chicken Boone talking about."

The laughter continued until Boone interrupted. "Don't work that way," he said, suddenly thoughtful again. "Nope. Those chemicals only grow the females. Look how scrawny Ali Baba is. His chest look like the cage that there Tweety Bird flew out from. Matter fact, this got me thinking they trying to *stunt* our boys. Keep 'em from becoming men."

"Oh, here we go," Cuffy said. "Can't leave well enough alone."

Boone scoffed. "Leave well enough alone? This jackass acting like he ain't heard of COINTELPRO. Start there and go back, and keep on going. You tell me if you can think of a time when war wasn't declared on us. Same as it ever was. At least we used to have the good sense to know."

The men fell silent. I was still stinging from being laughed at, but Sidney leaned closer to me and held his can of beer out over the fence. "Go on," he said. "This'll get you right."

"Man, this diluted piss won't add a solitary hair to that boy's stones. Much less spring him up any."

I ignored that comment and bit my lip to keep from smiling. Over by the rusted monkey bars, a group of kids played a rough game of tag. A young father with braided hair was trying to coax his son off the swings. The boy poked his lips out in protest until his dad promised ice cream and pie after dinner. I took the beer. Beside me Omari stuck his hand under his beak. His widened eyes watched me.

"Go on," Sidney repeated.

The wet can, nearly full, had soaked through the paper bag and softened it into a flimsy brown skin. I tilted my head back and drank deeply. Though watery and tepid, the beer was the best thing I'd tasted in a long time.

"Boy tryna get polluted."

"He already polluted. Look at him."

"He grown folks now."

"Even got a little bitty mustache."

"Hey Baba, what about your friend? Tweety Bird, you want some too?"

I wiped the smear of moisture from the groove of my upper lip and raised my eyebrows at Omari. Pop must have felt like this at the parade when he told me it was okay to look at those half-naked women. He'd wanted me to look, so I did. I couldn't disappoint him. "How 'bout it, dork? I won't tell."

Omari shook his head vigorously, *no*, and kicked the fence so that the links shimmied. "I'm not a Tweety," he said. "I'm not a dork. And I'm not a fag." He raised himself from the fence and went back to the swings.

"Guess he don't give a hoot," Sidney said. The rest of us jeered, and Boone threw a fistful of crumbled oatmeal cookies at him.

Soon Omari was the only kid by the swings. The young father and his son had long since left for dinner and ice cream and pie. One boy from the game of tag remained, hanging from the middle of the monkey bars. He swayed almost imperceptibly and scowled at his own dirt-hardened face. As the sun rolled down and marked the slope of the sky, a slight breeze picked up, but the air was still thick and hot. The men had invited me to sit with them, to take the place of a homebound man the others said was hopelessly pussy-whipped. It was a bit past six o'clock—we were already late—but I walked around the fence and sat. Pop was never whipped and I wouldn't be either.

The men showed no signs of slowing down. They kept calling me "Ali Baba" or "Grown Folks," and they gave me more to drink. Finally I got my own can, and then another, and I tried to imitate their pace in sipping, the unselfconscious way they hid the beer between their thighs. For a while they talked about the president, mandatory minimums, and "three strikes." They traded quips about O. J. Simpson. Then they were on about the number of black men in prison and how everything was out of balance. Sidney had taken the lead.

"Y'all know Portia Brown?"

"Who?"

"You know who I'm talking about."

"Nope."

"The megastructure. Need a special license to operate that kind of machinery."

"Man, that could be anybody."

"You mean *Paula* Brown."

"No, man, not her. Paula's good from afar, but far from a good."

"I know who you mean. Portia. Live over on Vernon Ave."

"Yeah, I'm with you."

"Caboose on the loose. That's a fine woman."

"A *good* woman," Sidney continued. "But you know her man's doing a twenty-year bid for some petty shit. Portia's, what, forty? From where I'm sitting that's young stuff. So what's she supposed to do?"

The men shrugged and sipped.

"I'll tell you what she *is* doing. Wednesday night I was over at the Lowdown, having me a quick taste, and who do I see creeping in the corner but Portia, lit up like a Christmas tree, eyes rolling around in her head. She got some Joe standing between her knees, dragging her skirt up. Ugly motherfucker. Cockroach-looking motherfucker. And guess what? Portia Brown wasn't wearing no drawers."

"Damn."

"I know. And on a Wednesday too."

"*Damn.*"

"I know," Sidney said, "*I know*. But hell, man, what's she supposed to do?"

"Maybe she could stop acting like a skank," I said. I didn't like the way my voice sounded, broken in places. In the quiet, as the men watched me, I took another sip of beer and held the warm, bitter liquid in my mouth for a long time before swallowing. I set the can, nearly empty now, on the concrete chess table. It was my third one.

"What you say now, Grown Folks?" someone said. I wasn't sure who.

"When I get locked up," I said, "I don't want my woman acting up like that, no matter how many years I get. Not if she supposed to love me."

Cuffy set his hat farther back on his head. "So, you *planning* on going to jail?"

"Might as well. If it's in the cards like you say. If everybody's there."

He looked around. Sidney cleared his throat and said, "Every black man don't go to prison, son." His tone had changed. "I mean, *we* ain't there." He spoke as if I was very small and sitting on his lap.

"Lucky you," I spat. I realized I was standing.

They all stared. I had forgotten how I looked. They continued to stare, and it felt like a coordinated effort to humiliate me. The breeze warmed my bare chest. On my head the T-shirt felt bloated and heavy.

"You ain't no better than the ones who are," I said.

"Nobody said that, little dude. There's no reason to be yelling."

My eyes found the man who had spoken. "Who's yelling?"

"You need to calm yourself down, boy."

"People need to quit telling me to calm down." I slapped my beer can off the table and it flew off to my left, toward the entrance. Without another word I stomped after it. I began to kick it along and, with a sudden feeling of permission, followed it out of the park. Before I had gotten very far, someone called after me: "Boy! Hey, boy! Little man!" I turned. It was Cuffy, standing behind Omari, his hands on my brother's shoulders.

"Left your bird," Cuffy said with an uneasy grin.

Omari moved away from him and stood out of anyone's reach.

Cuffy's gaze shifted back and forth between us before it settled on me. "Something ain't right. Why you got that mess on your head?"

"Me?"

"Yeah, what's the story?" he said.

Why was he asking *me*? I thought about his question for a moment, but there was no good place to start and no good place to end, and every simple answer had a truer, more perplexing one coiled within it. It all seemed impossible to explain. My hands came up and found the T-shirt already half-collapsed, a soft loose crumple of cloth. I pulled it from my head and put it on.

Cuffy's eyes widened at the sight of my hair. Omari breathed openmouthed under his beak.

"You got people locked up?" Cuffy said.

I nodded.

"Your daddy?"

"He didn't even do anything that wrong," I said. It was true. Just possession of a little bit of stuff he shouldn't have had.

Cuffy didn't respond. He knew better than to offer any words of sympathy.

Abruptly I said, "Tell me what you know about J'ouvert."

"J'ouvert?" He scratched his nose. "Why?"

"Just tell me."

"Well, call me boring, but that ain't my kind of party." He removed his trilby and examined it. His creased shaven head was shaped like a peanut—Pop would have said so. After a moment Cuffy held the hat over me and slowly lowered it. The size wasn't right so it drooped nearly past my eyes. An odor like mint and sweetened coconut oil emanated from its crown. "I got an agitated soul," he said. "Most of us do, I think. Not from no conspiracy or nothing. Just from being black and alive. So what we need is rest. To relax and let shit slide."

He gripped my shoulder, told me to keep an eye on my bird, then walked away, but not into the park. I stood there, confused and a little drunk. He seemed to move in slow motion. What he'd said in his destroyed voice suggested he'd once been a very different man.

"You not going back in?" I shouted.

"I got family, little man. I'm going home," he said. "And so should you. It's time. Those fools in there? They ain't got no place else better to be."

I knew home wasn't an option, and it didn't make sense to stay in the neighborhood, so we left and wandered into unfamiliar areas. I enjoyed feeling drunk. My arms slackened as we went, and my feet struck the pavement in a brutish, unpredictable way that made me smile. Cuffy's hat didn't make me forget about the Knicks cap, but I felt grateful, even though I had to tilt it back every few minutes to keep it out of my eyes. I marveled at some of the subtle differences I noticed as we walked. The way the buildings changed and the people also changed depending on whether they passed in and out of low-rises or high-rises, brownstones or houses.

Ma and Pop had been so happy together once, hadn't they? All of us had been, I was sure. Now she wouldn't even take me to go visit him. From the minute he'd gone inside she had refused to take me, and she kept saying I could go one day on my own. The last time Pop wrote, almost a year ago, he ignored what I'd written in my most recent letter, about the big march in DC, a million black men strong, and how I wished we could go together. Instead, he told me to stop sending pictures of myself. Despite his efforts, all he could see when he read my letters or tried to reply was one of the versions of me he had taped up, "stuck there on your bed, on the couch, on the corner," he wrote, "or stuck to the wall of my cell, not able to move at all." He wrote that his mind was getting smaller, getting stingy, squeezed into the squares of the photos I sent, trapped in the patterns of whatever shirt I wore. "Trapped in the lines the photos make of your face," he said at the end. He didn't even sign the letter.

For a long time Omari trailed behind me without complaint; now and then, as I sobered up, he would murmur to Angela. It was still hot, even after the sky started going dark, so when people weren't looking I fanned myself with the trilby. Soon my feet began to hurt, so I'd stop to sit on stoops. Omari sat too, but always at a distance. He followed me into bodegas and watched me stick my head into the freezers and coolers. "He's gonna get in trouble," he told Angela, and sure enough, at the very next store, I was yelled at and told to leave. Outside, Omari sat on the curb, hunched over his belly. He looked like a sack of stuff waiting to be thrown away. It was way past time for us to be home.

"Ma's gonna kill us," he said.

"She ain't even thinking about us."

"She said six."

"Mike's still there."

"So what?"

"He's gonna stay over," I said. "Ma don't have work tomorrow, and I bet he don't even have a job. Remember the first time he stayed? You want it to be like that again?"

Omari looked up at me and then lowered his head, took a deep tremulous breath.

"Let's have an adventure," I said. "Keep this thing going. You and me. And Angela too." He'd be more persuaded if I included her.

I extended my hand to help him up, but he stood without taking it. When we started walking again, he stayed a little closer behind me.

"Sea horses don't have legs, and mermaids don't have legs," he said at one point. "So if you got revenge and chopped off his legs but then felt bad about it after, you could throw him into the ocean."

Other than the occasional line like this, everything was quiet, dense and eerie and strange like the heat without the sun. I didn't like it.

"So, tell me about Angela," I said.

He thought hard about this. "I found her," he replied.

"She got lost?"

"The paper keeps saying it. 'Angela Adams is missing.' But she's not, you're not. Found you," he sang, "found you found you found you. And she found me too."

More questions, the vague shapes of them, spread like a rash in my mind. I searched for something, anything, to say. "Hey, have I told you about where we're going, about J'ouvert?"

"Oh," he said. "No."

I began describing a fantastical version of the West Indian Day Parade, with floats that moved like clouds down the street, and music that caused you to dance as soon as you heard it. I said that there was food everywhere, any food you could think of, and that there were people like him, bird-people who had feathers and could fly.

The feeling of being there, I said, was the best in the world. Someone would always look out for you and take care of you and let you know you could do anything.

For a little while he got excited, and apparently Angela did too. But eventually he began to whine that they were hungry and thirsty and tired. I ignored his complaints. When it seemed late enough, long after midnight, we headed to Eastern Parkway. I'd convinced myself, even though it was just a thing I'd blurted out a few hours ago, that Pop actually had been at J'ouvert back when I was seven. I'd always known he must have had a good excuse to stay out that whole night. It was wrong for Ma to yell at him. I understood why his eyes were bleary when he came in to get me. He'd been out experiencing something even better than the parade itself, something I hadn't been ready for back then.

At the parkway, metal barriers lined the parade route, but there were no bursts of music, no floats, no smells of meat cooking on a grill, no crowd, no bird-people, hardly any people at all. We walked along the barriers and I felt more exhausted than I'd ever been. I had been sure this was where J'ouvert happened too.

"We're so hungry," Omari said.

I was already past that point, as if the part of the body that feels hunger had given up and just eaten itself. At the next bodega I used Mike's quarter to buy a bag of potato chips, and we walked on. Every once in a while, from behind me came a sudden rustling of the bag followed by an unsettling crunch. Otherwise it was so damn quiet and lonely. Even Omari and Angela had run out of things to say.

Finally I stopped an old woman clomping along in heavy boots, but I didn't know what to say to her. Omari used a wet finger to get at the potato chip dust in the corners of the bag, watching me, and then he asked her where we were supposed to go for J'ouvert. The old woman squinted at us and laughed, showing her missing teeth, then said in a heavy Haitian accent, "Grand Army Plaza."

When we got to the plaza there was already a crowd spilling from the steps of the Central Library. Each individual was faceless one moment, familiar the next. The faces I thought I knew, from school or our neighborhood, flitted from body to body or disappeared outright. There was a man who could have been Mike, and even a woman, not far from him, who could have been Ma. Almost anyone, it seemed, could have been there. A crush of voices rose with anticipation. Then came the soft rollicking peal of steel drums, faint strains in the distance. The people, odd and ragtag, wore their shabbiest clothes and held musical instruments that looked homemade, nothing like my memories of the crowd on Eastern Parkway. They were waiting for something. Or maybe this was all there was to it.

But then came the sound of a horn, several horns. On the street, raised pitchforks prodded and tickled the air. A cluster of people wielded them, yelling joyfully. They were blue—*blue people*. Faces and bodies streaked with the color. They hopped around behind a van, and as it began to move along the avenue, pulling a creaky metal skeleton of a trailer, full of fidgety musicians, they moved with it.

Following the loose organization of people ambling down Flatbush Avenue, we walked on the outside edge of the street alongside Prospect Park, but most threw themselves into the middle of things. They proceeded in a kind of squat dancing, a slow gallop, a low roving strut matched to the risen rhythms of steel drums and cowbells and the flourishes of horns. Groups rolled and surged within the mass, people wearing T-shirts in the same bright color, or gyrating women in mere strips of cloth, or men with bells around their waists and rhinestones patterned on their slacks, faces raised, questioning and answering in song. Or the arrangement might have been according to the flags waved high or worn as capes or printed on cloths tied onto the head and worn over the nose and mouth in the style of desperados. Many of the flags I recognized. Trinidad and Tobago, and Jamaica and Barbados and Haiti, and Puerto Rico and Cuba and the Dominican

Republic too, but there were many I didn't know. It was the full array of them that I loved.

In and out of various cones of illumination from streetlights and from lamps fixed to police generators, we moved and watched. There was a frayed quality to the procession. Many people had masks on, just as cheap-looking as Omari's. A wolf man wound his way around the slowest people. A fat Pocahontas stumbled ahead in a ratty fringed dress. A woman in a shower cap lifted one leg and then the other, displaying the flecks of glitter on her inner thighs. Plastic helmets made pyramids of people's heads. Someone on stilts, wearing a yellow coat and a top hat, three times the height of a normal man, hopped on one false leg before he longstepped his way ahead.

Our forward movement stopped all of a sudden and people danced and strutted in place. Women of every size, in the shortest shorts I'd ever seen, gyrated their hips alone or with other women or with men. We joined a circle of spectators that opened for a woman in a dirty blond wig. She had a large belly and sagging breasts that bounced as she humped the air. The circle broke for a shirtless muscular man pulling a chain with a second man on all fours at the end of it. They looked like twins, but the man on the ground had painted his face to look like a hound. He went right up to the big-bellied woman and put his nose in her crotch. She turned around and bent over and he stuck his hound's nose up there too. "It's okay," I said, as Pop would have. "It's okay. You can look."

As we pushed on down the avenue, more figures with pitchforks, devils oiled slickly black, rushed at us and began to fling paint or grease or powder or dye. They targeted us, the ones who lingered on the edge and observed, stirring and scattering us, splashing the liquids from crusted detergent bottles and roughly smearing the oil from their own skin. I held on to Cuffy's hat as if the devils were a wind, and as they whipped us blue and white and orange and black, and as breathing felt like drowning in color, they seemed to be saying, *There are no observers here.* As if to confirm this, an old woman, maybe the same Haitian we had seen earlier (could it be?), but now dressed like a French maid, started screaming, "Dance or go home!" She shouted it again, "Dance or go home," and then said it once more with grave seriousness as she looked me in the eye.

And then I was grabbed by it, pulled into it, twisted up in the songs and yells and laughter, and in the flatbed trailer ahead the drums glinted, and I was squatted low and driven to dancing. When the current stalled again a woman twice my size backed her tremendous ass into me and began to grind and bounce me with it. I laughed and groaned and fought to stay on my feet and tried to hold on to her waist as I had seen others do but my hands slid on her glazed flesh. When the mass spasmed and advanced again the big woman gave me a hard bump, a final toss of herself, and I fell and was jabbed by elbows and knees, but then people reached and caught me by the arm and neck and lifted me and urged me on. I laughed and danced under the sky's slowly paling light, squatting and rubbing and strutting past the impassive eyes of watching policemen until my thighs started to burn. Then I thought I saw Trip's jeering face bob past. My father's cap. It looked as though he was wearing it. I shoved my way past several people as I pursued him, keeping the orange and blue colors on his head in view, reaching with my toes to maintain contact with the ground. I struggled out of the barrier made by one trailer's music and plunged into the faster tempo of another's. Despite my best efforts, though, I couldn't reach him. Trip, if it was Trip, got farther away, became obscured in the crowd, and was gone.

At that point, I noticed my naked head. Another hat gone, my head exposed again for everyone to see. But I realized I didn't care. I didn't care that my haircut was bad, or that my feet hurt and thighs burned and empty stomach growled. My stature wasn't important. I didn't feel small. I felt the weariness in my eyes but I liked it, and I imagined I must have looked just like Pop when he was here years ago. Of course a man like him, who loved his body and loved to dance, had stayed out that night, and was willing to be screamed at by Ma, not just on the morning of that day but the many days that followed until the screaming and fighting drove him away. He was never the same after that, but even where he lay now, in some hard little room at Otisville, he must have held on to that night and to the feeling, now coursing through me, of being shamelessly alive. Who wouldn't give everything for that?

There was a sudden surge within the crowd that held me now, and then came a strange shout, a high sprung note. I spun around and people brushed past me with their cowbells and horns. I didn't see my brother. I ran up a little ways, in case he had gone on ahead. A sign said we were close to Empire Boulevard, which meant only that I didn't know where I was. I turned and went back, moving against and alongside the procession now, calling Omari's name. There was another shout, and I knew for sure this time it was his. In the crowd a rowdy group of masked men were whirling and shoving and yelling, throwing themselves around. Within this group, in the quarterlight, I spotted Omari's mask, the stunned circular eyes of the owl. He was being jostled about, was struggling to keep his footing, and he shouted again as he was swept in a direction he couldn't see.

I pushed my way back into the crowd toward him. I felt ready to fight these men if need be, but when I reached them they absorbed me like a churning pool of water. Hugged by their bodies, I saw their masks up close and the human features within them, the hysterical eyes and cackling mouths, and the distress of Omari's shouts was lost in the ecstasy of theirs. They were enjoying themselves. They didn't mean to be scaring him but they were; they didn't mean to be hurting him but they might have been. I grabbed the back of one man's neck and pulled myself closer to my brother, but then a hand reached up and yanked me down hard by my shoulder and I lost all sight of him. When I regained my balance, at first I didn't see him but then, moments later, I did. He had been spat out of the large wave of men to the edges of the crowd. He got to his feet and began to run. By the time I wrestled my way out and ran after him, he was already far ahead.

We were going back the way we had come. The procession gradually thinned, became a few stragglers, and then was gone. With a hand held out to the side, Omari gimped along, like there was something wrong with one of his legs, but he still moved fast. I called after him and he glanced back. He looked again and kept looking when I called a second time, as if to verify, as if he couldn't believe it was me chasing after him and saying his name. A moment later, he brought his hands up to his head and pulled off his mask. Then he held his free hand out again. He picked up speed now, like this was a game he wanted to keep going.

I ran after him in the predawn half-light with an ache in my stomach that was something other than hunger. The air was heating up. Pigeons were beginning to fly. The rough, thick shadows of trees began to emerge on either side of us.

Omari veered left. He looked back again, his features opening at the sight of me. He dropped his mask on the ground and then clambered over a section of sagging fence into Prospect Park.

When I got to the fence, I stopped to catch my breath and rested my hands on my knees. The sun had risen, and in the full light of day I looked down at the vacant eyes of the owl mask. It was smeared with powder and paint. My sneakers and socks and calves were also filthy, my shorts and shirt too. My entire body had been marked.

That Labor Day morning when Pop came home to Ma's anger, his eyes were bloodshot and he stank a little of sweat, but his clothes, I remembered, they weren't dirty at all. What did this mean? What could it mean? I didn't know exactly, but he must have been somewhere else. Pop was no observer, so he must have been someplace else. There must have been another reason. Ma's voice from that morning, years

ago, came to me. *Where were you?* she kept shouting. *Where were you?*
When I saw him again, if I did, I would make him tell me. But what
if this wasn't even the right question to ask?

I went over the fence and into the park. It didn't take very long to
find my brother. He was in the middle of a small clearing. He had his
arms extended in front of him and was spinning around and around
in the hazy morning light, another game. I caught glimpses of his face
as he spun. It had been so long since I'd seen his face. It was a shock to
see it, with his eyes again among its features. His cheeks and forehead
were blotched, but he looked happy, struck dumb with joy. From the
trees, where a faint wind fingered my scalp, I reached toward him and
waved but he didn't notice. He laughed without making a sound, still
spinning, arms out, hands folded as though grasping onto something.
It was Angela, I realized; his hands were holding hers. He kept spinning with her, around and around, faster and faster. I waited before
approaching them. I wanted to see if she would let him go.

I Happy Am

When Freddy became a robot, a special map appeared in his mind. It alerted him to obstacles and told him the fastest way from here to there. One morning, instead of waiting for the elevator, he flew down the dozen flights of stairs, careful to leap over a big puddle of urine on the landing of the fourth floor. Outside, he ducked through the hole in the busted playground's fence. In the alley behind the liquor store, a homeless woman with a shopping cart shuffled into his path. He closed his eyes and clenched his metal fists as he crashed into her. The woman's stink exploded like a bomb, but it couldn't harm him. As he sped past, she yelled a lot of bad words, an enemy wailing in defeat. St. Rita's Day Camp was only a few blocks away, but by the time he arrived it was already past nine o'clock.

The other kids in his group had boarded the van. Sister Pamela stood in front of the day camp, her back pressed against the gate of the squat building. Her habit, made of plain white cotton trimmed in blue stripes, fit perfectly around her pale sweating face. She narrowed her eyes at Freddy and bared her brownish teeth. She'd been making this face at him throughout the summer, whenever he was late, but as usual it wasn't his fault. His mother had forgotten to sign her name. It had taken a long time to wake her up so she could do it.

"Where's your permission slip?" Sister Pamela said.

For a moment he didn't know. He couldn't answer her.

She glanced down. "Just give it to me."

It was right there in his hand, folded in half and crumpled, see-through in one spot from the moisture of his palm. She pinched the slip by a dry corner, tugged at it until his fingers understood and stiffly opened. Previously Freddy had been a wizard, an angel, and a knight. Lately, whenever he felt nervous, it seemed best to imagine he was a robot. He liked the ones he watched on TV best.

Sister Pamela held the permission slip away from her and examined it for a long time. Earlier, at the apartment, Freddy's mother had gripped the pen in her trembling fist like a toddler with a crayon. She'd gazed up at him from the couch with her one awakened eye, disappointed again, it seemed, that he wasn't the person she dreamed about, whose name she murmured in her sleep. Her signature was worse than the one he'd begged her to make on the camp registration form months earlier, little more than a thick wandering line dragged off the edge of the page. The tip of the pen punctured the couch's plastic covering, near the other holes and burn marks from cigarettes. His mother asked him then to call her job, to say she wasn't feeling well and would be late again. But he hated her boss's grouchy voice asking all those questions, and there was no time to waste, so he didn't call. In such lonely moments Freddy wished he had a sibling, a younger brother he could conspire with or boss around, forcing on him every unpleasant task. He felt now as if Sister Pamela could see everything from earlier that morning, including his thoughts and feelings, right there on the permission slip.

"Well?" she said finally. "Get in the van."

There was an open seat next to Santos, because the other kids avoided him. They said he had bad breath, that the little rattail on his otherwise shorn head made him look dirty, but Freddy didn't agree. He liked the fuzzy nub of braided hair and even wanted one himself.

And he thought Santos's breath smelled good. It was richly sweet like the bruised peaches his mother sometimes got for free at C-Town, from the old man who said he was in love with her. Those peaches were so overripe they were almost liquid, syrupy in their skins.

Freddy was nine. He couldn't make sense of the way opinions suddenly changed about some kids. The opinions about Santos hadn't shifted—not yet at least—so there was no danger of losing his friend to other boys.

Santos began imitating Sister Pamela, making the same face he used when mocking Chinese people. Freddy laughed.

"What an old bitch," Santos said. He whispered because they were sitting near the front.

Freddy laughed again. "You can't talk that way about her."

"She's just a wrinkled-up raisin wrapped in a sheet."

He was being a friend when he made fun of her, but Freddy wanted to change the subject anyway. He didn't like it when Santos said such things. Before she got sick, Aunt Ava had been thinking about becoming a nun.

When the van pulled into the street, the twelve kids, all boys, clapped and cheered. Sister Pamela sat beside the driver, looking back when it got too loud or when one of the boys said a bad word.

"What do you think the pool will be like?" Freddy said. "And the house. And what will they make on the grill?"

"The food's *always* great," Santos said. "Burgers, hot dogs, whatever you want. There's even steak. You can get seconds, no problem. Thirds too."

His know-it-all tone annoyed Freddy, but he smiled anyway. He'd been looking forward to the trip, imagining it for many weeks. This was his first summer with the camp, his friend's third. The sisters of the Missionary of Charity ran St. Rita's, and a few times every summer they'd take a van out to the suburbs, in New Jersey or Connecticut or Westchester, where some friendly white people would welcome the city kids into their house. It must have been their way to feel closer to God, or at least to Mother Teresa. She had started the Missionary. Last summer she had come to visit the Bronx. Even Freddy's mother had gone to see her. It had been important for her to spot Mother Teresa with her own eyes, as if that would improve things for her younger sister, Ava.

"The house is great too," Santos said. "Really freaking big."

"How big?" Freddy said, though he had asked this question before.

Santos grinned. "Wait till you see. I know."

"Liar."

"Your mom."

Freddy sucked his teeth. "How could you know?"

"I *do* know. I heard Sister Spamela say we're going to Scarsdale. I've been there before," Santos said. "Twice," he added, holding two fingers up in Freddy's face. "If it's Scarsdale, it's the Johnsons' house. We always go there."

Freddy had pictured the Johnsons' house before, and now he imagined it in more detail. As the van made its way out of the city, he saw the house's open garage like the ones on TV. Inside, two cars were parked side by side, their hoods shiny in the sun. The lines of bushes leading him to the front door were shaped like animals: a squat baby elephant, two fat pigeons, and a panda lying on its back. The house was white, it was true, with blue shutters and roofing, but different kinds of white existed, and this one was special, like a patch of new snow. In the kitchen, half the size of Freddy's whole apartment, the refrigerator was silver, not brown; it stood tall and wide, and didn't make a sound. It was dizzying to go down to the basement, where the floors and walls were like gold, and back up to the first and then the second floor, where he peeked into the bedrooms, before going back down again to change into his bathing suit. The path out from the back door, made of weird pale stone, felt warm on the soles of his feet. To his right, the garden had almost every color he'd ever seen and the flowers nodded and shook from the movements of fat bugs. He and the other kids fit easily into the pool—it could have fit almost twice as many of them—and there was no need to worry or watch out when anyone jumped into the deep end or flew down the slide into the cool, clear water. At lunchtime, they all sat under an outdoor shelter, like a little house itself, and its roof and the trees protected them from the sun and from summer rain. They breathed in the smoke of meats grilled over charcoal. Then they ate tender slices of steak and laughed, and their laughter was even louder and more relaxed than the sounds they were making on the van as it sped away from the city. And through it all, Mrs. Johnson floated around them like a spirit, a gentler sort than he knew in his world, her hair gold like the walls of the basement, her face softened by a smile.

But the house they arrived at wasn't white and blue. The place was painted a dull yellowish-brown, the color of old ginger cookies. Santos cursed when the van stopped. Sister Pamela turned and gave him a harsh, but brief, look. She also seemed concerned about where they were. Freddy told himself not to worry. For a robot, there was no such thing as an unwanted surprise.

"This is it," the driver said, scratching underneath the brim of his cap. He showed Sister Pamela the address written on a piece of paper and then pointed with the same thick finger to the number on the door. "This is definitely the place where I drove the other Sister."

After a heavy breath, Sister Pamela told the boys to sit tight, then got out and shuffled between the ugly hedges toward the house. Before she got there, a woman emerged from behind the front door. Freddy knew right away that the woman couldn't be Mrs. Johnson, but he wasn't aware until she appeared that he had still been holding out hope.

Against the protests of the driver, the boys slid open the heavy door and poured out of the van. They stood in a group on the sidewalk, and Freddy moved away from everyone's groans and whispered complaints, closer to the house so he could hear what Sister Pamela and the woman were saying. The woman was black, no different from him. Her skin was the same dark shade as his. She didn't seem like a maid or anyone else who would work in a big house in the suburbs. She looked older than his mother, but healthier, and wore a dark floral-printed robe that went down only to the middle of her broad thighs. The straps of her pink sandals matched the little shocks of color on her nails. Her eyes hid behind a large pair of sunglasses, and whenever she raised and lowered her arm, thin silver bracelets shimmied down her wrist. Her shoulder-length hair had been set and curled in a fancy way. It shone like hair he had seen in TV commercials, much nicer than his mother's had looked in a long time. Otherwise she could have been one of his neighbors in the South Bronx, the kind of woman his mother, in her ugliest moments, would call a bitch and tell him to avoid. The only thing unusual to him about these women was the way they dressed, in clothes that looked very expensive. Whenever he saw one of them in the elevator, it seemed like a mistake. He wondered where they went all day in their nice clothes. He wanted to ask why they didn't know where they were.

Freddy got even closer to the house. "Ain't no mistake here, Sister," the woman said. She was loud like his neighbors too. In response, the comments of the boys behind him rose above whispering. Sister Pamela looked back at them sternly before she resumed the conversation, asking about the man of the house.

The woman nodded and said, "But he's away, on business. He goes away on business a lot."

Then Sister Pamela mentioned the Johnsons.

"Yeah, just like you say. Him and the Johnsons go to the same church."

"Your husband, you mean?" Sister Pamela said, her voice rising.

"What are you asking?" the woman cried. "Hey, I got religion *too*,

Sister!" She leaned to the side and stretched her neck to look at Freddy
and the others. "Anyway, these boys here," she said, "they might as
well be my own sons."

Before letting them inside, the woman lined up the boys shoulder
to shoulder and made them repeat their names until she could recite
each one. She paced in front of them, cooling her sweaty face with
a handheld fan, and got irritated at herself the few times she confused one boy for another. Freddy's hands began to stiffen like metal
when she stopped in front of him and stared through her dark glasses.
After a few moments she smiled and guessed his name correctly. "My
name is Arlene," she told the boys, "but if you want you could call me
Mrs. Clinksdale."

The inside of the house was like a bigger version of the apartment
where Freddy lived: couches covered in plastic, a bible on the coffee
table, a big wooden spoon and fork hung side by side on a kitchen
wall. In one way it was even worse: there was no TV. The boys took
turns with the bathroom on the first floor. As Freddy waited, Sister
Pamela stared at an image on the wall. He was the last to go in and
change his clothes. On the rim of the tub, he found bottles of the
same pink lotion his mother used to moisturize her hair.

Back in the living room he stood alone, fidgeting in his swim
trunks. He held his elbows tightly. He'd had similar feelings at home.
A few months ago, his mother had let in a maintenance man while he
sat watching cartoons, wearing only his loose Superman underwear.
She'd allowed him to walk right past and stare at Freddy's body. That
man had been the first visitor to set foot in the apartment in a long
time, and no one else had been there since.

The other boys were already out by the pool. With his telescope
vision, Freddy could see them through the sliding glass door. He felt
reluctant to join them and further ruin the picture he still held in his
mind, but he didn't like the sensation of having driven an hour from

home only to arrive at a bigger version of the same place. Before he went outside he told himself there was still a chance it could all turn out great.

But the pool was small, a plain rectangle of cloudy water, and it didn't have a slide or diving board. Several boys, in up to their chests, splashed each other or bobbed around, already shiny with play. Between the pool and the house, dingy umbrellas on rusted white poles shaded a few circular tables. Sister Pamela sat at one of them with her hand pressed to her mouth. She yelled for order once in a while but no one paid her much attention. Arlene stood behind her and smiled at the boys in the pool, a hand resting on the left hip of her avocado-shaped body. With her other hand, she fanned herself. She wore a sun hat now, also pink, and the fake-looking straw of the brim drooped over her face. As her head turned from boy to boy, her lips formed soundless words. Freddy had seen his mother do something like this as she wilted into sleep.

"All right, everybody," Arlene announced. "I'm about to get these burgers and dogs on the grill!"

"What?" a few boys said. They looked at each other in confusion and then fixed their pleading faces on Sister Pamela. It seemed this wasn't how things normally went.

"You know," Sister Pamela said, "we arrived at your home only a short while ago."

"My fault for not having the grub ready when y'all got here," Arlene said.

"But it's ten thirty, Mrs. Clinksdale. Not even that."

"Who you telling? I know. We get peckish around here if we don't have lunch by eleven. Have you seen how skinny these pups are? Look like they haven't had a decent meal in weeks. Can't have that, not in my house anyway."

She went into the house and brought out two pitchers of lemonade. Next came uncooked hot dogs and fat-laden patties of beef on an aluminum tray. A few yards from the two tables stood a small grill. It looked cheap and was hidden by a low-hanging tree branch and a tall growth of hairy-looking plants. Freddy got closer. The grill was electric, not charcoal like the ones he'd seen some white families using at Van Cortlandt Park. Arlene, humming with pleasure, began to cook, but the backyard didn't fill with the flavor of fragrant smoke. Freddy wasn't hungry at all, and he could tell the other boys weren't either.

Freddy hardly ate the sides of mustardy potato salad and microwaved kernels of frozen corn. He didn't even like steak, but felt disappointed that there wasn't any. The boys were done with their food before eleven thirty, but Arlene said they should wait an hour or else they'd get cramps. Sister Pamela pressed her lips together and then said she was certain that was a myth.

"Can't take chances," Arlene said. "Plus it's so hot out today."

"Is it?" Sister Pamela replied. "Last week was hot. It feels nice today."

"Says you. Anyway, can't take any chances with our children."

The boys remained around the tables for that hour, not even snacking from the bowls of greasy potato chips, afraid of extending their forced idle time. Aside from a few minutes of fun, they had been sitting the entire morning. Arlene hummed again as she cleaned up. Before she was done, she exhaled and began to mutter, asking herself where she had put her water bottle. As she looked around, her shaded eyes met Freddy's—he felt them lock onto his, felt her regarding him.

After the hour was up, most of the boys began playing again, but Freddy wasn't interested. He drank a glass of the tart lemonade and then walked around to the far edge of the pool, where he crouched and slid his hand into the water. It was lukewarm, like used bathwater, and smelled strongly of chlorine. Santos waded over, pushed himself up, and sat next to him. He lifted his goggles onto his forehead and slowly kicked underwater.

"This sucks," he said.

Freddy didn't want to admit it, but it was true.

"Those hot dogs? The worst."

"The burgers too. Everything."

"And the pool. The deep end don't even go past my chin. What kind of deep end is that?"

"Nothing's what it's supposed to be like."

"Sucks," Santos replied. He kicked faster, his feet breaking the water's skin.

"How did this even happen?"

Santos shrugged. "Don't ask me."

"You said it was a big white house. You said there was a slide and a garden and animals in the bushes."

"Animals? What are you even talking about?"

"You told me," Freddy said.

"I heard her say Scarsdale. Scarsdale always means the Johnsons."

Freddy glared. "Why'd I even listen to you?"

"Me? It's not my fault!"

"There probably isn't even a real Mrs. Johnson."

"There are a *million* Mrs. Johnsons," Santos said. "They only brought us here so *you* wouldn't get all excited and jumpy and piss yourself like a baby."

"Don't call me a baby."

"You *are* a baby. Your mother stopped raising you as soon as you were born. Everybody says so."

"Liar!"

"Call me a liar again," Santos dared.

Freddy curled his shaking hands into fists. They felt solid, heavy, and strong. "You're a liar and you smell like garbage and that's why nobody else ever hangs out with you."

Fear made him hit Santos then, as if this act would somehow erase the startling violence of his words. But smashing a fist into the side of

Santos's head didn't help the way Freddy had hoped. Instead he found himself tangled up with his friend, arms and legs knotted and flailing as they both fell into the pool. A rush of warm water poured into his mouth, and it tasted like bleach. His left knee scraped against the coarse pool wall. Santos elbowed him in the stomach and Freddy's eyes flew open to the murk of the water, ribboned with gray-green strands. Santos kicked wildly to right himself, forcing Freddy to inhale more water and open his eyes even wider so that he saw the shadow and substance of the other boys in the pool. When he felt other hands on him, he reached his toes for the bottom. His head broke the surface and he found himself gasping and spitting where he stood, with shouts swirling around him, his stung eyes attempting to blink away the world.

Arlene had pulled him from the pool. With a towel wrapped around her still-wet body, she listened as Sister Pamela scolded them, then interrupted and ordered the boys to shake hands. Santos seemed sincere when he said sorry, but Freddy didn't even make eye contact while muttering his apology. He didn't so much shake the offered hand as nudge it away. "Well, forget you then!" Santos yelled. Arlene got upset. She started to scold them much worse than Sister Pamela had, then stopped and touched her face. She shook her head slowly and mumbled that she was feeling dizzy. After a moment she said, "Maybe I should lie down for a while," and went inside the house.

Sister Pamela said the boys' punishment was to sit for the rest of the afternoon, at two different tables, and watch the others at play. She perched herself on a chair between them to prevent any more fighting. When Sister Pamela wasn't looking, Santos caught Freddy's attention and silently imitated an ugly sobbing child. His eyes weren't red, but Freddy could feel that his own were. He drank more lemonade, kept his gaze fixed on the sweating glass as the crescents of ice within it melted.

What Santos had said about Freddy's mother wasn't true. She'd been good at raising him once, at least as good as the white mothers he saw on TV, the ones who made steak for dinner on Friday nights. When he was a smaller boy, she taught him that the world was a huge bear, but that you could beat it if you imagined you were bigger than you really were. She would tell him you could always do more than you thought you could, and she lived that way, finding money to pay for things they needed when it appeared impossible, helping distant cousins and aunts, and even neighbors sometimes, when it seemed she wouldn't even be able to provide for the two of them. But that was before Ava, his mother's sister and only real friend, got so sick.

As the boys played tag in the pool, Freddy picked an old scab on his knee. After considering what would be best now—maybe the wizard or the angel—he imagined again that he was a robot. Robots didn't cry or feel lonely. It didn't matter at all to them if a pool had a slide or a diving board, or if a disappointing lady served overcooked burgers instead of steak. Robots didn't care about the difference between a Mrs. Johnson and a Mrs. Clinksdale, and they didn't care when their friends told lies. They didn't feel achy chests or sick stomachs, and for them, sitting all afternoon next to Sister Pamela wasn't a punishment. It was just a fact.

When Freddy's mother told him Aunt Ava probably wouldn't get better, that this was one of life's meanest bears, she hadn't yet lost her attitude about being strong in the world. She kept Freddy away from Aunt Ava, getting someone to watch him while she made her visits to Newark. Before leaving and when she returned she said hopeful things about her sister that Freddy found confusing, given what had to be true. Since she said them so often, he asked, and then begged, to go visit as well. She gave in and brought him along one day, less than two months before the funeral would be held. When they arrived he was scared by how thin Aunt Ava was, by the shadows and hollows that had replaced the fleshy sections of her face. Freddy's mother looked scared too, as if this face and this body weren't at all the ones she had seen the previous time. Her complaints to the doctors and nurses went ignored, so all she could do was hold her sister's hand and direct the force of her attention there, slowly rotating the rings now loose on Ava's fingers. That visit, in that room, would form the first of Freddy's many memories of his mother crying, shaking as if very cold, and during the train ride back to the city he kept waiting for her to re-shape her lips into a smile.

Freddy intended to sit by the pool until it was time to change clothes and leave, but he had to use the bathroom. He kept telling himself that robots didn't have to use the toilet, didn't have to worry about hold-ing it in. Still, the feeling got worse. Unable to endure it any longer, he stood and said he had to go. As he walked toward the house, Sister Pamela watched him with hard eyes, her face taut with frustration, but she didn't try to stop him. Instead she tried to quiet Santos, who was laughing at Freddy, and then she shouted at some boy misbehaving in the pool. No one paid any attention to her.

Santos's laughter followed Freddy into the house. When he came out of the bathroom he explored the first floor. He searched for any-thing interesting, something he could show Santos to make him jeal-ous, or make him beg to be friends again. He tried a door that might have led to the basement but it was locked.

Above the couch in the living room hung the image Sister Pamela had been looking at earlier. It was a framed painting of a brown-skinned man with thick dark hair and a full beard. A faint light en-circled his face, and he gazed gently skyward. It took several moments before Freddy realized that it was supposed to be a painting of Jesus. This was mysterious. He'd seen plenty of these images—one hung in the hallway of his apartment—but never a Jesus who wasn't white. He looked behind him, and felt both relieved and sad when no one was there. He didn't want to be caught, but he also didn't want to be the only witness to what he was seeing.

Outside, Sister Pamela was still shouting at the boys to listen to her. Freddy stood at the foot of the carpeted staircase. Was a black Jesus different from the other kind? Was he easier to talk to? What kind of person would even have a black Jesus? What else did she have? From where he stood, it appeared very dark upstairs, even though it was daytime.

In the cartoons and movies, robots could see through walls and across long distances or sense a body by its heat or detect the smallest thing that was wrong. Freddy tried to open himself in this way, as he did when his mother locked herself in her room or stayed out at night a lot later than she said she would. He made a map of what surrounded him: Santos laughing and Sister Pamela yelling out by the tables, the other boys getting wild in the pool, the basement behind the locked door, the mysteries upstairs. He listened for the glass door sliding in its track and for Sister Pamela calling his name, but heard only the continuing shouts and laughter. Then came something from upstairs, a small and familiar sound, a cough that was also a moan, a tiny cry.

He thought about ignoring it, as he did with such sounds at home, and was close to just going back out by the pool. But what was the big deal? He was already in trouble. Who knew what would happen when his mother found out about the fight? If she cared, she might not sign the permission slip next time. She might not allow him to go back to St. Rita's at all. The map in his mind told him there was some danger upstairs, but he wanted to be brave, not afraid and always wondering about what he hadn't done. He put one foot on the first carpeted stair and was surprised how easy it was then to go up the rest of the way.

Freddy crept into a room that made him gasp. It had no furniture and was painted in two clashing colors. The right side was a delicate yellow, with an image of a tall white tree on one wall. White paper flowers hung from the branches or fell from them in a pretty pattern. Leaning against this wall was a long, narrow cardboard box, unopened and unmarked. The left side of the room was painted pale green, and it had words in curvy white letters:

> *What shall I call thee?*
> *I happy am*
> *Joy is my name*

He kept coming back to that second line. He used to make dumb mistakes like that when he was younger, misspelling words or writing them out of order. His mother would help him with his homework back then, correcting his errors before he got to school, but she didn't do that anymore. Since Aunt Ava's passing she looked at his notebook the way she looked at everything, including her own reflection, including him: with dead eyes, as though she was tired—bone-tired, as she liked to say—and what was left in the world simply had to wait. So now when Freddy got to school, he sometimes embarrassed himself.

He stared at the two walls for a while and tried to set his mind free to play in the room. He expected the words to rearrange themselves or something amazing to leap from the image of the tree. Nothing happened. It all remained still. He walked around the room, sensing something invisible. But there was only a creepy sensation, like feathers all over his body.

He peeked into the next room. In it, Arlene was lying on a bed, already facing him in the doorway.

"Come on," she said. "No monsters in here, nothing evil. Just me." Her voice was more soft but less steady than before. "It's Freddy, right?"

He nodded and took shy steps into the dim, curtained light. Her head rested on a mass of pillows, her hands folded below her chest. She wore the same clothes as earlier, aside from a pair of loose khaki shorts, and her feet were bare. Her dark glasses lay beside the lamp on the night table. He hadn't seen her eyes before now. One was opened a bit more than the other.

"Have you calmed yourself down yet?" she said.

Freddy nodded.

"You're a good boy, aren't you?"

He studied the floor, still feeling the feathers from the other room on his skin. He didn't know if he was good.

"You like snooping around in people's houses?"

Freddy shook his head.

"At least tell me what you think of it."

He thought about what he should say. "It's fine."

Laughing, she held herself as though she might break into pieces. Sit at the foot of the bed, she told him, and he did. "Tell the truth now, child. Would you want to live here?"

"Mrs. Clinksdale, I—"

"Arlene."

"I already have a place," he said. "We all do."

"Oh, I know *that*. But if you and your family could trade—"

"It's just me and my mom."

"Okay. How about if you and your mama could trade for just a little while, like a week, would you?"

Freddy shrugged. "It's a nice neighborhood, right?"

"Not the very best, but it's nice, yeah."

"Do the Johnsons live here?"

"Close enough," she said.

"I heard they have a real nice house. I heard they're real good people."

Arlene smiled and slowly nodded, like she was saying, *Well, all right then* to a spurt of pain. "They do have a lovely home," she told him.

"I'd trade for that," he said.

She grimaced. "But Freddy, you ain't even been there."

He shrugged again. "I don't know." At first he wasn't sure how else to reply, but then he said, "I don't want to live in the ghetto no more. Ghetto people live in the ghetto."

Arlene's eyes widened until they were the same size, then went back to normal. She made a face like she was thinking hard. "Come here," she told him.

He stood closer to the head of the bed.

"The Johnsons . . . Well, they have these pictures up in their parlor, shots of all the groups from camps like St. Rita's who have been up to visit and use their pool over the years. So many boys—brown boys, like you—just smiling all big and giving the thumbs-up, every one of them, like they were told to." She gave a thumbs-up herself. "The pictures are in these fancy wood frames and hung right beside the plaques and trophies and awards. The Johnsons show these pictures to all their guests. Did you know that?"

"That sounds nice, Mrs. Clinksdale—"

"My name's Arlene."

Freddy frowned.

"What're you thinking, child?"

He asked the simplest question he had. "What's a parlor?"

Arlene laughed again and wriggled her toes. "Shoot, what *is* a parlor?" she said. "A room where you keep all the stuff you're mad to show off to certain people, I guess. Something this house don't have."

On the night table, faceup next to her glasses, lay a photograph in a plastic frame. Arlene was in it, a bit younger and thinner. She smiled in the arms of a man with a mustache, a white man. Was this Mr. Clinksdale? He was handsome and tall, like the men Freddy's mother had liked to watch on soap operas, but this man held himself in an odd way, so that only the very top part of his body made contact with Arlene's.

"Don't worry," Freddy said, "you'll get a parlor one day." This was the kind of thing his mother used to say to quiet him as he dozed off at bedtime.

Arlene's smile was similar to the one in the photograph. "I'm forty-one years old," she said, as though talking to herself, or to someone who wasn't Freddy. "Forty-one. There's things I used to want and just don't no more, even some of the things I have now. There's other things I want with all my heart, and if I don't get them soon I never will."

Then she parted her robe, fully exposing her shorts and the top of her bathing suit. Between them rose the little round of her belly. It was slightly larger than the paunch his mother had developed since she started staying out late, but it sat differently on Arlene. Seeing it and the parts of her body not covered by her shorts and bathing suit made Freddy aware of his own near-nakedness. He wanted to leave, but he wanted to stay too.

"You don't think my baby will like this house?"

"It's a *baby*?" Freddy said.

"Of course it is, silly. Fifteen weeks of one anyway. Never made it this far before."

"Is it a boy? Or a girl?"

"You know," Arlene said, "I was thinking girl all the way this time, but just before you came in here I decided it could be nice to have a little boy too. But not if he's gonna be fighting like you and Santos. Not if he can't forgive and mean it when he says sorry. He's gotta act right and do better."

Freddy tilted his head downward.

"I'll admit it though. I got plenty of boy names running through my mind."

He stared at her belly. "Is that man your husband?" he asked.

Arlene looked at the framed photo on the table as though it was something she had forgotten to put away. "He's a person who takes care of me. Or used to. I don't think he wants to anymore." She seemed to be talking to someone else again.

Freddy was still staring at her belly. He wanted to hide his fists between his knees, but he couldn't move.

"Why don't you touch it," Arlene said.

"What—?"

"Go ahead."

"I can't."

"Sure you can," she said. "I read somewhere it's good luck. Need a lot of luck in this terrible world. Could be there's some kind of way it works the opposite too. A little luck for you and maybe some for me. Me and my baby. Here, give me your hands."

Freddy's hands were so tightly clenched they trembled and ached. He got closer, hesitating at first, but then gave them to her. In her hands his fell open, and then she turned them over and placed his palms on her belly. It was softer than he'd expected, and warmer.

"Well, what do you think?" she said.

He wasn't sure what she meant. All he could think about was his mother lying half-awake on the couch, telling him and the old man with peaches and the rest of the world to wait.

"What do you think it is?" she asked. "You tell me. Boy or girl?"

He stared at her belly once more, but it didn't reveal anything to him.

"Boy or a girl?" she asked again, and the question seemed to echo from her, from the bed, and out from the room.

Freddy's imagination could turn him into an angel or a wizard or a knight. Through it, he could become a robot, one that created maps he used to protect himself. The robot also knew what was happening and what would happen next. It was quiet outside now, by the pool. Sister Pamela was in the house below them, calling his name. At any moment she would decide to come upstairs. She would peer in the first room and not find him. He would hear her approaching, and when he looked up at her startled eyes and brown teeth, his hands, by a shared choice, would still be open on the curve of this woman's belly.

But it wasn't Freddy's imagination to which Arlene spoke, and which continued to fire with every passing moment of contact with her skin. She spoke instead to what his imagination guarded. It was lost in thoughts and feelings about mothers and babies and parlors and the dark brown face of Jesus, and could only begin to make sense of them. This part of him, not yet grown, didn't know the answer to her question, or to any questions that hid behind her question, and so it didn't know how to reply. It did know that this, what was happening, was a thing he might never forget, but for now it could hardly speak.

Everything the Mouth Eats

I've started this story many times and deleted the pages many times. The reasons aren't a mystery. I keep seeing the face of my brother, to the exclusion of anything else, and I keep getting lost. But perhaps there's no other way it can be written. The face of my brother, which resembles my face much more than I've ever been willing to admit, in many ways *is* the story. Also, if I'm going to be honest, I have to confess from the outset that I've always been terribly lost. I want to tell this story, and I want to tell it honestly.

The trip to the capoeira event that morning, years ago now, should have taken less than an hour, but somehow I ended up driving us west of Arlington and I messed up again near Springfield. My brother, Carlos, sat in the back with baby Rosa. His girlfriend, Sulay, beside me in the passenger seat, was growing increasingly baffled. Her hazel eyes waxed full, mouth opening and closing as she reluctantly surrendered to the strict silence Carlos and I had sealed into the space of the car. She probably felt every single effort we had made, to first create the germ of silence and then to cultivate it, conspiring to be cruel to each other.

We drove in their beat-up black Honda. Energy bar wrappers, water bottles, juice boxes, and flat orange peels were strewn all over.

The red corner of a children's book and a library copy of *In Our Time* peeked out from the gap between the passenger seat and the console box. Next to Carlos, three pairs of unlaced sneakers had been tossed on top of a pile of folded pants and T-shirts. On the rear deck behind his head sat musical instruments, or parts of them: three painted *cabaças*, some *caxixis*, and a few coils of unused *arame*. The strong sweet and sour odor of a small child, an odor Carlos and Sulay probably didn't notice anymore, infected the car's cooled air. Beneath this hung the stale, heavy smell of cigarettes.

When I'd insisted on driving, Carlos had immediately announced he would sit in the back with their daughter. I had claimed I knew the DC area and could get us from there to Prince William Forest Park in Virginia. This on the basis of trips I'd been making from New York down to Northeast to see a girl I couldn't bring myself to love. But I'm a terrible driver. I get especially nervous on highways. Something seems apocalyptic about them. It's difficult to see other people clearly in their cars, and the speed of it all recalls the desperation of escape. I'm awful at figuring out when to change lanes. The deceptive monotony gets to me, and the arrows point all over the damn place. My eyes dart from mirror to mirror, and I end up misreading signs or not seeing them at all.

I somehow failed to get us onto the interstate, and Sulay couldn't contain herself any longer. She turned to Carlos and her face asked him for help, but none was forthcoming. Despite her harried appearance, Sulay sounded calm when she turned back and spoke to me in her lilting voice. "Eric, are you sure you don't want one of us to drive?"

I shook my head stiffly, slicing the air twice with my chin. My grip on the steering wheel tightened as Carlos, whom I had seen grinning in the rearview mirror since we left their apartment in Takoma Park, seemed to decide on his line of attack. For a moment, our gazes met.

"You know 95 is pretty big, don't you?" he said, not to me but to Sulay. "One of the longest interstates in the country, if I'm remembering right. Main artery of the East Coast. But I'm not telling you anything you don't already know."

He had lifted one hand from the car seat to carve shapes in the air—a conductor of his own voice—and then settled it somewhere near his chin. The tip of his finger played in the patch of fuzzy hair under his bottom lip. His other hand was agitated in his pocket, jangling keys and coins as Rosa sneezed herself awake.

"Your uncle is just like me," he said to his daughter. "Got those fat, juicy veins in his arms. A doctor's dream. But every once in a while you get one of those who doesn't know what he's doing, and he stabs your arm all to hell trying to draw blood. Meanwhile there's a fat, juicy vein sitting *right there*."

"What are you talking about?" Sulay asked.

Carlos gave a short laugh. "I swear, one time I nearly grabbed the damn needle and stuck it in myself. No lie." The rhythmic ring of metal in his pocket had stopped. "Life is hard enough," he said. "It pains me— it physically hurts—when people fuck up what's easy and obvious."

I inhaled deeply to stay calm and then smiled at Sulay. "So," I said, "he's still smoking, huh?"

Carlos winked at her. "Babe, tell my brother it's actually been months. No, no, tell him this: it just takes a long time for old stink to go away."

I hadn't had a talk—a real talk—with my brother in many years. Maybe we'd never had one. In any case, I wasn't sure either of us even knew how. The truth was, I didn't really want to talk to him, but I felt guilty, or duty-bound to our mother. So on this trip I kept trying to persuade myself that I would try.

The only way Carlos and I were going to speak to each other right now was to argue. Since I didn't want to start a full-on argument in the car, I didn't ask Sulay about his drinking or his search for a steadier job. The relatively "good" terms of our relationship were a new and tenuous development. Surely he felt as much as I did the strain of

proceeding—word by word, gesture by gesture—with so much deli-
cacy. We'd been rebuilding things slowly, ever since I'd found out
from our mother that he'd been, essentially, homeless. Going to the
capoeira conference together was a part of that rebuilding. I was trying to show that my interest in him and in the things that mattered
to him was real. Also—and I never would have admitted this until
now—I wanted to understand how the hell he, with all his troubles,
had ended up with a woman like Sulay.

Since we'd started talking again, Carlos would go on and on about
what he called his "blessings," which he said had saved his life. At first
there were two, Sulay and capoeira angola; Rosa became the third. He
would go on and on, and the repetition was something he could rely
on in the strangeness of our attempts to communicate. One day, over
tea in a chilly Dupont Circle café, when I was tired of him repeating himself, I stared at Sulay—I'd been staring at her all afternoon—
and asked about capoeira. I knew a little about it. I worked as an
adjunct literature professor in downtown Manhattan and had seen
a circle of people doing capoeira in Union Square Park, or, rather, I
had seen other people crowded around the people doing it. Amid the
clamor of Fourteenth Street traffic, the pedestrian multitudes, and
the constant noise of my own thoughts, came the half-heard music—
wah-wah sounds interspersed with vague buzzing and high-toned flut-
ters. My question was for Sulay but my brother was the one who spoke.

"First of all," he'd said, "you don't *do* capoeira; you *play* capoeira.
And you live it." He started talking about African martial art traditions
and enslaved Africans in Brazil, the development of the form there, and
its spread to the United States and other countries. He talked, more
rapidly now, about music and rituals and perspective. After mention-
ing "antagonistic cooperation," a phrase I associated with the writer
Ralph Ellison, he went on to philosophize about what it meant "to see
the world upside down." He wasn't answering the question, he was
lecturing.

"Just tell me what the hell it is," I said.

He reached over to Sulay and held one of her blue-mittened hands. *"A capoeira é tudo que a boca come,"* he said, to her, and then became quiet. His silence then was supposed be as profound as the one he settled into now in the black Honda, after successfully having the last word. It would be a relief to finally arrive and escape the space of the car, which felt increasingly small with every passing mile.

Carlos and I refer to each other as brothers, but technically we're half-brothers. I was born to our mother in Fayetteville, North Carolina, and he was born in New York City. Our mother met the man who would become my stepfather, Carlos's father, in Brooklyn, when she was struggling and unhappy with her job at Montgomery Ward. He was a career counselor then, and in those days, though I find it hard to believe, he treated my mother with great kindness. She says he gave her sound advice, but, more important, he took an interest in her beyond her employment, an interest that alleviated her loneliness. Soon enough they were seeing each other, and then we were leaving Brooklyn for the Bronx to move in with him. My own father is a man I have no memory or evidence of.

The first clear images I have of my stepfather are from the day we moved, when I was four. He lived near the top of a housing project in the South Bronx, in the same apartment where he had grown up. I gawked at the sheer size and formidable brick of the building, and of the buildings that stood around it, throwing down enormous shadows everywhere, and so he too became impressive. He was an overweight but striking Puerto Rican man, with large hands, light skin, and wide, active eyes. With his thick black horseshoe mustache, he was trying to approximate or even surpass Willie Colón, whose face would appear again and again if you flipped through the sleeves of his record collection. I was so impressed, which is to say frightened—by these buildings, by this man, by this new scale of being—that I peed my pants, just as we were about to board the elevator that would take us up to our home.

The projects seemed full of frightened, nervous people like me, because the elevator always smelled of urine. Sometimes you could see where the splashes had gathered into a puddle, and you would ride up or down with your back pressed against the elevator wall, pretending the fresh puddle wasn't there, pretending that some frightened, nervous person, someone you knew or saw everyday, hadn't recently been in that elevator relieving himself.

When it wasn't broken, that elevator took us to and from our home, on the tenth floor, for over ten years. In the first of those years, my mother became pregnant with my brother. I don't remember anything about his birth or his first appearance in our apartment, but I do remember feeling vaguely indignant that I would no longer be an only child. I also remember that Carlos was a fussy baby, not allowing anyone but our mother to hold him, though later, with no effort or enthusiasm on my part, he suddenly warmed up to me. One of his first words, frequently yelled from his crib, was "Ba-dee," the nonsensical pet name he had invented for me. There was something antic and skittish about him, however, so I didn't feel whatever connection I was supposed to. It was from observing him, who was conceived in that tenth-floor apartment and breathed much of his first air from that elevator into his tiny lungs, that I came up with my theory about what the projects could make of people.

Rain from two days earlier had pulled a sweet musk from the soil that seemed trapped below the forest canopy of yellow poplar and Virginia pine. Carlos and Sulay had voiced their worries about bad weather interfering with the conference, but sunny days were in the forecast. It was less humid than it had been earlier in the week, and the clouds had completely spent themselves during Tuesday's cool rain. Carlos started grabbing our things from the car. Holding Rosa in her arm, Sulay stood in her camouflage pants, leaning on one leg. She pointed a brown finger up at a stand of red maple and then, below it, on the other side of the car, she showed her daughter Solomon's seal, a flowering dogwood, and sassafras. Sulay's mouth seemed to caress every syllable. Rosa pointed in wild imitation of her mother and squealed with laughter.

I started to walk off, down a path beneath the maples, but Sulay called after me. I was going the wrong way. We followed the line of parked cars for a while until the high singing of a lone *berimbau* filled the air and a sign appeared for Camp 5, nicknamed "Happyland." A few yards past this sign hung a yellow banner with black letters: 6TH ANNUAL INTERNATIONAL CAPOEIRA ANGOLA ENCOUNTER. Above the letters was a simple but elegant picture of a man and a woman facing each other while standing on their heads. After Sulay informed me that she had painted the picture, Carlos kissed the corner of her pouting mouth, which seemed ready to pronounce the names of more trees.

We came to a clearing where people milled around a cabin camp. The berimbau player sat with a few other people on the steps of the largest cabin. In the stretch of grass before them stood a woman pulling lengths of wire for arame from the inside rim of a tire. Without a word, Sulay pressed Rosa into my arms, leaving the camphorous scent of her own hair with me as well. She ran into the grass and smacked the woman's bottom. After shrieks of recognition and greeting, the two embraced with a long, tight hug and then stood apart to regard each other, holding hands like schoolgirls about to skip around. Abruptly, with a smile still playing on her face, the other woman pulled Sulay in toward her and tried to butt her with her head. Sulay slipped her hands from the woman's grasp and her body went soft, boneless, and she evaded the *cabeçada* by melting into a low defensive posture. In a way, she became a part of the strike, pulling herself through and ahead of it in the same sleeve of motion. Without getting hit, she appeared to absorb the attack's energy and dissolve herself perfectly into its time.

The berimbau player on the steps began to play at a faster tempo, with complicated variations, and another man accompanied him with the tapping and slapping of a *pandeiro*. The two women danced in front of each other as they pivoted counterclockwise, feinted with implied sweeps and kicks, and spun on the heels or balls of their feet, smiling and laughing the entire time. Sulay moved sinuously, like a slick eel swimming through water, and stood tall with her elbows close to her waist as she shifted around. By contrast, the woman's dance, her *ginga*, remained consistently low, vigorous, and angular, with heavier footfalls and jabs of elbows and shoulders that declared the power of her thicker body. They went through a series of attacks, evasions, and counterattacks, observing the rule that only hands, head, or feet ever touch the ground. The attacks—spinning kicks and straight kicks— became more intelligent and forceful, many appearing from pockets of just-vacated air. After a particularly fluid and flexible sequence, they both executed slow, achingly beautiful cartwheels. This, holding the inversion, became another kind of contest within the game, so they both settled into steady handstands, Sulay with one leg unbent, pointed skyward, and the other wrapped prettily around it, the other woman with her knees tucked into her chest. They tilted their heads and grinned at each other, comfortable as though on their feet, waiting to see who would lose her balance first.

As always when observing capoeira, I could concentrate on only one player at a time. The experience resembles reading a poem with clever line breaks and complicated syntax: my sense of the dynamic between two players corrects itself retrospectively, deferred until a second or two after the surprise of a noteworthy exchange. Sulay calmly lowered herself into a headstand and then let her legs fall behind her, slowly arcing into a back bridge. I was blind to what the other woman was doing then, and with Rosa starting to fuss in my arms, I missed the end of their impromptu game. Carlos glanced over and heckled me with a laugh. When I set Rosa down, she tottered over to him and grasped the knobs of his knees. And then Sulay was with them, soaked with sweat, shoulders heaving as she breathed, her face like burnished wood. My brother lifted Rosa onto his hip, and Sulay wiped the sweat from her forehead onto his cheek.

Carlos's father had a game he liked to play, especially during the time our mother was taking evening classes in accounting, when we, the two boys, were alone with him. He began it as soon as Carlos could talk. He would take one of us onto his lap and say, *"De quien tú eres?"* We quickly learned that the correct answer was "Daddy," but the speed of our learning was less important than the speed of our response, and we could never respond quickly enough. As soon as he asked the question—even if it seemed that the answer came right away, even if the answer interrupted the question—he would begin relentlessly tickling whichever boy was sitting on him. Countless times, his thick fingers would clamp onto my narrow rib cage, and no matter how many times I screamed the word *Daddy*, I would be left gasping and nearly crying. Carlos was also a subject of this regime of laughter and filial affection, yelling and thrashing until he slid from his father's lap and shared with me the mercy of finally making it down to the floor. Afterward we would often be forced to massage his feet. He'd be on the couch and we'd still be on the floor, each of us with a bare foot. I remember the sour smell, the hard skin on his sole and under his big toe.

We were only slightly menaced by this game; if he came home from work and sent us trembling to the floor, then it meant he was in a good mood. On such evenings, he might also play some of his pop records. With this music blasting out of the speakers, he would dance, his brow knitted, his bottom lip sucked into his mouth, spinning and sliding in his thin dress socks. I would join in mostly by jumping up and down.

Carlos moved with more grace and sophistication. He understood his limbs and his hips, and he understood time. Even then he was a skilled and intelligent dancer.

At that point, Carlos's father was working as an officer with the Department of Probation. Once, when my brother and I were out of school for some odd holiday, my stepfather took us to work with him for the first time. The building where he worked, in lower Manhattan, down on Centre Street, was imposing and severe, a place that supposedly handled matters of justice but which nevertheless looked merely like a prison. The three of us went through a metal detector and rode an elevator to one of the highest floors. It was morning, but my brother and I were allowed to get potato chips, red licorice, and soda from the vending machines. As we made our way down the hall, Carlos's father had us peek into certain offices and cubicles so he could show us off to his coworkers. After we got to his office, a middle-aged white woman with a long neck and her hair in a tight bun came in to chat.

She pointed to my brother and said, "Oh my god, is this your son?"

"They both are."

"Well, this one looks just like you—the same smile, the wavy hair . . . Look at his adorable baby fat!"

"These are my boys," he said.

"But this tall guy, he isn't your biological, right?"

He looked at her then in that familiar way, his eyelids parted as far as they could go, the orbs themselves seeming to have moved a full inch out of their sockets. She appeared to be the sort of person who walked around the office saying things she shouldn't say. If he'd had the proper authority, he might have fired her on the spot. Instead, he stood behind me and put a strong hand on each of my shoulders.

"Yes, he is," he told her calmly. "They both are, like I said."

Everyone in that room, except maybe Carlos, who was very young—though even he may have sensed it—knew this was a ridiculous statement. My stepfather's colleagues had to be at least somewhat familiar with the basic facts of his home life. Also, I looked nothing like him, and at the time, I looked nothing like Carlos. His hair was curlier and softer, mine lighter by a few shades; only later would a few similarities of nose and cheek from our mother become apparent. It was possible, and less absurd, that I had been grabbed off the corner of Centre Street for the purpose of an office gag. The woman pinched her mouth shut and then went out the door, leaving us alone in the room with my stepfather's lie.

"You *are* my son," he said, not gently. "You know that, right?" The look on his face wasn't very different from the one he had given the woman, and his voice was a double voice. I heard the unmistakable command in the lower one, so I nodded. He sat down in the chair next to his desk and made Carlos and me stand together before him. A distance from my brother opened suddenly, as if each of the years between our births were a tract of desert now stretched between us.

"De quien tú eres?" he asked us. There was no threat of tickling this time, which somehow made things worse.

"Daddy," we said.

People, mostly men, sat on the steps of the big cabin, where we would all eat our meals at Happyland. People kept busy inside, carrying kitchen items and hanging decorations and signs from the exposed beams. The berimbau player was a middle-aged Brazilian, his hair stippled with gray and cut in an outdated flattop. He smiled often but still looked malicious. He turned out to be a famous *mestre* I had seen in photographs and videos, a capoeira angola teacher lauded for his mastery of the form's movement, music, history, and philosophy. The people sitting with him, other mestres and teachers, spoke in lilting Portuguese, a teasing song directed at Carlos and Sulay. I couldn't comprehend most of what they said but detected something almost flirtatious in it, a longing heard in the way their mouths massaged the vowels. Most of the attention focused on Sulay, maybe praising her for the beauty of the game she had just played, or for her own beauty, restored and even augmented so soon after pregnancy. They praised the beauty of Rosa, shy behind my brother's legs, as well. From the way a couple of the men stroked their chins, it was obvious they were poking fun at Carlos's beard. He'd been growing it out, and it was patchy and unkempt on his face.

After recognizing the famous mestre, I muttered his name to myself in surprise. Carlos glanced at me and chuckled. He stroked his own chin and then introduced me to the mestre, speaking slowly in Portuguese. I caught the first words. He said that I was his "*irmão de Nova Iorque*" and that I had been "*treinando na capoeira angola por um ano, mais ou menos.*" But then the pace of his speech quickened and he kept gesturing at me, with a conniving look on his face.

The mestre seemed bemused. He turned his flat, brown face at me, sizing me up, as Carlos spoke. With an expression almost like a sneer he shook my hand and held on to it as he said, "*Você quer jogar comigo, rapaz? Hm? Eu acho que pode acontecer.*"

The other people sitting on the step hooted and snapped their fingers, waiting for me to respond. I understood what my brother had done. It was an impossible situation. Neither yes nor no was the right answer, so I said nothing. I just shook his hand again and smiled.

A year earlier, I'd started taking capoeira classes in Harlem, with an old, shrunken Brazilian nicknamed Big John. I was drawn to the art's historical and philosophical elements, and I wanted a dynamic form of exercise to counter all the hours spent immobile at my writing desk. I supposed it would also give Carlos and me something in common to talk about, but we hardly talked about it. While the training was hard on me, it was much easier than exchanging words with my brother. Not long after I first started, I was in the men's dressing area one evening after a strenuous class. The movements had been full of twist-

ing backbends and headstands that made me dizzy. I had changed
out of our white uniform and was bending, slowly, to tie my shoes.
In the hair of time it took me to blink, there was an extended foot
an inch away from my face. The foot belonged to a longtime student,
a Rastafarian from Jamaica whose long, thick locks of hair filled an
immense tam. He stood over me and pointed to his eye. "You gotta
watch," he said, "or else you get a foot in your mouth." In most con-
texts this would have been cause for a fight, but on that same evening,
after we dressed, the Rasta offered to treat me to a vegetarian dinner.
En route to the restaurant, he scolded the way I walked and shared a
bit of our mestre's wisdom. "Slow down," he told me, "stay alert, make
wider turns on the sidewalk. You never know what could be around
the corner."

Part of entering the world of capoeira angola is a constant training in vigilance, and not just during the actual playing of the game.
Feints and trickery are generalized into a capoeira player's worldview
such that they are revealed to be an unavoidable part of the texture of
life itself. I realize now how strange it is to exist otherwise, especially
in a big city, and I marvel at people rushing, rushing, headlong into
things, how full of trust they are, how they can't see what often lurks
behind the floating vapor of a smile. But isn't the family the first arena
of such knowledge? Isn't it family that, in so many ways, determines
our approach to life's deceptions?

After Carlos's father insisted in his office that he was my father too, I
warped my laughter into screams whenever he tickled me. I no longer
looked him in the face when I answered, "Daddy."

In addition to taking evening classes, our mother had also started
a day job, which meant that I had to walk Carlos to and from our
nearby school and babysit him until an adult got home. In those un-
supervised hours after school, we never had much to say to each other.
We played, however, and I began to play rough with him. Back then

we watched professional wrestling on television, and it was easy to persuade him to let me try out the moves. When we played this way, I always took on the role of the villain, the heel. I'd pick him up and slam his body onto our dingy couch, bend his spine against my knee, apply various choke holds, pretend to smash his head into the wall. We both knew that pro wrestling was fake, at times barely on the threshold of convincing physicality, and we played in the same spirit. This usually extinguished the aggression that flared within me.

One day, when I was in eighth grade and Carlos was in third, we wrestled for a long time, until I had him in a choke hold called "the sleeper." I was behind him with one arm wrapped around his neck and the other cradling the side of his head. This was routine for us. I would pretend to squeeze his windpipe and he would pretend to gasp for breath, swinging his arms stiffly in the air until he feigned unconsciousness. But this time all I saw in my mind was my bicep. Carlos flailed as I kept flexing it, and I was fascinated by the way a part of my body could be hardened into stone. Even when his weight sagged against me and he stopped flailing, I kept on with the routine, now acting as the referee. I let him slump against the front of the couch, then lifted his arm by the wrist and let it drop. I lifted it again and it dropped, and he fell onto his side. If his arm dropped a third time it would mean I had put him to sleep and that I had won the match. But I never won this way. Carlos had never let his arm drop a third time. He'd hold it in the air to signal consciousness and his eyes would pop open, and then he would go on the attack. That afternoon, however, his arm did drop a third time.

I raised my fists in victory and stomped around the living room, jeering at the imaginary crowd that surrounded us as my brother lay on the floor. Full of uncaged power, I laughed and pointed at him to show the crowd how weak their hero was. I planted my foot on his hip and raised my fists again, but when he didn't move I began to get scared. His fingers were curled like shriveled leaves, and one of his legs was bent at an unnatural angle. I nudged him with my foot. Was he breathing? I squatted beside his heaped body and began to shake him. Tears ran down to my nostrils and my jaw. "Carlos, I'm sorry, please wake up," I kept saying. "Carlos, wake up. I'm sorry. Please wake up. I'm so sorry."

When he finally woke up, his squinting eyes blinked with confusion. Maybe it was because he realized what had happened or because he saw my tears, but he started crying too. He held his arms out toward me, but I backed away, afraid. In this moment how could either of us think touch was a good thing? I wiped my cheeks. "Why didn't you breathe?" I said. "You're not supposed to stop breathing. Why didn't you say something?" He kept nodding, accepting the blame as he cried. "But you can't tell," I said. "Carlos, you can't tell what happened. We'll get in trouble. We *both* will. We'll get a beating, so you can't tell."

Carlos never did tell on me. He was convinced that I had saved us from a beating, and he may have even thought I had saved his life. In gratitude, he built a little religion and installed me as its godhead. This went beyond a younger sibling's normal admiration for his elder. In a way, I had once again become "Ba-dee," the alpha of his first and most private language. He was so single-minded in his devotion that, thereafter, when his father tickled him and asked, *"De quien tú eres?"* it was a shock that he didn't respond by naming me.

He seemed especially eager to show his love for me at school. We attended the parish school of our neighborhood's main church. It was a three-story building made of red brick and trimmed with sandstone, next to the rectory. The sixth, seventh, and eighth grades used classrooms on the first floor, and the younger students were upstairs. Once we got to school, there was no reason for Carlos and me to see each other until it was time for dismissal, but he found ways. He knew the grades on the first floor switched classrooms between periods, so he started to sneak downstairs, bathroom pass in hand, in order to say hi to me in the hall. It was funny in the beginning, and, indirectly, I won a bit of attention from the girls. "Oh, your little brother is so *cute*," they'd say, but in their minds his cuteness had nothing whatsoever to do with the big brother. The gap-toothed smiles and hugs and devotional dances he improvised made the girls no more likely to peel back their mysteries for me.

I was a good student, and would go on to became salutatorian. Mr. Taylor, my favorite teacher, called me "exceptional" and said I was "blessed with talent." He told me constantly that I had a bright future, that I was one of the lucky ones who would get out of the South Bronx and make something of myself. In spite of this, I had decided that the true purpose of eighth grade, my last year at the school, was to figure out girls. Most of them had begun to roll up the waists of their plaid skirts, and nothing any teacher said in class, even Mr. Taylor, could be as interesting as the legs of a fourteen-year-old girl. In Taylor's math class, what my friends and I enumerated on any given day were the newly exposed inches of blooming thigh. We especially loved Ms. Nelson's English class. She had us sit in a circular formation, so we were able to look directly across at Evelyn Martinez, who, as far as we were concerned, was already a woman. The girls weren't always careful about crossing their legs, so sometimes we would catch a flash of underwear, or pretend that we had. Darius would convulse in his seat whenever he claimed to see something, as though the effect of such a glimpse were a blast of electric current. Sheldon couldn't contain his laughter. Ms. Nelson caught on to the fact that we were up to no good, so she kept a closer eye on us. She must have shared her suspicions with the other teachers. They became more vigilant with us in their classes too. We came up with other ways to satisfy our curiosity, but without the safety of our classrooms, we had to deal with Carlos, my annoying shadow.

The school's cafeteria was in the basement. We figured out that it would be easy to get our blasts of electricity if we lingered at the back of the eighth-grade line after lunch while the girls proceeded to the first-floor landing. We got to enjoy these lightning storms for a few days before Carlos, with his shirttails untucked, ran over to us from his seat at the raucous third-grade table. He'd seen me peering up at the girls and giggling, tugging at my clip-on necktie, so he peered up into their skirts too. His initial look of bafflement gave way and he laughed as though he had heard the world's funniest joke. It was an ugly and gratuitous laugh, and it made him look like a small, frightening clown with a painted-on mouth. I dragged him by the arm back into the cafeteria and told him he had to stay with his class.

"Be good," I said, too rattled to think of anything else.

I don't have children, and at this point I doubt I ever will. But I have a brother, and there are enough years and other distances between us for me to understand the vanity of saying those two words to anyone, especially a small child. To this day, I can clearly see the expression of near pity on his face.

Carlos and Sulay wanted to assist with the final preparations for the conference—setting up the registration table, getting the instruments ready, bringing crates of food and bottles of water to the kitchen. It was determined that Rosa and I would just get in the way, and the people who would run childcare for the conference hadn't arrived yet. Sulay had insisted her daughter would warm up to me, but it appeared this might never be the case. All my attempts to get Rosa to play with me by the campfire circle failed. Despite my efforts, she whined and whined for her parents until I gave up and brought her back to the big cabin. She was such a shrill annoyance to everyone there that one of the mestres, a dreadlocked Brazilian with a high, scratchy voice, got fed up. He rested his hands high on his narrow waist and, in broken English, told all four of us to just go away for a while. Two hours remained before the opening ceremony.

A creek ran not far from the camp, and we decided to take our swimsuits and wade in it. The hike was brief and easy. Midafternoon sunlight shot through the leaves of the forest canopy and spilled like tossed clutches of coins along the ground. Flutelike cries, *ee-oh-lay*, rang through the air. Rosa eyed me warily over Sulay's shoulder as Carlos and I followed them on the trail. To our left came sounds of rustling in the briers.

"I hope there aren't any snakes here," I said.

Carlos snorted. "The snakes he needs to worry about are back at the camp. Hope big brother's been training hard."

I had taken classes a little more frequently in the three weeks leading up to the conference, but I'd found they taxed my mind more than my body. Capoeira angola remained a puzzle to me, no matter what, and when I played the game, I tended to think my way through it. A *jogo* can be played slowly, especially in the opening minutes, but not always. I preferred the slow game, found it beautiful and chesslike. The sweet agony of controlled and unhurried movement appealed to me. When I played in a game that started to speed up, I got flustered. I couldn't *think* quickly enough. Snakes of any kind would be an issue.

Quantico Creek was a narrow sheet wrinkling in the breeze. Reflections of the trees danced in its shimmer. Farther along, the water quickened and frothed white over rocks; near us it fed into a still pool. Sulay treated this visit to the stream pool as though she were at her favorite beach in Leme. As soon as we reached the south bank, she set Rosa down and was out of her clothes in a snap. Sulay stretched her long arms upward, then back, and made some futile adjustments to the scanty bottom of her suit. In a moment, Rosa was also in her bathing suit, back in her mother's arms, and the two made their way into the water. Carlos stripped down to a pair of tiny swim trunks, which Sulay must have chosen for him. Even though mine were much longer and looser, I removed only my shirt and shoes. I sat in my jeans at a reasonable distance from Carlos, both of us perched on a circular formation of warm, smooth rock, our feet pointing toward its center.

"Porra!" Sulay yelled. She proceeded more gingerly into the pool, taking lighter steps on the gravels. The water came to her hips now, and Rosa's toes skimming across its surface made splashes and spray. Carlos and I watched without speaking. A band of sunlight traced a white line along Sulay's cheek and shone on her head of gathered curls, reddening them, blanching the loose, trembling strands and the wisps at her nape. She waved to us and convinced Rosa to do the same. Carlos, on my right, watched me now, with a strained look on his face.

"So what's happening with that girl in Northeast?" he asked. It had taken him a lot of effort to ask.

"She has a sad face," I said.

"I think she's pretty. At least she was the *one* day you let me get a look at her."

"I just can't stand her sad-ass face anymore."

"And here I thought you were gonna dedicate your damn novel to her."

"It's not even like that."

"But she loves you," he teased, "doesn't she?"

I ran my thumbnail along a groove in the rock. "Women fall in love too easily."

His laughter, a loud shot, silenced the nearby songbirds and sent them darting from the branches and leaf litter. They filled the sky with yellow flight. "I don't think the easy part is what bothers you," he said.

Upstream, a mysterious shape moved with the current. The creature—or was it a shadow?—slid near Sulay, who was squatting to dip herself and Rosa up to the shoulders. She came up laughing with the girl. Her clavicles were bare in her strapless suit and they made fine shallows that each held a little teaspoon of water.

I pointed downstream. "Think the lake is that way," I said.

My brother's eyes bored into me. "Nope. This way's the Potomac. Lake's the other way." For a while, we were quiet again as mother and daughter communicated in Portuguese and gibberish. Then he said, "So how about it? What happening with what's-her-name—Millie, right? Big brother's not getting any younger."

"What kind of name is Mildred anyway?" I said. "*Mildred*. Who the hell would give a newborn baby a name like that? Just out of the womb and already someone's ugly grandmother."

"That girl is not ugly. She seems nice, and sensible, like she knows what's what. You *were* hauling your ass down to DC every few weeks to see her. You definitely weren't coming to see me."

"Nobody knew where you were."

"Nobody cared," he said.

"Come on. Mom tracked you down."

"Oh, we're doing this? Okay. You're right, Mom cared," he said, his voice a little louder now. "But you know how she is, light as a feather. Sometimes things get to where you need care to come down hard. Sometimes shit gets so bad, hard is all you feel."

I didn't respond and he allowed our silence to linger. The sun was over the lake now, pulling bits of green and amber to the surface of the water.

"Hey," he said abruptly, "remember that time we got into trouble at St. Francis? I know you do. Man"—he laughed—"that's one of my most vivid memories, but I didn't understand a thing about it until later. Girls, sex . . . But I didn't *really* understand it until a lot later."

"Understand what?"

"Well, how angry you were. How angry we both were. Remember?"

"Guess I blocked it out," I said.

"What? No way, Eric. How could you forget that?" A bittersweet smile played on his face. "This is gonna sound crazy, but I think that's the closest I ever felt to you. You initiated me, buddy."

The sky, in that moment, resembled an open, waiting mouth.

"You remember. You have to," my brother said, his voice full of excitement. "Come on, help me out with the details. Who was the one—?"

"Why you gotta talk about old shit?" I said. We watched each other for a moment.

"Don't yell at me, man," he said.

"I'm not yelling. I'm just saying. We're here, right? I'm here with you now, *right*? I don't want to talk about Millie or St. Francis or the Bronx. None of it. Let's just enjoy this."

He shook his head and stood. His body had become muscular, I noticed, his skin glowing with health. He waved at Sulay and Rosa, who were returning now. Sulay again took careful steps, dragging the length of her body out of the water, which pulled the bottom of her suit down slightly along her hips. Her belly was marked by Rosa's birth, and at this moment a strange expression marked her face.

"Eric," Carlos said. He glared down at me. "You see that woman there—my wife, my daughter's mother? Yeah, I know you do. You might not be able to tell though, 'cause she's got that nice smile and looks the way she does in that suit. Got those pretty eyes and that hair, the accent, a name that makes your mouth feel good saying it. But don't get it twisted. That woman's as solid as that rock your ass is sitting on. She knocks me upside my head the way I need her to, know what I mean? She loves me hard, but she loves me."

He seemed like he wanted to say more, or maybe he was waiting for me to reply. I didn't say a word. He squinted up into the sun and shook his head again, then walked until his feet were in the water, his arms held open for his family.

How would my brother tell the story I'm about to tell? What words would he use? Why was he so excited that afternoon by the creek? What he said wasn't true, or was it? But how could that have been the time he felt closest to me?

The end of my last year at St. Francis approached, and for my friends and me, the sap, as they say, began to rise. All of us had troubles of some kind at home, or claimed to, so we stayed out after school as much as we could. We'd go to the corner store after our last class and get boxes of Ferrara Pan candy. We'd walk around eating it and talking about what next year would be like. Darius, Sheldon, and I were all going to different high schools.

Our madness for girls intensified, but we couldn't talk freely about them because Carlos was always there with us. It was easier for us on warm, clear days. We'd stomp over to the playground by PS 49 and send him off to the monkey bars or the slide. One afternoon, however, Carlos wouldn't leave us alone. He kept making unreasonable requests. Finally, when I promised to go with him on the seesaw later, he let us be.

My friends and I discussed the girls at school whose panties we had seen that day, or wanted to see again. This went on for a while until I announced I was tired of just looking. It wasn't good enough anymore. I wanted more. I told them about an incident that had happened the other day.

At school there was always a big show at dismissal time. Since the oldest students had class on the first floor, we were the first ones to gather at the entrance to the school, where the principal stood grinning at us. The younger kids pressed in behind us or crowded into the stairwell. The principal would wait until it got quiet and then she'd say, "Good afternoon, St. Francis!" We'd reply, "Good afternoon, Sister," and then she and the vice-principal would open the doors. It wasn't unusual for us to jockey for position to be the very first ones out. I explained to my friends that as I worked my way through the crowd, the back of my hand accidently, or so I said, had rubbed along the back of Kayla Valentine's skirt. At first they called me a liar, but I insisted that I had touched her. Showing the hand I did it with seemed to convince them. When Sheldon asked what it felt like, I smirked at him. "Soft," I said. "Like heaven."

They both wanted to do what I had done, and I wanted to do it again too. So for over three weeks it became our everyday routine before the school doors opened to worm our way through the crowd and touch girls with the backs of our hands. All we could talk about was the thrill of dragging our knuckles along those skirts. When we gathered on the benches in the PS 49 playground after school, each of us bragged about which girls we had gotten, especially the prettiest ones, the ones who ignored us. Sometimes we planned targets for the next day. Carlos was always with us, observing everything, but it no longer mattered to me. I wanted to get even bolder.

"I'm gonna palm one," I said. "Get me a handful."

In response, my friends told me I was crazy, and that I was going to get caught. "Chill," Sheldon added. "Your brother."

But I didn't care. I'd grown lax about shielding Carlos from our "grown-up" talk. Glancing at him, I said, "He's so pressed to be around me, I'ma let him. He's gonna hear what he's gonna hear. See what he's gonna see. You won't say nothing—right, peanut?"

I had decided Beth would be next. Beth was a grown woman, one of the kindergarten assistants, whose daughter was a second grader in the school. She wore the tightest pants we had ever seen, and her body reminded us of the exaggerated drawings of heroines in comic books. To us, she far exceeded the skinny white girls on the covers of magazines. She was at the apex of our adolescent desires. We dreamed of her, claimed her in our fantasies. At my urging, Sheldon and Darius promised they'd go through with it too. Tomorrow was a Friday, and I insisted it had to happen then. I didn't want to go into the weekend without having done it. My desire felt violent, like a fury.

After dismissal the next day, the three of us, followed by Carlos, raced down the front stairs and hung out by the school gates. Beth came down the stairs, swaying her broad hips as usual. She stood on the sidewalk talking to some of the kindergarteners and looking around, probably for her daughter. The crowd was a little sparse but I still went right away, before I lost my nerve. As I approached, I commanded my hand not to shake. I slid my palm against the seat of her jeans and, as I did, a fuzzy sensation glided along the entire length of my own body. After several more steps, I turned around with a big grin, but then my face fell. Beth gripped Carlos by the arm, almost shaking him, and she pointed at me and yelled. Darius and Sheldon were nowhere to be seen.

Carlos and I were brought to the principal's office. Mr. Taylor and the vice-principal sat across from us, black men facing black boys. Mr. Taylor never lost his cool, but when I looked up at him from underneath my brows, he seemed to be trembling. He told me I was a good kid, *exceptional*, one of the best he had ever taught, and so he was deeply disappointed in me. Didn't I know I had a responsibility to be an example to my brother? Helplessly, he said he knew my body was going through changes and my hormones were raging. When he asked if I understood why what I did was wrong, I nodded. The vice-principal knelt in front of Carlos and sternly reminded him that you never ever touch anyone's private parts. My brother started to cry.

They brought Beth in so we could apologize to her, but it was clear she didn't even want to look at us. I didn't want to look at her either. When she left, Mr. Taylor and the vice-principal talked about calling our parents. Mr. Taylor sighed and said he'd better be the one to do it. "Eric's had math with me for three years now. I know their folks pretty well. I'll call this evening and break the news."

I would get the worst beating of my life for this. I'd probably be on punishment for months. And the thought that Mr. Taylor would be the one to deliver this message made it even worse. On the walk home, Carlos kept glancing up at me. He took my hand when we crossed streets, but mine, shaking, stayed limp. Neither of us said anything until we got to our building. In the elevator, which, as usual, smelled of urine, Carlos said, "We're gonna get pow-pow?" He hadn't stopped calling it that.

He had calmed down some by the time anyone got home. We sat around looking sad and silently ate our dinner. When asked what was wrong, neither of us said anything. We wanted to delay our fate as long as possible. We kept expecting the phone to ring, waiting until evening turned into night. But Mr. Taylor didn't call that evening or any other evening. At school on Monday, during homeroom, he gave me a curt nod. Nothing more was ever said about the incident. I don't know why he didn't call, or maybe I just don't want to think about it. I was so grateful at the time—we, Carlos and I, both were—even though it wasn't the right thing for him to do.

I notice how many times I've just used the word *we* in what I've just written, and I wonder if the frequency of that word somehow indicates the closeness that Carlos talked about that afternoon by Quantico Creek. I don't know. What I do know is that the story I've just told isn't the only story; it isn't the real story that needs to be told. I try to imagine it. I'm trying to understand.

Around this time, before my brother and I got in trouble at school, our mother began taking the last of her evening classes. They were on Mondays, Wednesdays, and Fridays, and on those days, Carlos's father would get home from work, exhausted, and he'd go straight back to their bedroom. Carlos and I would have our homework done by then, and we'd play video games or watch television in the living room. After a while, Carlos's father would call me, just me, and I'd go back to the bedroom.

The man would be lying supine on the bed in his underwear and he'd tell the boy to close the door. It would always start with his feet, the boy massaging them, the man correcting the boy. When the boy was doing it the way the man wanted, he'd tell him. That's good, he'd say, like that. Your brother's not strong enough yet, he'd say. So you have to take care of the family, you have to take care of your old dad. *De quien tú eres?* he'd ask. (Daddy, the boy would say.) The meaning of feet is work, he'd say. That's why they're like that. Hard. Use your nails, use your knuckles. Good, now higher. Be careful with the bones, the ankles and the shins. Be careful with the kneecaps. Rotate them, gently, gently. Good. Higher. The man would often fall asleep when the boy's touch reached his thighs. Or the man, still awake, would tell the boy to come up to his face. Feel my face, boy, he'd say. Feel that? That's the face of someone who's been stepped on by life. The human head gets hit every day, he'd say, whether you realize it or not. Put your fingers at my temples and press. There, good. Now your thumbs, put them lightly, lightly, on my eyelids. Circles, make circles, he'd say. You feel my eyeballs underneath? Are they hot? That's because of all the shit they see everyday. Make little circles, good. Very good. *De quien tú eres?* (Daddy.) You'd better believe it. God, do you feel the knot in my shoulder? Press down with your thumb. Yes, good. Your mother, she used to do this, but now she's never home, he'd say. You might be stronger than her anyway, son. Let me see your muscles. That's good. Okay, lower. *Coño*, be careful with the hair on my chest. That's better. A man's shoulders and chest are the things that say wimp or warrior. A man who can puff his chest out and draw his shoulders back will win half his fights before a single punch is thrown, he'd say. And you have to suck your belly in. Not as easy for me these days. Don't worry, just grab a handful of that belly. It won't hurt, don't worry. Good, now grab another handful. Keep going. You'll earn your belly in this life, and if you're lucky you'll have a woman who's around to rub it for you. Good, that's good. *De quien tú eres?* (Daddy.) Sometimes this was when the man fell asleep, mumbling words about the woman while the boy's hands were kneading the fat of his belly. The man always talked about the woman, and it may have been that the boy's trembling hands reminded him of the woman's trembling. It may have been that the boy's face reminded him of the woman's face, and if the man were still awake and opened his eyes, he would see her questioning face in the boy's, the constant *why* that seemed to churn the man's guts. The man didn't believe in *why*;

he believed only in *yes*. The woman's mouth used to ask *why* of her circumstances, but the man said things to the woman and saw to it that her mouth asked no more questions. Only her face asked now, and the boy's face did too. When the man beat the boy, when he beat both boys, it may have been that he was beating them with the mother's questions pounding in his head, churning his guts. But it seemed he couldn't beat her questions out of the boy; they were on his face, in his eyes, and the man would feel the insistence of *yes* welling up inside of him. So on the evening when the man stayed awake and felt the boy's trembling fingers on him and saw the boy's questioning eyes and the sky dimming in the window, his guts churned and churned, and he kept saying *higher* and *lower*, the words edged with threat, and there was the restrained swelling and the unrestrained tears and then the spillage of *yes*.

I didn't see much of Carlos or Sulay on the first full day of the conference. He seemed to be avoiding me since we'd returned from Quantico Creek, but it could have just been that there were so many people. We were also divided into groups according to level. I stayed in the classes for beginners, while he and Sulay were with the advanced students.

Up to that point, I had never been through a more strenuous exercise, and I had never taken a class with live music. There is always music in a capoeira class, but in Harlem we used CDs. The teachers here made us stay in a low defensive posture called *negativa*, holding our bodies just above the floor until our arms shook. We crouched and jumped up and down like frogs until our thighs burned. We did ginga, the base of capoeira, the shift, the dance, the sway, for what felt like forever. To make matters worse, at the same time we also had to sing along to the music, which throbbed at us from the *bateria*. I'd have to catch my breath, but the mestre who had been playing berimbau when we arrived at the camp would get in my face if I stopped moving or singing. "When you go to the disco," he yelled in English, "you can dance all night, hm? You don't get tired there. Dance! Listen to the music! Relax your body! Dance! Sing!"

By the end of our training that Friday morning, my shirt was completely soaked through and my limbs were noodles. I couldn't imagine what Carlos and Sulay had done in the advanced class. I didn't see them at lunch either. During that time, the students from the group hosting the conference held a meeting. After lunch there was a *bate-papo*, a chance for us to listen to the wisdom of the mestres. They kept bringing up the words of Mestre Pastinha, the father and patron saint of capoeira angola, our most important ancestor. The words were the same ones that my brother had said to me almost two years earlier: *A capoeira é tudo que a boca come.* I didn't understand what the words meant, even after translating them into English. I still puzzle over them now.

After music class and the afternoon movement class, I was spent and sore. I lifted my fork slowly to my face at dinner, avoiding conversation with anyone, and then skipped that night's *roda*, the capoeira circle, and went to sleep in my cabin. When I woke up Saturday morning, my body had stiffened and every one of my cells seemed lit by small, intense flames. I contemplated leaving the conference as I stood under the spray of the shower. At breakfast, I stared at my plate for a long time; it felt as though someone would have to feed me. The room was buzzing with conversations in English and Portuguese. Near the end of the mealtime, Sulay set down her tray and sat across from me.

"Carlos is outside getting the instruments ready for morning classes," she said. "If you're looking for him."

"Fuck these classes. I'm dead."

"You were not at the roda last night."

"Fuck the roda," I said. "This place is a cult."

"Come on," she urged. "You come all the way here for the weekend. *Mais forte*, Eric. Stop being such a punk."

I took a bite of melon and chewed it deliberately as she watched me.

"You come all the way here to see your brother, to play capoeira," she said, singing in her accent. "One day and you give up?"

"I've got nothing to prove here," I said, glaring at her.

Sulay squeaked, incredulous. "*Wrong*," she said, dragging out the word. "You do have to prove it."

I exhaled heavily. "Quit the nagging, okay? You're getting on my damn nerves."

Her mouth tightened. After a moment she said, "See that guy over there, in the red shirt? He's from Chicago. He comes to see Carlos and to train, and sometimes we go there. We cook and eat together. We talk after we put our babies to sleep. The guy next to him is from Philadelphia. Same thing. They are his brothers. That guy there, in the yellow shirt? He's from Baltimore. When Carlos was having his difficulties he would come in to watch the roda in DC. The door is open at our *academia*. That guy from Baltimore noticed him, went over and talked to him. He helped him. He taught Carlos his first ginga. He took him in, his *irmão*. He helped him. *We* helped him. This is capoeira. We took him in because we knew he was *família*, and look at him now."

I glanced around the room as if my brother were there. "Sulay," I said, and then fell silent. There were flecks of steel in her eyes. Carlos had had lots of trouble, at times nearly violent trouble, with women. He hadn't treated them well. He hadn't treated himself well. But he was with this woman now and he wasn't the same person. "What the hell do you want me to do?" I said.

She rose with her tray even though she hadn't eaten a single bite. "Be his brother. You have to prove, Eric. The cost is big."

I have a memory of something our mother said that always gets mixed up in my mind. There are two possibilities of when she said it. One is from our time in the South Bronx, and the other is from when she called some fifteen years later to tell me Carlos was in DC, and that he was in trouble.

The night in the South Bronx, my mother and I sat at the kitchen table as Carlos slept. He had started causing problems at school. His teacher reported that he was being inappropriate with girls, hitting them and touching them. I thought my mother wanted to talk to me about that.

She had yet to separate from Carlos's father, but he was visiting relatives in Puerto Rico, so that night it was just the three of us in the apartment. I'd been so angry lately, because of my stepfather, because of the awful things he did and made me do when he called me back to the bedroom. Earlier that day, I had argued with Carlos, who was twelve at the time. I told him he was going to grow up to be a fat, useless, perverted bastard, just like his father. He had already gained a lot of weight and was becoming self-conscious about it. My words seemed to hurt him even more than I had intended, and I had intended to hurt him a great deal.

My mother took off her glasses now and looked at me. She was tired, with dark patches under her eyes and unkempt hair. The pads of her glasses left indentations on both sides of her nose. "You can't talk to family that way," she said.

"He was bothering me," I told her. "He's always up my ass."

"You watch your language, boy. And I don't mean that curse word that just came out of your mouth. You can't say things like that to your brother."

"He's not even my brother. He's only my *half*-brother."

She struck me in the mouth. I was used to being hit—beatings were happening more and more often recently—but this was the first time my mother had hit me since I was a small child. With her hand to her cheek, she stood and walked over to the window near the sink. Then she opened a kitchen drawer and took out a knife. She placed it on the table in front of me.

"Which half?" she said. "Take this and go into that bedroom and show me which half you claim."

I wanted to laugh at her getting all Old Testament with me, but I didn't. She had never looked at me so hard. I didn't know whether she would hit me again or collapse into tears.

"Ain't no half, Eric. Are you out of your mind? Half? You go on in this life fixed on half and you'll end up with nothing."

I stared at the blade of the knife until she started to speak again.

"I had a brother," she said. "You know your aunties, but you don't know about Junior. That's what we called him. He was named after your grandfather, Henderson. When I was born he was already a teenager. Junior always did whatever he wanted to. No one in the family could tell him nothing. It seemed like he was always leaving. He left the house, left the town, and then left the country. He went off to Vietnam and it seemed to be that he never came back. He did though. He did come back, but we didn't have any hands or eyes on him. We didn't reach out. It wouldn't have been easy to find him, but that's an excuse. We didn't look. We didn't even call his name." She shook her head. "Junior died almost a decade ago in Jacksonville, Florida. Didn't find out until last year. My brother, dead and gone with no ceremony, in a place where I never even knew he'd been."

Next in my memory come the words she may not have said until the later time, or it may have been that she said some version of them to me both times.

"Keep your eyes on your brother," she said. "You might see terrible things—you *will* see terrible things—but you can't look away. Stay close. He's got to know that you're watching out for him."

But I didn't stay close. I refused to. My mother wanted me to attend college in New York, and Carlos did too. She said I was a man now and that the family needed me, that my brother needed me, but I didn't apply to even one school in the city. After all, I was "exceptional." I had an opportunity to get out and there was no way I wasn't going to take it. I applied to places in the South and on the West Coast, as far away as I could think to go. When schools in California started sending letters of admission, I was as good as gone. It didn't matter which of them I went to. Every acceptance, every distant *yes*, confirmed my sense of my fate.

By then, my stepfather was at his worst. He was still calling me back to the bedroom when our mother wasn't around, even more frequently, and he had begun calling Carlos back to the room too. I knew this, but I didn't care. I was so ashamed and angry, so desperate to save myself, I didn't think twice about leaving my mother and brother behind.

I left the dining hall not long after Sulay did, but I didn't go to any classes that day. I returned to Quantico Creek and managed to find the exact spot where Carlos and I had talked two days earlier. From that rocky place I headed east along the water toward the Potomac. I walked about three miles toward the eastern edge of the park, and made it to the visitor center. I considered leaving the park entirely, hitching a ride with some strangers, but I just sat outside the center, for a very long time. When the sun started to go down, I began walking again. I got turned around a few times, but I found my way back to Happyland. It was a shock that I didn't get lost forever.

By the time I arrived, all the classes were over and the bateria was playing for that night's roda. I was exhausted from all the walking and sore from the previous day's classes. My first impulse was to just go to bed, but I headed in the direction of the music. It was coming from the big cabin that served as our dining hall. I went inside and stood by the door. The tables had been cleared away to make room for the circle of people, and the sounds of the berimbaus leaped under the roof. A single voice was raised in song:

> *Deus que me deu, Deus que me dá*
> *Capoeira de angola pra nós vadiar*

The chorus, everyone else in the circle, responded, "*Deus que me deu, Deus que me dá*," and then the back and forth continued:

Tudo o que eu tenho é deus quem me da

Deus que me deu, Deus que me dá

Na roda da capoeira eu quero jogar

Deus que me deu, Deus que me dá

Carlos was playing, and from his clothes and his sweat it appeared he had been at it for a long while. I had never actually seen him play capoeira. Though he had a large, strong body, he was incredibly fluid and flexible. I remembered when he was a little boy and would dance to please me.

The man Carlos played with was overmatched. Everywhere he tried to go, my brother was there. He was telling the man, *I know this place; I've already had that thought; no, there's a better way.* He showed the man all of his vulnerabilities, just with the placement of a foot, a beautifully timed sweep to put him gently on the floor, letting him know that it isn't such a horrible thing to fall down. There was pure joy on my brother's face, but I could also see that he was full of mischief and that he could be cruel—spinning slowly into an easily evaded kick, and then spinning immediately into the kick again with much greater speed, stopping his foot just short of the man's stunned face. As the people in the circle murmured and whistled in admiration of the implied strike, he mouthed some words and seemed to be arguing with himself. It became obvious that he'd had a desire, just barely contained, to go ahead and hit the other man. Making full contact with that kick would have deeply gratified him in some way.

Carlos ended the game, shook the man's hand, and hugged him. He began to walk out of the roda, but the famous mestre stepped in. One woman yelled, *"Opa!"* and several people exclaimed in delight. Sulay was on the bateria, playing the *atabaque* drum, laughing now. When the two men crouched facing each other at the berimbaus, she led the next song:

Valha-me Deus, Senhor São Bento
Buraco velho tem cobra dentro

Valha-me Deus, Senhor São Bento

Quando vê cobra assanhada

Valha-me Deus, Senhor São Bento

A cobra assanhada morde

Valha-me Deus, Senhor São Bento

They shook hands and began to play. It was my brother's turn to be overmatched. The mestre, a true snake, had probably been playing capoeira longer than Carlos had been alive, and now he was the one who knew where the other would go. His footwork was incredible, and his feints were so layered that it was hard to know when a real attack might come. He began a kick now, and Carlos tried to sweep his base leg, but this kick was also a feint and my brother was the one swept to the floor. The mestre strutted around in the roda and everyone laughed, my brother too. They shook hands again and the game continued. In this second phase, after the fall, my brother became more alert and seemed more comfortable. He used his flexibility more and danced as he had in the last game. He and the mestre had several beautiful and intricate exchanges, and while the mestre still controlled the game and pressed him, Carlos played well. After a few more minutes, they shook hands and embraced, ending one of the best games I'd ever seen. The mestre stood with his arm around my brother in the roda, as if showing him off, and people began to applaud for them. I applauded too. My brother noticed me then and, tentatively, I raised my hand to him. He pointed me out to the mestre, but before anything else could happen I slipped out the door.

"We are all apprentices in a craft where no one ever becomes a master." This sentence, frequently quoted by writers, is attributed to Hemingway.

I still teach his work sometimes, though I've grown somewhat cold to it. Perhaps, for writers, what he says is true. It certainly seems true for me. With my brother, however, it's a different story. Watching him that night, I knew that he would one day become a mestre, a master of the small roda as well as, in some ways, the large. As I lay in bed later, in my otherwise empty cabin, listening to the distant sound of the berimbaus humming in the air, I wondered about mastery. What it took to achieve it. The drive to attain it, to constantly correct oneself, the ceaseless drive to be complete. It struck me as such a hard life. Masters of an art are magnetic figures, yes, and we are drawn to them, fascinated by them and their hard-won talents. With rare exceptions, though, they must be lonely too. So few of us know what they know, or have their capacities. So few of us feel truly worthy of them. Our astonishment also keeps us at bay.

The next morning, near the end of the conference, I walked into the noise of the big cabin for breakfast. Carlos was already there, sitting with the men Sulay had called his brothers. I got my food and sat alone at the end of a half-empty table. The heat and sweat of last night's roda were still present in the room. Carlos came over and sat at my table, next to me. I ate, and for a while we sat in silence and stared at the same empty space.

"You ran away last night," he said with a grin. "Mestre was looking for you."

"I don't think I can deal with that," I said. "But you looked good—you looked great."

We were quiet again, lost in the chatter of the room. Then, somewhat disingenuously, I said, "What happened to us?"

He sort of chuckled. "I don't know what happened to *us*, big brother, but I sure as hell know what happened to me."

I nodded, thinking of the terrible things I knew about and might have prevented. I also wondered at the things, known and unknown, that in some way I might have caused.

"Actually," he said, and he looked at me then, "there *are* things that

I know have happened to both of us." He wrung his hands roughly and stared at them. "I'm ready to talk about it if you are, and if you're ready to hear it."

"Yeah, we should do that," I replied, too quickly.

After a moment, he stood and said, "Hey, I want you to be at the closing roda tonight."

"Sure."

"I mean *in* it," he said, "not just watching from the damn door. Can you deal with that?"

"Think so. Just keep that old snake away from me."

"Can't make any promises, buddy."

"You know," I added, "I learned a few things in Harlem that might surprise you."

He laughed deeply and gripped my shoulder. "See you there," he said, and went back to sit with his brothers.

That evening, everyone wore white. The circle was beautiful, a bright and solid ring. The famous mestre held the *gunga*, the largest berimbau, and presided over the roda the entire time. He led all of the songs too. One of the reasons for his fame was his singing voice, and I'm tempted to say that it was the most impressive thing about him. There was something of the ocean in it, or below it, a quality like sonar, like the wailing of the many drowned and gone. His voice was a vessel too, driving into you the way a prow slices through water.

Carlos sat next to me in the perimeter of the roda. He closed his eyes for a while, also enthralled by the mestre's voice. He leaned over and said, "It just transports you, doesn't it? Takes you all the way *there*."

Soon he was next up to play, but instead of going with whoever was opposite him, as one typically did, he took my hand and led me into the roda. He gestured for everyone around us to move in, and they contracted the circle, leaving much less space in which we could move. I saw how Carlos wanted us to play, low to the ground, our bodies close. This intimate, and dangerous, style of play was known as "the inside game."

My heart pounded at we knelt at the largest berimbau, at the feet of the mestre. He rested his voice for the first time that evening, and Carlos began to sing:

> *Camarada, o que ele é meu camarada?*

The chorus responded as one, "*É meu irmão*," elongating the second word to fit the phrase into the rhythm of the song. Carlos continued to lead it. He too had a beautiful singing voice—coarsened over time—and the weight and texture of it pressed against me. The surrounding chorus encased us in a pillar of sound, sealing us into the space of the tightened circle. After Carlos's next call, "*Meu irmão do coração, camarada*," I joined in with the response, and the song continued:

> *É meu irmão*
>
> *Na roda da capoeira, camarada*
>
> *É meu irmão*
>
> *Irmãozao de coração, camarada*
>
> *É meu irmão*

He passed the song to the mestre, who led it now and drove the words so that they cut deeply into me. I understood them. Carlos and I bowed our heads and reached for each other's hands. We leaned into the roda to begin.

A Family

Curtis Smith watched from across the street as the boy argued with Lena Johnson in front of the movie theater. She had probably bought tickets for the wrong movie. Or maybe Andre didn't want to see any movie with his mother on a Friday night. Her expression went from pleading to irate. The boy said nothing more. With his head taking on weight, hung as though his neck couldn't hold it, he followed her inside.

It was a chilly evening in November, and rain threatened the sky. Curtis blew warm breath into his cupped hands. Obedience, he thought; he could talk to the boy about that. He'd been making a list of topics they could discuss. The question of obedience felt right for a boy of fifteen, when the man he would become was beginning to erupt out of him, like a flourish of horns. Though sometimes it was important to *disobey*. Curtis had known this since he was younger than the boy was now. Twelve years in prison hadn't changed that, and so Curtis was here, doing exactly what his mother had asked him that morning not to do anymore. He'd been seen watching Andre and Lena, and his mother's friends were gossiping about what they saw. Maybe Curtis still had a grudge against Lena, they said, or maybe he simply couldn't let go of the past. But he didn't care what his mother or her friends said. A man decided his own way, and there came a time when a boy growing into his manhood had to as well. *Unless your balls haven't dropped yet.* Curtis could say that to the boy, teasing him the way he and the boy's father, Marvin Caldwell, used to tease each other when they were young. Marvin dreamed most vividly of everything he would do for his mother one day, but even he knew to disobey her.

Curtis took a last look at the names of the movies and tried to guess which one Andre might have wanted to see, and which one Lena would have chosen instead. He counted his money. He'd spent only twelve of the forty dollars his mother had left for him, so he decided to get a bite to eat while he waited for the movie to end. At the Downtown Bar and Grill, an old favorite, he ordered a hamburger and a soda. Refills were no longer free, so Curtis kept asking for glasses of water. From where he sat he could still see the brilliance of the marquee.

The rain began before Andre and Lena came out of the theater. They took a walk anyway, and Curtis followed. Lena opened an umbrella that was large enough for two, but as they strolled along the promenade Andre kept drifting away from her, exposing himself to the cold drizzle. Lena stopped at a bench and used a piece of newspaper to wipe it dry. Andre maintained a distance from her when they sat. Curtis stalled for a few moments, and then settled near the middle of the next bench. A large trash can partially blocked his view of them, but he could hear their conversation.

"Your daddy liked to come out here," Lena said.

"You told me that before," Andre replied. Curtis had been following them for weeks, but had rarely been this close. He'd never heard them talk about Marvin.

"Well, it's nice, isn't it? Look at that view."

Andre stood and gestured wildly at the rain. "Hello? I can't see nothing."

Curtis had been out on the promenade several times since he'd been released from prison. There was plenty to see, he thought. A great unseen hand depressed the keys of the city and sounded notes held constant in the many windows, a thousand little squares of humming light. These seemed to float independently, since the tall buildings themselves, their outlines obscured, were indistinguishable from the black enamel seal of the sky. The night grew more thickly clouded by storm, but in the shifting bands of reflected light from the bridge and the city Curtis could see the surface of the river alive and puckered like so many restless mouths. Given all the nights he'd spent here since getting out, it felt like a triumph that he no longer thought of feeding himself to the water.

"Why we out here, Ma?" Andre asked, sitting again. "It's wet. I'm cold."

"It's not so bad under the umbrella."

"Can we go?"

"I just thought you'd like to stay out awhile longer. Might as well enjoy it now. I need you to be at home tomorrow."

"For what?"

"You know how the girls go out to Temptations after work," Lena said. "Well, this time they finally invited me."

"Tomorrow's Saturday, Ma."

"I know what day it is. And I need you to be at home. For my peace of mind."

"While you out shaking your ass at the club."

"What'd you say, boy?"

"Nothing," Andre said. "I'm cold." He stood again and started walking back the way they'd come.

Lena chased after him, sounding pathetic as she called his name.

Curtis didn't follow them. After a while, he got up and strolled along the promenade in the direction of the Brooklyn Bridge. The only other person he saw was a man with an unsettling face. The man's bouts of muttering formed clouds that flowered like visible emblems of his secret language before being pulled apart by the wind. But it was the way this man's hands jumped within his dirty coat as he shuffled along that marked him as dangerous and insane. Curtis had been both of these things, in those months after Marvin died in the fire. Those months before Curtis went to prison. It was danger lurking in the man's left pocket, he suspected, and insanity leaping around in the right. He liked the feeling of their passing him by.

Curtis huffed the name of his long-departed friend—*My dead friend*, he told himself soberly—so he could see the wind take it. He imagined that it too, along with the words steaming from the man's mouth, drifted off and seeded the East River. The river was badly polluted, but he liked it anyway. It flowed in either direction, reaching both ways until it licked the sea. As the man prattled on, now some distance away, Curtis again said Marvin's name, which rose from his lips and hovered there for a moment, clean as an unstrung bone.

He might have also said the name of the dead woman, the one he had struck with his car, the one who intruded on his dreams. But his life was for other things now, he'd been desperately telling himself, beautiful and wondrous things.

The rain began turning to sleet, the sound of it an exhalation steadily hushing the world. Curtis indulged his sense of feeling contained but not trapped. Under the capacious dome of sky he was free, but bounded, so his newly freed limbs wouldn't fly apart. As much as he wanted to stay there on the promenade—often he stayed until the spell of night began to break—the sleet was penetrating his slicker and the thin coat he wore underneath. His hands and feet were already numb. Curtis shivered. It wouldn't make any damn sense to get out of the clink just to turn around and catch his death of cold. He walked quickly to keep the chill from settling into his muscle and marrow.

The next night, Curtis walked along Atlantic Avenue, not far from the movie theater and the Downtown Bar and Grill. It was eleven o'clock and he enjoyed the bustle and breadth of the thoroughfare. He was still amazed at how much had changed: the number of fancy restaurants and wine stores now. Then again, many of the old bars remained. And the new nightclubs were just the old nightclubs with different names.

An empty bus made its way past, the driver lit against its dark frame like an insect stuck in amber. On the corner stood a white woman trying in vain to hail a medallion cab, and Curtis stood beside her, as though waiting to cross the street. She wasn't dressed for the weather, with only a scarf and a trim jacket over her short dress. Her uncovered head twitched, shaking her cropped hair from her lips; her legs were thin but shapely, the color of rich cream. She was what Marvin used to call "a slim goody." Curtis imagined how soft the inside of her thighs would be. He imagined her open mouth.

It had been a long time since he'd had sex with anyone but himself, his own clutching hand. In those first years in prison, he kept an old black-and-white picture of the actress Marpessa Dawn taped to the wall. Following those years of her smiling in the swimming pool came explicit pictures of women opening their shiny, hairless bodies to the camera. When he got out of prison he bought a couple of magazines with centerfolds, but then he discovered how easily videos could be found on his mother's computer. He still liked that picture of the actress in the pool most of all.

The white woman's phone began ringing, and she greeted the caller, apparently her mother, the simple words strained by her tone of heavy familiarity. The second Curtis heard her speak, a feeling of exhaustion overcame him; she reminded him, for some reason, of the woman he had struck with his car. But if that woman had been white, Curtis knew, he would still be in prison, with many more years there ahead of him. To get away from the voice now whining into the phone, he jogged across the street.

In front of Temptations, three men were lined up behind a black velvet rope. The bouncer wore dark glasses and appeared to have no intention of letting the three in. Curtis took his place in line as the first man began to complain.

"Come on now, chief. We been waiting out here for a minute."

"Damn near a half hour," another said. "Say it straight."

"And the hawk is *out*, big man. Come on."

The bouncer said nothing. Another man got in line behind Curtis as a livery taxi pulled up. Three women got out and were followed by Lena Johnson, an afterthought. The bouncer wasted no time letting them in.

Waiting in line with the other men gave Curtis plenty of time to reconsider going in. In fact, he tried to change his mind, calling up reasons he should leave—images of the promenade, of the white woman on the corner—but it was Lena's nyloned legs emerging from the taxi that were lit up on the stage of his mind. Moving slowly in a sapphire dress, she trailed the other women. The shock of seeing her dolled up was slight, but after she vanished through the door, every scene that proceeded on the stage of his mind featured the nylons and the sapphire dress and ended in foolishness. He kept thinking about Andre imagining these scenes unfolding or trying to decipher his mother's face tomorrow during the broadcasts of Sunday afternoon football. The boy needed to be spared his mother's small tragedies.

About fifteen minutes later, the bouncer announced to the men that it would be a ten-dollar cover to get in, speaking as if they had only just arrived. He examined Curtis's clothes doubtfully before admitting him. Curtis wore jeans, but they weren't that dirty; the real problem was that he had on work boots instead of what Marvin would have called "slippery earls." This outfit wouldn't have gotten him into the places they used to frequent, back in the days when they used fake IDs.

"Good luck, playboy," the bouncer said. He stepped aside to let Curtis through the curtains. "Your broke ass gonna need it."

The nightclub had two floors. Curtis didn't spot Lena on the ground level, so he went down to the basement. He took a seat at the bar that gave him a good view of the room and recognized certain features: the low ceiling with its copper tiles, the four pillars that marked the boundary of the dance floor. He and Marvin had been here before, back when there was only a basement level. The place used to be called Nelson's.

Curtis had extra money from an odd job helping his mother's neighbor move some boxes, plus what was left of yesterday's forty dollars. It was easier than he thought it would be to order a bourbon. The words didn't get stuck; the bartender didn't stare. The taste of the drink closed his eyes and warmed him from his throat to his navel.

The music blasting in the club sounded like pure racket, but this wasn't new. While he liked some of the rap other boys listened to when they were growing up, Curtis was always drawn to older music, songs from the sixties and seventies. *All right, old man.* Marvin had a great time teasing him about this. *Look at the old head tryna get his groove!* He'd mock Curtis by bending over and holding his lower back, two-stepping with an imaginary cane.

Lena and her friends were already out there shaking their bodies, each with a drink in hand. Some new dances must have caught on from the music videos. As he watched, Curtis felt he was a man true to better times. He returned to the problem of Andre, how he'd manage to talk to the boy and what his first words would be. After a while, a tall man in a suit came up behind Lena and began to whisper in her ear. She laughed. Soon she had backed herself into him and they became fused in body and rhythm. She pursed her lips and slapped her thigh with her free hand as they danced. Although he and Lena were the same age, thirty-five, Curtis was upset to see her carrying on like this. Feeling sorry for the boy and, somehow, for Marvin, he wished he had just gone to the promenade. He ordered a second bourbon.

Lena and the man in the suit talked for a while at a different side of the bar. He had bought her another drink, but the smile was gone from her eyes. She seemed much less engaged now that they weren't dancing. The man must have noticed this too. He tried to pull her back onto the dance floor, but she refused. The man tried a few more times and then his mouth turned cruel. He appeared to curse at Lena before he walked away.

She stood at the bar for a while, staring into her drink. Then she tossed it back, the entire pour, and drew a thin cigarette from her purse. She said something to one of the women she'd come in with and went past Curtis upstairs. It seemed for a moment that her gaze had fallen on him, but in places like this people's eyes darted everywhere. He followed her. From the entrance, he saw her smoking out near the curb. Her coat was still checked inside and, with her purse pinned under her arm, she held herself, trembling against the cold. She dropped her cigarette and watched it smolder and die on the ground. She could have been some kind of bird staring down from a high perch, wings pinched against her blue body, refusing to fly.

"Hey, playboy," the bouncer said. "You leaving or what? It's in or out, my man."

As Lena took out another cigarette and began the drama of lighting it, Curtis walked back into the club. He stayed on the ground floor this time, where the music seemed not quite as loud. Sipping from his third bourbon, he thought about how easy it had been to go from his first to his third, and beyond, on the night the girl was struck by his car. Dismissing this, he wondered instead about what Andre was doing, if he too was taking advantage of his freedom or compounding the little tragedies of the night by sitting timidly at home. A boy his age should be in the world, seeing as much as he could claim or aspire to. He should be terrified by the new sensation of a girl's modest breasts in his hands, by the new sensation of her hands in his jeans, not by thoughts of his mother in a short dress playing at youth out here in the drunkenness of night. They were thirty-five, yes, but they were old. The boy was still young and he had his father's face. Curtis had gotten close enough to see that. His face was the same, but his fate wouldn't be.

Curtis smelled the rank tobacco on her breath before he felt her cold hand on his shoulder.

"You might as well come on," Lena said.

When he spun around on his barstool to look at her, she grabbed his drink and finished it in one swift motion. "Come on and dance with me," she said.

He allowed her to lead him to the dance floor, less crowded than the one downstairs. He bent his knees, searching for their bodies' fit—it turned out he hadn't forgotten this, how to accommodate the body of woman. They danced to old lovers' rock. Her breasts were crushed against his ribs, his leg planted between hers. She held his shoulder and rode his hip. He touched a hand to her back and found skin there, exposed and sweaty. He could smell the cigarette smoke in her hair.

She was clearly drunk and he, with the bourbon at work in his blood, had the impression that he was anonymous to her. He wished he could vanish on the spot and leave her to her phantom, but something he couldn't name begged him to stay. It didn't seem sexual—his body had yet to respond in that way to hers—so, he told himself, it had to be his obligation to the boy. But it felt like something more bewildering than an obligation. The yearning didn't belong to him, and it didn't belong to her either. It was beyond either of them, he felt, so it claimed them both. It was as though a bright, delicate object they couldn't see, some filament, were held between them, along the length of her sapphire dress stretched taut by his thigh, the spark of it hot where he carried her on his hip, moving her in the rhythm of his stationary stride, and they had no choice but to pull each other close, to preserve the object between them, otherwise it would drift free and fall and lose its light. The exhilaration of her breathing and her slim clutching thighs and her hand pulling on his shoulder were the forces she exerted on him, and he carried her with his hip and his knees bent and his back dimly aching, but all that mattered was the fragile wire pressed between them, lit by something they could neither face nor abandon.

This feeling of being stuck persisted and Curtis was horrified by it. When the long set of lovers' rock ended and released them, he averted his eyes from the sapphire dress going loose again between Lena's thighs. He knew of nothing else to do but go back to the bar and order another drink, and when she followed him there he ordered one for her as well. It was what anyone in the role of her phantom would do. Her drink was cooled by a sculpted sphere of ice that had the look of perfection and permanence, a little moon displayed in glass. When Lena drank she did so deeply, and the moon slid, and it wet the tip of her nose. Curtis's drink had no ice. When he took it up he tilted it so the liquor fell just short of his lips and he could inhale its heat before drinking.

What did she see when she looked at him? Added weight had rounded his face and a beard darkened it. His hair had receded above the temples so that a blunt arrow pointed down at his nose. What would Marvin look like now if he were alive?

Curtis avoided Lena's eyes, hoping the rest of their time together would pass like this—in silence. He tried to lose himself in the music that was playing but it wouldn't permit him access; its borders were dense, its patterns impossible to predict.

"I know who you are," Lena said. "You."

Curtis was overcome with a feeling that by entering this place he had once known, he had also elected for so much more. He sat, helpless. Everything around him—the music, the carnal laughter, the spinning stellar lights—all of it was a frenzy. He'd forgotten this basic truth, that freedom was a wilderness.

There was no place for them to go. He explained that he was living with his mother for a little while, listened as Lena said that her son was at home. Then she surprised Curtis by suggesting they get a room. Just for a couple of hours, she said. She was lonely. It wasn't all that late yet. The nightclub itself would be open until four, and her son knew not to expect her home until after that. He'd already be asleep anyway, and she'd still wake up before he did. "All that boy's worried about is having his breakfast ready in the morning," she said. She told him she made pancakes and bacon on Sundays.

Curtis hadn't expected the drinks to be so expensive, so only six dollars remained in his pocket. His dignity would have been one reason to tell Lena no. Andre was another, but he was a reason to say yes too. Getting mixed up in her night wasn't a good way to get closer to the boy, but it might be the only way.

"I spent all the money I had on me," he said.

"Don't worry," Lena said. "I got it."

Their motel was called the Galaxy Inn. A strange scent hung in the air of their room, which was nearly as small as his cell had been. A coat of silver paint had recently been applied to the walls, but there was something else, an organic pungency. Little effort had been made to mask the presence of former occupants. Useless dials studded the walls, mysterious blinking lights. Curtis felt trapped in some television show from the sixties, a science fiction program he had watched in syndication as a child.

Lena lay with her back to him, abruptly calm, abruptly still. Curtis couldn't even hear the sound of her breathing. He'd been surprised by her wildness, which exceeded his. The rough sheet covered her to the waist, displaying her long neck and the slick coins of her spine. Curtis felt the urge to yank the spine out of her, to scatter those coins all over the bed and catch a true glimpse of her inner workings under the room's dimmed bulbs of winey light.

Lena sat up. "I should go soon. See about my son."

Up close, even in this light, Curtis could see how dry her skin was, the blemishes on her forehead and cheeks. "Tell me about him," he said.

"Now?"

"That boy's asleep. You got time."

She studied his face. "What's in that head of yours?"

Curtis shrugged and made himself hold her hand. "Come on, tell me a little something."

When Lena grabbed her cigarettes, Curtis complained, but she ignored him and lit one anyway. She began to speak about her son, hesitantly at first, but her initial vague description of him eventually turned into a long complaint about her challenges with him, how easily she seemed to make him upset. He was a good child, she said, but their relationship was worsening and it was difficult to manage things on her own. "It's not just that he's a teenager," she said. "It's more than that."

"He's probably just girl-crazy," he said.

"Uh-uh, I don't think so," she said, and went on, speaking with more kindness about him now.

Then Curtis insisted on giving his view of things. The question of obedience was still on his mind, but nothing he said was profound. Lena listened to everything he said anyway, and she seemed contemplative when he fell silent again.

"You know," she told him, "if it was my boy you were interested in, there were easier ways than sniffing after my behind. You could've just walked up to him on the street and told him who you were."

Curtis straightened against the headboard. To him that sounded like the most difficult thing in the world. "I was just looking out for Marvin's people, that's all." He felt embarrassed, a little angry. "I know it's not the usual way," he added.

Lena shook her head. "Look at you," she said. "I know you been gone, but you not invisible. People talk. I got eyes."

"How long have you known?"

"Long enough to think plenty on whether to do anything about it."

Curtis gestured at the blinking walls of the room, a tired old version of the future. He gestured down at the bed. "This what you decided to do about it?"

"Well, you were there, sniffing as usual," Lena said. "I had my notions, and you just happened to be the one. I knew you were safe. And I figured you'd go along with it."

He yanked off the sheet and exposed the full nakedness of his body. He sprang from the bed and glared down at her.

"I'm all done with that," she told him, "so you can put it away now."

"I'm not somebody you know," Curtis said. "I never was."

She rubbed the edge of the sheet between her fingers. "Look, I'm gonna go. You can stay the rest of the night if you want, if you don't wanna sleep at your mama's house." She rose from the bed and watched him for a few moments, frowning. "You don't know me either," she said, and began to dress.

Curtis left not long after Lena did. No need to stay and stare at a dead end. Night was starting to drain from the edges of the sky, but he didn't go directly to his mother's house. Walking restored him when he was upset, helped him regain his focus, even before he went to prison, and now he savored it much more, despite the times he was harassed by cops. As adolescents he and Marvin would often stay out late, sometimes until dawn, romping all over Brooklyn. Marvin preferred walking or taking the bus to the half-blind underground careening of the subway. He liked taking different routes, favoring the slightest deviations or even dangerous blocks or neighborhoods over what he would have called "the same old, same old." But he did enjoy the promenade.

When the two boys went there together and gazed out at the protruding jaw of the city, they spoke most openly of their desires. Marvin spoke as if the days and years to come were nothing but a cycle of restoration. "I'm gonna get my mother a house," he'd always say. This was his favorite thing. Not only would he pay off her considerable debts, he would do this too. The house he imagined buying for her was like a place he'd already been in, stepping past furniture bought from her catalogs and out to the little vegetable garden she'd keep. Looking up with her past the white slats to the blue roof where the birds would be rebuilding their nest. "She wouldn't want the birds there," he said once. "But I do. They do all the things I like."

Marvin spoke of girls as if he weren't a virgin, as if he knew a thing about the frightening business of female nudity and of sex, which Curtis understood was animal and floral: the odd nosing around, the smells and the sap, the near-violence of fingernails and coarse hair, the peeling back of language to a hard core, like the spiked stones of peaches the boys used to throw at stray dogs.

Then, for reasons Curtis never understood, Marvin got stuck on the idea of Lena Johnson. He talked about her constantly, and soon the boys' wanderings through the borough began to circle her old neighborhood, not far from where Curtis was walking now. There was the basketball court—still there, Curtis knew—where Marvin kept insisting they go, despite the busted rims.

One spring day they saw her there. She came from across the street and began to stroll the sidewalk along the length of the court, lifting her hand to take languid pulls from a cigarette. Marvin raced over with an odd look on his face, his hands in loose fists. He was carrying little rocks baked and blanched by the sun, as though he wanted to roll them at her like gifts through the openings in the chain-link fence. Curtis followed, smelling the opportunity for mischief. The boys caught up and then kept pace with Lena on their side, daylight flickering in their faces, blinking madly through the diamonds of the fence. The flashing light did not transfigure Lena's appearance. She was still just a skinny girl with pointy elbows and spooky eyes, whose shirts and sweaters were always linted-up, whose flat ass made a pair of jeans droop and frown.

When Marvin greeted her, she blew out the smoke that had been held in her lungs. She was inhaling from a joint, they realized, not one of her usual cigarettes. Kids made fun of her at school for having stale breath. Curtis laughed at these jokes. Marvin used to laugh too.

"My mama told me not to talk to strange boys," Lena said, without looking at either boy.

"What? It's me, Marvin Caldwell. From school."

"I know who you are. Don't mean you not strange."

"But you talking to me anyway."

"Do *you* always do what your mama says?"

And that was it. She kept going without another word and left Marvin standing with his long fingers clawed into the fence, exactly where Curtis stood now. Marvin somehow turned what she'd said into a genuine mystery, one he considered, on that day and afterward, by wondering aloud about her life. Had anyone ever seen her mother at the school? Did they get along or did they argue all the time? Did they look alike? He let Curtis know how deeply he imagined her. As Lena gradually became a part of Marvin's life, he talked less often to Curtis about her. And when they became a couple, he hardly talked to Curtis at all.

It took a long time, but Curtis finally got him to go on a walk, like they used to, one Sunday afternoon in Prospect Park. When they got near Drummer's Grove, alive with sound, he confronted him. "We supposed to be boys," Curtis said.

"Then be happy for me," Marvin replied.

"I can't even remember the last time we hung out."

The shaking of gourds decorated the sound of the drums. Marvin said, "Man, you know how it is when people first get loved up."

"You don't even talk to me no more."

Marvin laughed. "It's not like that. You're my boy. Trust. We'll be good."

"So it's just a phase?"

"Nope, it's real. Be happy I'm happy."

"What about me?" Curtis said. The drumming got more layered and complex. A strange instrument that looked like a bow and arrow made high twanging noises.

"Okay, I see," Marvin said. "You want it to be about you."

Curtis frowned. "I just can't believe you let a bitch get between us."

Marvin stopped walking. He narrowed his eyes in the direction of the music. The head of a dancing man jerked up and down. Sounds from a wind instrument wove between those of the drums. "Don't ever come out your mouth like that," he said. "I'm serious, you hear me?"

Curtis laughed wryly. "But that's what you did though."

Marvin closed his hands into fists and then opened them. Curtis watched them close and open, close and open. Marvin got in his face. Their noses almost touched. Curtis tried not to blink.

"I'm out, man," Marvin said finally, and gripped him in a firm lengthy hug.

Curtis let his arms hang limp at his sides, hands loose. As time passed, until the fire and the death, he mostly kept his arms and hands that way, until he used them again to drink.

When Curtis came in, his mother was asleep in the easy chair again, the glow from the television in the living room bluing her form. He didn't switch off the old sitcom and he didn't wake her. Instead he listened to her dogged breathing. On the small table beside her were peanut shells on a paper towel and a cup with the dregs of tea. When Curtis stayed out until seven or eight in the morning, his mother would be awake when he got in, looking tired as she sipped strong coffee and stretched her sore back at the kitchen table. Otherwise she'd be where she was now, floating on the merest shallows of sleep. When he told her not to wait up for him, she said this was nothing; she'd been waiting for him to come home for twelve years.

A little time remained before sunrise. Curtis would often read in such circumstances; he'd become an avid reader of Walter Mosley's novels in prison. But he liked the feeling of being near his mother now—he liked her when she was asleep—so he sat with a tall glass of water and forced his gaze onto the television screen. The off-hour commercials for ridiculous products held his attention better than the show itself, though the canned laughter was a kind of murmured grace. Despite his efforts, his body slumped against an arm of the couch and he fell asleep.

Curtis often slept during the day, so his dreams were full of light. At least, this was how he made sense of what happened. Each dream brought him to a city of houses and water and clear sparkling glass. Every inhabitant wore white, against which their brown skin was beautiful. People smiled and held the hands of their lovers, their children, and their friends. The strange thing about these light-filled dreams was that Marvin never appeared, not a piece of him in the fragments Curtis could gather upon waking. He told himself that the grandness of the dreams—the pristine landscapes and spacious houses, the variety and richness of color—was a symbol of Marvin's presence, or that the diffuse light, the kind you see in old paintings, was the gold of his friend's fantasies. But he knew his claims were suspect. He felt stung by Marvin's disregard for his dream life.

It was not yet morning now, however, so his dream had a different character. Aside from the darkness of waking life seeping into it, there was the dim, gray shadow of the woman he'd hit with his car all those years ago. The woman sprang into the dream the same way she'd sprung out onto the street; she was faceless, voiceless, and pale, gesturing woodenly at the edge of his vision. As she had been in the last few moments of her life, she was barely a smudge, nothing more than a faint mote in the air before suddenly looming. That night she seemed to fall upon the car like a burden dropped from the sky, and in the dream she acted the same way, flying at him, shocking him out of sleep. He jerked awake, shaken and afraid, with a metallic taste on his tongue. The taste offended Curtis, reminding him of the pit his mouth had become after Marvin's death, in those months of heavy drinking.

In the kitchen Curtis's mother spread butter and cherry preserves on slices of toast. "Glad it's Sunday," she said. Her job at the hospital gave her Mondays and Tuesdays off, so she was on the cusp of her weekend. She pushed his breakfast plate across the table and got up to place more bread in the toaster and fork scrambled eggs from the pan on the stove. She was already dressed for work. A saltshaker pinned down two folded twenty-dollar bills, the amount she'd leave for him a few times a week to eat lunch and get around as he searched for jobs. While waiting for the toast to pop up, his mother hummed old gospel songs, something she'd never done when Curtis was growing up. She must have learned them as a little girl back in North Carolina. Now, as she drew closer to her life's other edge, the songs must have come back to her again.

When she sat back down with her plate, she watched Curtis, nearly done with his eggs, toast, and sausage patties, before touching her own food.

"Want some more?" she said.

Curtis nodded and grunted yes.

His mother gave him one of her hot triangles of toast and began to scrape some of the eggs from her plate onto his. "Go on and eat it, Curtis," she said. "Shoot, I'm getting fat anyway. I need to start back with my exercises."

Remembering his private vow, that his life was now for wondrous things, he accepted what ended up being almost all of his mother's breakfast so he could see her lips closed and smiling and her eyebrows settle back down to a sensible height, so there would be the satisfaction of silence. It was true that she was getting round in the midsection, but he knew she would never return to her exercises. She'd never started in the first place.

Curtis felt her watching him eat the second portion of food. She'd be late for work if she didn't leave right away. She was sixty and he wasn't surprised by how old she was starting to appear. The visits she'd made upstate to the prison each month revealed the rhythms of her decline, and in the intervals he guessed accurately where and when age would touch her next. Her brown skin was somehow darkening. She had a soft pouch under her chin. At the cheeks and around the eyes the skull was beginning to show itself behind her face. She was nothing to write home about anymore, but a man her age probably wouldn't complain. When she and Curtis's father decided their relationship just wasn't going to work, she was still a young woman, and quite pretty. She made only half-hearted attempts at romance though, as if she believed you got just one real try at it in life.

She used those energies to dote on Curtis and fuss over him the way it seemed Lena fussed over Andre. As soon as Curtis set his fork down on his plate, his mother snatched them up, along with her own, then went to the sink and began washing them.

"I was telling Shirley what we talked about on Friday," she said. "She thought you were gonna give me lip, but I said, 'Oh no, my boy gets it.' Look, I know you loved Marvin. He was like kin to you. But following his people around ain't what's right for you. I know you know it. Can't look back. It's like the Bible says: *Let thine eyes look right on, and let thine eyelids look straight before thee. Make level the path of thy feet, and let all thy ways be established. Turn not to the right hand nor to the left—*"

"Ma, don't you gotta go?" Curtis said.

She waved him off with a gloved hand, flashing yellow, flicking suds and drops of water across the kitchen. "My baby is home," she said. "Ain't no thing to put some soap and water to a couple dishes."

That's right, he thought. Your baby. Can't get a job, can't get my own place, can't open a goddamn bank account. You wouldn't even care if I pissed the bed.

His mother snapped off her rubber gloves and glanced up at the clock. She blinked slowly, keeping her eyes closed a beat or two longer than necessary, and opened them as she took in a great draft of breath. Curtis steadied himself for what was coming. This had the look of one of her speeches, the ones that began, *Baby, you know the Lord has forgiven you. Now you just need to forgive yourself* . . . Curtis wasn't sure God had forgiven him. He wasn't sure God agreed that the accident couldn't have been avoided. He wasn't even sure about God. If God was true and had forgiven him, then why did He keep sending the woman into his dreams at night? Curtis had to do it the other way. If he forgave himself first, maybe then God would follow.

He steadied his breathing, thinking of beautiful things and filling his head with their music: The words of the man on the promenade, grabbed by the wind. "The Payback." Freedom on his tongue like the taste of curry chicken and macaroni pie from Culpepper's. "Someday We'll All Be Free." A pretty woman opening her legs and arms for him. *Devil in a Blue Dress.* "Ruby." Marpessa Dawn taped to the wall. "A Felicidade." Marvin, his friend. Andre, who looked so much like his father. "They Reminisce over You." "Little Ghetto Boy."

Curtis followed Lena into a bank one afternoon that week. He tried to make the encounter seem like a coincidence, but could tell she knew better. They talked uncomfortably for a few minutes, both averting their gazes. Then he apologized for the other night and told her he wanted to see her. After some hesitation, which seemed to him like ceremony, Lena gave him her phone number.

Whenever they got a room together on weekdays, Lena would tell Andre she was working an extra shift, but they usually got rooms on Saturday afternoons. Curtis brought her home once, while his mother was at work, but only after he made her promise not to smoke there. After they arrived, Lena told him it was fine, but he felt humiliated being with her on such a small bed, in a room filled with his childish things. He was morose after they slept together. Even the scent of their sex couldn't distract him from the pervasive smell of his mother. When Lena tried to comfort him, he asked her to tell him about the night Marvin died.

She flinched. "Y'all were like brothers," she said. "You know all about it."

"I wasn't there."

"I wasn't there either," she said. "You had to know that much."

"But tell me about the last time you saw him."

Lena chewed the insides of her cheeks before she spoke. "I was waitressing back then too," she said. "The late-night shift at a diner over by Coney Island. I like waitressing. You get to know folks and they get a kick out of you remembering them and they tip you good—well, as best they can."

"What about Marvin?"

"Like I said, I was working the third shift, and that started at midnight during the week. Marvin had already lost his construction job. Then he lost his side gig too. You know how hard things were for him."

"I didn't know."

"Well, he couldn't handle it. Poor thing was always beat from pounding that pavement all day, every day, but he liked to stay up and watch me get ready for work. Tried to keep himself awake with a book of all things. Can you imagine? He *was* one to think reading in bed would keep a tired man awake."

"What was he reading that night?"

"I don't remember," she said.

"How about Easy Rawlins and Mouse? Did he like that?"

"I don't know."

"And the fire?"

She looked at him for a long time and then studied her hands. Her voice, when it came, was flat now: "You must've heard how it happened, Curtis. It was just like that."

"Tell me."

"I told him not to smoke in the bed, especially when I wasn't around. But the man was tired, always, and with every job telling him no, he was a bundle of nerves. I kept telling him to ask for help, but he had to do things all by himself. Too proud. He wanted life to be different for us, and for his mama. All that debt . . ." She shook her head. "He thought we deserved to be in a better place."

"I heard his spirits were low."

"Sometimes."

"You'd know better than me." Curtis tried to say this with some tenderness, but she flinched again. For the first time she seemed beautiful to him, like a woman grieving calmly in a painting. He pressed on: "Do you think he . . . ?"

"What?"

Curtis looked at her.

"Took his own life? Is that what you mean?"

He nodded. He knew he was being cruel, but couldn't help himself. He wanted to hurt her.

"What—in his right mind he just lit a match and let it fall on the damn pillows? You asking me if he meant to destroy his own self? Why would you say such a thing? Why would you even think it?"

Curtis sometimes imagined that his friend would understand what it was like to feel that blue, but he knew Marvin had loved life too much to take his own. "Maybe you're right," he said. "Maybe you're right." The faded Knicks poster on the far wall hung askew. "I guess he wouldn't have done that with Andre on the way. He knew about the baby, right?"

Lena seemed baffled. "Whatever did or didn't happen, it wasn't because of what was growing inside of me."

Curtis nodded, but meant nothing by the gesture. "Tell me the last thing he said to you."

"I don't know, Curtis," she said. "As far as we were concerned, it was just another day."

"Last time *we* saw each other, he gave me a hug."

Lena lay with her back pressed to him, her knees drawn up and touching the wall. "That's no surprise. I never heard him say a bad word about you, not once." She inhaled loudly. "What in the world happened between you two?"

Curtis didn't reply. After that Sunday afternoon by Drummer's Cove, Marvin eventually reached out to reconcile, but Curtis ignored him. He met any attempt to talk or spend time together with silence. When they finally talked on the phone, Marvin begged to borrow some money.

"I lost both my jobs, man," he said, "and nobody's trying to hire a brother. Can't catch a damn break right now."

Curtis cleared his throat but otherwise stayed quiet.

"And you know how it is with my mom . . . I'm having a real hard time, man."

Before he hung up, Curtis said, "Well maybe that bitch you got can help you out."

He didn't tell Lena any of this now, and it was obvious that she didn't know. He listened as she breathed, the steady in and out, the deepening. He closed his eyes. In a while he was startled awake by his recurring dream, and then startled again by a cold hand on his shoulder. Curtis saw it had taken a great effort for Lena to reach out to him, even though they had no space between them on his bed. Her reddened eyes, taut mouth, and fingers roughly scratching at the points of her elbows meant she knew she could never be loved by him—he had told her as much when they talked before falling asleep. Maybe she already knew she couldn't love him either. He held her though, in the little bed, and then she held him too. As they lay there, he decided he would never bring her to his mother's house again.

Curtis and Lena stopped getting rooms and he moved in to her apartment. This took a while though—almost six months. They both danced around the question in such a way that both of them could claim the other had come up with the idea. When Curtis told his mother it was happening, she cried, almost as much as she had when he was sentenced to prison. He invited her to visit them, but she said she would need some time.

Before the move, Lena would invite Curtis over only for meals: dinners or late Sunday breakfasts, when he got to see the boy. On Sundays, the pancakes were dense. Lena piled the bacon in the pan, so it always came out soggy. It was greasy and almost sweet on the tongue. As it slid down his throat, Curtis held his hand to his mouth and gave Andre a funny look, but the boy seemed to like the food. He didn't seem pleased with much else.

Lena had told Andre the simple truth, that Curtis was his father's good friend. "He's like your uncle," she'd said, but the boy rolled his eyes. When he called Curtis "uncle" after the move, he said it with a hint of derision. The two of them got along well enough though. Curtis pretended Lena had never called him the boy's uncle, but Andre went on calling him that anyway, still with a mocking tone. He liked to say it in the mornings when Curtis emerged from Lena's bedroom, or right before he went in at night. "Morning, Unc," he'd say, or "Have a good night, Uncle Curtis."

In bed, Lena would rub her cold feet along Curtis's shins to signal her desire for sex. He had never liked the way her tongue tasted, but the first few times they'd slept together, he had been surprised by how much pleasure her skinny body gave him. He wasn't gentle with her, and the things she whispered to him made it clear she didn't want him to be. But now he hated the little sounds she made, the words she said, loud enough that the boy would be able to hear. Sometimes, not quite meaning to, Curtis covered her mouth.

When summer arrived, Curtis took Andre to the basketball court in Lena's old neighborhood and watched him hang listlessly from the rims. They took long walks together, though Andre complained. "Why don't we just take the train?" he asked. They had macaroni pie at

Culpepper's, but the boy said Lena's was better. Curtis told him about his time in prison. Andre seemed uninterested until Curtis began to exaggerate, and then the boy asked if being locked up was the way they showed it in some movie Curtis had never even heard of. His reply was yes, exactly like that.

One of Andre's favorite things to do, because it made him laugh so hard, was ridicule his mother. It bothered Curtis afterward but he joined in anyway and complained about her bad habits. He made fun of his own mother too. When the weather was nice, he laughed with Andre on the promenade, tears wetting his eyelashes. Curtis often fell silent and made a show of watching the young women walk by.

"What makes mothers the way they are?" Andre asked one day. It was the first time he had posed such a question to Curtis, that of a boy seeking the wisdom of a man.

"They lose themselves and get all kinds of ridiculous," Curtis said. "Ain't no mystery to it."

But Andre was quiet, and it was hard to tell if he was listening. Curtis fixed his gaze on a jogger in tight red shorts, and leaned forward to keep her in sight as long as he could. He pointed so that Andre would look too. Then the joke from the old song leaped into his mind. "Goddamn," he said. "Do fries go with that shake?"

Andre turned to look out at the harbor, his eyes a bit dulled. His taut lips shifted from side to side, as restless as the river.

Curtis kept up the banter about the jogger. "You like that, huh?"

"If you say so," Andre replied with a shrug.

"Well, she looks like a college girl to me anyway, young buck," Curtis said with a laugh. "Might be out of your league."

"Man, I'ma be so glad when I go off to college."

Curtis nodded and listened as Andre continued to talk about his future, his life of success, of accumulation and bachelorhood. "There's one thing you gotta do though," he told the boy. "A house. When you make it big like that, you gotta get your mother a house."

Andre seemed taken aback, and was quiet for a long time as he considered the idea. "Ain't *you* gonna to do that?" he said. "I mean, I'll come visit and everything. But you're the one with her, right? You make it happen. She'd like that, wouldn't she?"

Curtis didn't say so, but he supposed she would.

"Hey," he said, "you never ask me anything about your daddy."

Andre shrugged again.

"I got a lot of good stories. Don't you want to hear them? You should get to know who he was."

"What for? He's still gonna be dead."

"Your father was a good man," Curtis said. "And—"

"I know, I know. You loved him like a brother."

"No," Curtis said. "That's what people keep on saying but it was more than that, a lot more." He was startled by the sound of his own voice, the force of it. He gazed down at his hands, unable to bear the gentle, curious way Andre was looking at him. He couldn't find the words to explain the affection he felt, still, for the boy's father, and in this moment he didn't want to be misunderstood. Another jogger went past but neither of them paid her any mind.

"What happened the night that lady got killed?" Andre said.

Curtis had a sour taste in his mouth. "I was drunk," he said. "They said she had some drink in her too. She got in my way. That's all." He rubbed his palms against the knees of his pants. "I did something I shouldn't have done."

Since no one would hire Curtis for steady work, he had lots of time to spend with Andre, when the boy allowed him to. Lena supported them all, sometimes working extra shifts at the restaurant. She stood aside and let Curtis try to deepen his relationship with her son. She put a smile on her face when Curtis, and sometimes Andre too, made fun of her Sunday bacon, picking it up by one end and wriggling it in the air. She must have noticed the way they both looked at her when she reached for her cigarettes. Soon enough she stopped reaching for them, and then Curtis no longer saw them in the apartment at all. She hardly ever took a drink, and in this way, he followed her example. She didn't buy tickets for movies on Fridays, unless she was going to the theater by herself. When the woman Curtis had struck with his car kept entering his dreams, Lena didn't put her hand on his shoulder. If she ever cried at night, she refused to be comforted by him. She still signaled him with her cold feet, however. She still made her little demands for intimacy, and sometimes he did too.

Before they slept, she lay beside him in bed and listened as he talked about Andre, unable to stop himself. "He seems happier, doesn't he?" Curtis asked one evening, and she agreed, as though he truly understood her son. It was true, Lena told him, and she called them her "men," her "two men," which she was in the habit of doing, as if they were all she had ever wanted.

"I think Marvin would be glad," he said, but wondered. Lena agreed again though, and appeared pleased at the thought of all her contented men. Curtis forced a smile onto his face too. He kissed her cheek, lightly, his lips barely making contact with her freshened skin. He and Lena wouldn't love each other, but there was love they openly shared, and that would be enough, for now, to make a kind of family.

A Lucky Man

Lincoln Murray sucked in his stomach on the crowded morning subway. He struggled to keep it from touching the young woman in front of him, whose throat was alive with perfume. Now in his mid-fifties, Lincoln withheld himself by habit. Only in the privacy of home did he allow his stomach to settle into its full hanging bulge. Until recently, his wife, Alexis, would tease him while reaching out in the same moment to soothe his paunch and his pride. Like his wife's scent, the young woman's perfume reminded him of bright citrus. A finger drawn lightly across her neck, an accident of that kind, and he'd have some trace of her to keep for a while.

The young woman's face was smooth, dark, and glowing. She looked maybe a few years older than his daughter, Tameka. The white plastic buds in her ears emitted a loud, constant hum, and the wires connecting them to her phone were caught in two tangles. The young woman had eaten a healthy cereal with almond milk for breakfast, he guessed, or maybe she'd taken the time to pack spinach and cucumber and apple into a machine for fresh juice. And she drank it wearing whatever she had slept in, something pale yellow or some other color good for springtime, something that floated around her thighs. Maybe she had a lover and had stood this morning drinking the juice in one of his shirts.

As the train rocked, Lincoln leaned forward to figure out what the woman was listening to. His job at the Tilden School, even more than his relationship with his daughter, meant that he knew the music of young people. All he could tell was that the voice was female. He imagined one of those new soul singers with respectable clothing and a bloom of natural hair. Alexis watched them with pleasure on television. This thought prompted him to smile at the young woman, but she kept her lids narrowed, eyes dull crescents, and her attention lingered somewhere beyond him. The faulty cooling system in the car wheezed as it pumped in warm air. Sweat pearled a little on the woman's nose and darkened her T-shirt at the chest.

They rode in the last car, which would let Lincoln out at the stairs closest to Ninety-third Street and Broadway, five blocks away from the school. The way the subway operator drove made the last car feel only loosely connected, as though dislodged from the rails. As it approached Penn Station, the train took turns he hadn't felt on other mornings, turns that seemed to belong to another route, and which knocked the commuters in the last car against each other. Through it all, they avoided making eye contact, as people in the city tend to do.

When the doors opened, the crowd thinned out a little and the young woman took one of several seats that had opened nearby. Lincoln stood over her. He held on to a pole and took his phone from his left pocket. It was a gift from Alexis, who had said when she gave it to him that it wasn't fun anymore to ridicule his old, dented flip phone. Lincoln was slow to follow technology. He held the phone close to his face— Alexis mocked him for this—and read the message from his daughter again, even though there wasn't much to it. He'd read it several times since it had been sent the previous night. *My bus gets to Port Auth at 4 tomorrow, daddy*, the message read. *Meet me? Can't wait to see you.* That was all. It was the end of Tameka's first year of college. She had a job on campus for the summer, but was coming home to visit for a couple of weeks.

He hadn't expected the sweetness of the message. The safe bet was that Alexis would have turned their daughter against him. In his mind, those two were always together. Even when their daughter misbehaved as a child, Lincoln was often alone. In the middle of a scolding, something would overwhelm his wife's anger—some deep pleasure, he sensed—and she would be drawn toward the defiance in Tameka's face. When he and Alexis talked in the bedroom before falling sleep, she said the quality was a kind of strength and argued that they shouldn't be so quick to discourage it in a little girl. But even before she said anything, he had felt her softening and drifting to the other side. He knew. She and their daughter were the same way.

The young woman on the train was the same way too. She could use her face like that, he thought. If she had a lover, she showed him that face. Something like a scowl, the expression seemed different on women of a certain beauty, like they never had to justify their use of it—they just assumed they had the right. Like some wealthy children, many of the ones at Tilden, who grow up making little effort in life, but demanding their share of it, or more. Lincoln could see the young woman fussing about any little thing or wearing an outfit too revealing when she went out to dance with her friends. He could see her being casually cruel to her lover, or doing worse things. The lover would forgive her soon, if not at once. But why? The secret had to be in that face, the way it ripped at its own symmetries, contorted its relied-upon beauty. It was a kind of threat and he, like the woman's lover, felt weak against it.

The train pulled away from the Times Square station, and more seats became available, but Lincoln saw no point in sitting for two stops. The train took an abrupt turn, and he fumbled his phone a bit. Pleased about not dropping it, he held it even higher than usual and smiled, showing off for the young woman. He noticed they had the same hard blue casing on their phones, so he said, "Would you look at that?" The young woman didn't reply. Still listening to her loud music, she exhaled heavily and turned her head toward the empty space on her left, as if to share a bug-eyed glance with a friend. As she turned, one of her earrings, a long and loose silver strand, made a brief spiral around one of the white wires and unwound itself. Lincoln then forced his attention back to his phone, touching the screen. The young woman looked up at him and there it was. He touched the part of the screen that activated the camera function and took a picture, without noise or the flash of light. He took another picture before thumbing the button that made the screen go dark. He slipped the phone into his pocket. Holding it there, as if it would leap out otherwise, he affected a serious study of the poem above him, where an advertisement would normally be. "Those Winter Sundays," he read, but couldn't get beyond the title. He felt the eyes of the young woman questioning him. After the Seventy-Second Street station, Lincoln moved away from her, stood for a moment facing the nearest doors, and then walked to the ones farthest away. In the tunnel, until his stop, he swayed with the movements of the train and shivered in front of the scratched glass, rapt in the darkness, oblivious to the passing streaks of light.

A feverish energy coursed through the avenues of the city that morning. After weeks of disappointing weather, it was finally spring. Rainclouds had been wrung away, leaving a clarity of unbroken sky and a sheen on everyone's limbs. Lincoln unbuttoned his cuffs and folded them back a little, exposing his wrists to the mild breeze. He walked toward the school while holding the phone in his pocket. As he passed the Goldfinch Academy, the all-girls school that obsessed the older boys from Tilden, Lincoln knocked on the loose pane of a window and waved. Sidney had been a security guard there longer than Lincoln's sixteen years at Tilden, and his hair was more fully gray. Over beers, he liked to use the authority of his tenure and his grayness to proclaim, in a heavy Bajan accent, that Tilden boys had always preferred the girls at Goldfinch to their own. For some reason he felt proud of this. His girls were prettier, he said. Smarter too. One day, after more beer than usual, he added that the Goldfinch girls were more likely to participate in those rainbow parties. Lincoln had heard about the parties. He heard lots of things from students, but he'd also heard about them from Alexis. Tameka had told her mother after transferring from Goldfinch to Tilden. She had called the parties "nasty," said that they were things mostly white girls went to. She declared that she would never go. Despite this, Lincoln wondered what Tameka did when she was allowed to have late nights and sleepovers in the city. He hardly admitted these thoughts to his wife.

The Tilden School was the second oldest private school in the entire country. Lincoln liked to walk past the doors of the upper school and place his palm on the dated cornerstone, still cool in the early morning, before he went inside. The kids addressed him by his first name, and he was almost popular among them. Three freshmen gave him high fives outside the student lounge area, already raucous with shrill laughter, deodorant, and young sweat. Boys hooted and girls lifted their faces to the fluorescent lights.

At the security desk, adjacent to the lounge area, James wasted no time starting to chatter, seemingly in the middle of a sentence. A younger man, still a bachelor, James kept his shirtsleeves rolled far past his ashen elbows, showing his hard forearms and the slopes of his biceps. He flapped his blue necktie as he talked, about sports or in barely coded language about his latest sexual triumph. In Lincoln's opinion, James wasn't bragging just for fun; he really thought about women that way. The younger man talked on, and Lincoln held the phone in his pocket as he halfheartedly listened. Whenever he took his hand out he rubbed the moisture from it on the thigh of his uniform's pants.

Before long he took a break from James's coarse jokes, and from chats with students who held him captive during their free periods. He went into a stall of the nearest boys' restroom and lingered there, sitting fully clothed on the toilet seat. He slid his thumb across the screen of his phone and studied the pictures of the young woman on the subway. The first image came out blurry, but the second one was clear: her rigid mouth—the scowl there—and tensed nostrils. Her earrings had managed to seize the light, and they formed two slivers of visible heat on either side of her jaw. But what disconcerted Lincoln was a kind of raw serendipity. He had caught her gaze at a moment when it shot into and almost through the frame. She stared from the phone directly at him. None of the other pictures on his phone looked like this. He'd taken about seventy now—mostly of women who appeared to be in their twenties or thirties, a few in their middle years—and in every one but this, the agitated faces had oblique and unaware expressions.

Two students burst into the restroom and Lincoln hastily put the phone away, as if the door to his stall weren't closed and locked. While the boys talked idly at the urinals, he stayed completely still. Alexis had been upset when she discovered the pictures, but why? They were all pictures of faces, not that other kind. He knew how easy those would be to take, trailing a college student, her long hair swaying in a braid as she walked in form-fitting workout clothes on sun-warmed streets, or behind a young wife coming up from the subway in her ladylike way, slim fingers pressing the billowing edge of her skirt against the backs of her thighs. Tameka said boys took these sorts of pictures all the time and sent them to each other. What he had done, or was doing, wasn't nearly as bad. Not even close.

After the two boys left the restroom, without washing their hands, Lincoln felt uncomfortable staying there. He took one last look at the most recent picture and tried to commit its details to memory. This might be the one. As he received visitors and checked IDs back at the security desk, the image would be there, fixed in his mind, and at some moment he might understand it: the power held by such a face.

It didn't take long for James to ask about Alexis. He made no secret of his fondness for Lincoln's wife, and she inspired many of his jokes. He said her first name in a familiar way, almost lewdly. Though she was forty-six, ten years older than James, she could have passed for his age or younger. Unlike Lincoln, she had kept her looks. She exercised to tone her arms and flatten her stomach. The years had only improved the shape and breadth of her hips. Her face remained smooth, marked by a few tiny lines around her eyes only when she lost herself in laughter. She liked to say, "Black don't crack." When James joked, she was the inspiration and Lincoln was the target.

"Lexi hasn't been by here in a while," James said. Lincoln had warned him before about calling her that. He thought it was a pornographic name, a stripper's name.

"She's off visiting her people down by Richmond," Lincoln replied, telling all he was willing to admit. He wasn't ready to say that Alexis might have left him.

"Man," James said, "I miss when she brings in those cakes."

Lincoln crossed his legs at the ankles and began tapping the blunt end of a pen on his clipboard.

"Chocolate frosting," James said, flapping his tie. "Or lemon frosting . . . Lemon's good too, better than vanilla, but you know brothers like that chocolate the best."

Alexis worked as one of two manuscript curators at the Schomburg Center in Harlem. Sometimes, on Mondays, she'd take the short taxi ride down to Tilden during her lunch break and bring in desserts from her favorite bakery. She liked to show her appreciation of the security and maintenance staffs, "the invisible folks," she called them. They seemed to be the only black and brown people in the school. Her notion wasn't far from the truth. After Tameka transferred in for high school, Alexis become known among some administrators as a rabble-rouser for initiatives related to diversity. Her Monday visits always caused a stir—not only among the men—but she hadn't been by in a month. It had been that long since Lincoln had seen her, that long since they'd last spoken. Before taking vacation days for her trip to Virginia, she had spent some time away, in Jersey City with her girlfriend Donna.

"You keeping her under lock and key, I bet," James said. "Can't blame a man for wanting those cakes all to himself."

Lincoln smiled and tried to be a good sport, but he was gripped for a moment by a reckless idea. He tried to think instead about the face of the young woman on the subway, to see it clearly enough to contemplate it.

"Hope to God you bring her to the end-of-year party though. She looked like a queen at Christmas. Finer than frog hair, as my cousins and them down home like to say. *Jet* Beauty of the Week status, you know what I mean. Tell her I said hello, all right?"

Lincoln gave an imperceptible nod and tapped his pen more rapidly. The woman's face was vague in his mind, then gone.

"Hey, tell sexy Lexi I said hello, okay?" James said.

Face burning, Lincoln threw his pen at James, a blind, broken gesture. The pen bounced feebly off the younger man's chest.

"What the hell, man?" James said, rising. "What the hell?"

A group of students nearby fell silent and stared at them.

"You could've put out my damn eye," James continued. This wasn't true, but his brow and the activity of his arms said he was ready for a fight.

Lincoln picked up the pen and held it in the space between his knees, rolling it with his fingers as he spoke. "Don't talk about my wife that way," he said quietly.

James's face softened to puzzlement and then consideration. He noticed the students and told them to go on about their business. He sat back down as the students turned or walked away. "Come on, man," he said to Lincoln, tapping him on the shoulder. He leaned closer and let his voice fall to a whisper. "You know I'm just messing with you, chief."

Lincoln acknowledged this with a nod, his head still heavy and hanging low. All that he held at bay from even the surface of his thinking sank to an unavoidable depth.

"I'm just jealous is all, chief; you know that. You're a lucky man. I wish I could get me a high-quality woman like that. A good woman."

"A good woman," Lincoln repeated, "but . . . but she's gone."

James sucked his teeth and shook his head slowly, commiserating as if Lincoln had already explained everything, or as if he didn't have to. *Men were men and women were women*, his gestures said. And that was that. He rose again and the students stared again. "I know how it is, man," he grumbled. Then he leaned over and wrapped Lincoln's slumping body in his powerful arms. Lincoln felt like he was held for a long time.

After that, James left him alone or, in a brotherly way, uttered vague expressions of support. "It's gonna be all right," he'd say, or "Don't even worry about it." He insisted on doing everything. He jumped to answer phone calls, hand out visitor passes, sign when the UPS man showed up with deliveries. He made sure the kids hanging out in the lounge area stayed under control. But if he thought he was doing Lincoln a favor, he was mistaken. Left with nothing at all to do, the older man had no choice but to confront his wife's face, which loomed at him now in a spectral way. Lincoln tried to read the *New York Times*, an article about a Cleveland man charged for his crimes against several girls, but he kept thinking about his wife and her face.

When Lincoln met Alexis, twenty-two years earlier, they were equals. He was as handsome as she was beautiful and bright, and despite their age difference he had as much to expect from the coming years as she did. Lincoln courted her in Richmond with a passion rooted in his certainty about himself. He'd been a good student, and had excelled at boxing and football; his life had been full of prizes, trophies, and scholarships. He'd had more than his share of attention from women and had enjoyed the warmth and cheer of many men. He thought often about the question of what lay ahead in his life, but when he tried to see its exact outlines, he couldn't—it was indistinct with light. It had been this way with her too. With other girls, there was no limit to how long his eyes could feast on the shape of legs glistening in stockings, on the coy retreat of a trembling hand, or on the flash of tongue in their laughing mouths. But looking at Alexis Campbell was like gazing into the sun. After just a few moments, he had to turn away. At Garfield's Bar he would tell his buddies how it hurt to look at her, and they would agree, mistaking his words for their usual hyperbole about women. On one of those nights at Garfield's, it occurred to him briefly that love was pain.

His father, who dispensed wisdom while rubbing his knees or soaking his feet, had always told him, *You better don't.* Better don't be fooled by the slenderness of a girl's waist or the roundness of her behind. Not if you're thinking about marrying her. If your heart and mind were inclined in that direction, he'd say, what you'd better *do* is have a look at her mother, because that's what she would become. It was lore—heard as often as *Stand by your man*—so Lincoln took it seriously. He would succeed where his father, for many years a lonely man, had failed.

He worried during the drive down to meet Mrs. Campbell. Despite the lovely and brilliant girl sitting beside him, he didn't expect much from a widow in a little unincorporated town called Hobson. "What's the name of the creek again?" he'd ask in the car. "Chuckatuck," she'd reply with a laugh. "And the river on the other side is Nansemond," she told him. "Named after some Indians. Then there's Nix Cove. Good fishing." All Lincoln could do was shake his head. When they got to Hobson, there were several men on Mrs. Campbell's porch, none inside. During the visit, he'd had to leave from time to time to sit out there with them. Men of a kind can bear only so much light. It might not have been true that Mrs. Campbell was even prettier than her daughter, but Lincoln couldn't tell because his eyes wouldn't follow her. Sitting out with the men, blowing steam from his cup of coffee as they blew it from theirs, he knew he had something in common with them—a small part of him had fallen for the widow too. He and the men shared this affliction but they wouldn't talk about it; as far as he could recall, none of them said a word. Better not to speak than tell a lie. On the drive back, Lincoln decided before they even got to Newport News that he had to marry Mrs. Campbell's daughter.

James kept busy at the security desk now, doing the work of both men while Lincoln sat there with his stomach on his lap. He felt a sort of bond with James now, a familiar gratitude. But one gets sick and tired of saying thank you. When he was engaged to Alexis, and during their first years of marriage, his friends would also tell him how lucky he was, but this was said as a joke. Lincoln would say thank you and agree, would tell them how grateful he was for her, but this wasn't true. He deserved her—this was what he believed, and he knew this was what his friends believed *in*. A man of a kind should get what he deserves, and if a man like him couldn't get a woman like her, then something was terribly wrong with the world.

James snipped withered leaves from the spider plants, a thing he'd never done before. Do her friends tell her *she's* lucky? Lincoln wondered. Has Donna said that to her? Has her mother told her to give thanks for her man? She might be saying it now as they picked out plums and nectarines at the fruit market, or sat out on the porch shelling peas. Surely this was foolish thinking, just as foolish as thinking Tameka would spend these years breaking the hearts of any eager Georgetown boy who wasn't like her father. Lincoln came to understand that this had always been part of his vision for himself, to have children who adored him—a son who resembled and worshipped him, a daughter for whom no other man would ever measure up. This was part of what he couldn't see before he married. But there was no son, and the years of Tameka's life had marked his decline.

She had grown up watching it. His professional gambles with the boxing gyms, and the attempts at training and managing, had failed.

His charm and stature no longer earned him opportunities, and in New York he had no reputation. He was lucky, he knew, to have his job at Tilden, steady and respectable work, but years ago he and his wife had deserved each other. Time had not treated them equally. Why did he expect otherwise though? With any two people one would get the brunt of it, and time had hit him worse than any beating he'd ever seen in the ring. He felt it had brutalized him. What did his wife think? Alexis had always been kind and supportive, but in her privacy she had to keep thoughts. A long marriage forced you to witness or suffer such brutality. Lincoln wondered, not for the first time, if this was exactly what marriage meant.

Across from the front desk, James pulled the director of security aside. Lincoln couldn't hear what they were saying, but the discussion had the look of seriousness. He approached, but the director stopped him short with a flat stony hand, which he closed into a fist before lowering it. Lincoln went back to his chair.

One day his wife's looks would go. Creases would line her face, the skin there would loosen and thin, pouches would form under her eyes, maybe little dewlaps like his under the jaw. And her mind, it would start to slip and show weakness too. Everything cracks eventually. But when? How long would it be his good fortune to have her? How long until he could just plain have her again? Her smooth face. Even after all these years he longed for it, to rub his cheek against hers and breathe hot words into her hair—there'd been no diminishment of that feeling. He still had those appetites, and she did too. Yet he also felt the urge to press the sharps of his teeth against her face, to bite down and place the first deep crack in it. When pulled by contrary desires, you often don't do anything at all. So on evenings and weekends he'd sit at home like a chastened boy, captive to her every small gesture. He didn't want to lose her.

But Lincoln was a man with luck—yes, he still had it, James had said so and he was right. Good fortune can change in an instant, however, or it might never, but whatever it does has nothing to do with you. For years it had persisted in following him. It went home from work with him, lived with his family, claimed a space between him and his wife in their bed. She still had her light, but his was his luck. If it left him, she would too. No one would blame her. Neither Donna nor her other girlfriends, nor her mother, nor their daughter. Nor James. Maybe James had been wrong earlier. Maybe Lincoln's luck had already abandoned him—his wife was gone for now, after all. Or maybe Lincoln was the one with wrong notions—maybe, slumped in his chair at the desk, unable to muster the little strength it took to hold in his belly, it was his luck that he was alone with.

The director of security came over with James smiling at his side. "Listen," he said, "why don't you take off early?"

"But I'm okay," Lincoln said. "I'm good."

"Cut the crap. You've looked like shit for days now." A few of the students nearby laughed. "People on this team take care of one another." He nodded to James and then fixed his light gray eyes back on Lincoln.

The director was a big man, a former marine and police officer. He had a hard, pasty face that splotched red in winter. When he'd started working as the director, Lincoln had had the impression that he was still learning how to be gentle again. The cushion on his voice had worn thin, and he didn't like it when his kindness was declined. Not knowing what else to say, Lincoln ended up thanking him, but the director dismissed this.

"Take tomorrow off too," he said. "A couple of days, if need be. Don't worry. The team will pick up the slack. We'll be fine without you."

Lincoln spent a long time eyeing the labels on the packages and randomly moving things around on the desk. With the director in a meeting, he lingered until dismissal time so he could be swept by the onrush of students out of the building. Outside, he kept looking back through the glass doors at James, who waved and then shooed him away. All three divisions of the school flooded the sidewalk, and SUVs had started to line up at the curb. As he approached Columbus Avenue, passing Tilden's more modern middle- and lower-school buildings, Lincoln had to take special care to avoid bumping into the youngest students. The next few blocks would be like this, as many kids from Tilden, Goldfinch, and two other neighborhood schools liked to intermingle.

He thought about tapping on the window at Goldfinch, but his leaving early wasn't something he could even pretend to gloat about. Sidney looked busy anyway, dealing with the girls and their mothers and caregivers. Lincoln made slow progress on the sidewalk between the avenues, but he didn't want to cross the street or change his usual route to the subway station. The girls' voices rose into a kind of keening and comforted him. He used to walk over here from Tilden to get Tameka at dismissal time, before she was old enough to cross streets by herself. She never liked it when he held her hand, and would snatch it away as soon as she set foot on the sidewalk.

The uniform the youngest girls wore hadn't changed much over the years. The jumpers were a darker shade of blue, and the shirts now had rounded collars; otherwise they were the same. A few familiar brown faces remained among the caregivers, though they were older now. Lincoln exchanged nods or smiles with even those he didn't recognize. Grinning high-school boys, some from Tilden, weaved their way through the crowd. One boy shouted to a tall Asian girl about the upcoming weekend. To Lincoln the weekend felt very far away. This moment appealed to him, and he didn't want it to end. As he stood there, he felt a stirring on his body, but it was just the vibration of his phone in his pocket. A couple of lower-school girls jostled by him, then he moved over to an open space near the curb and brought the phone high up, close to his eyes. The screen showed a message from Tameka: her bus would get in about half an hour early. He took a few idle steps as he typed his reply, then stopped because he kept hitting the wrong letters. He walked a few more feet and stopped a second time to correct another error. "Lord have mercy," he muttered. All that trouble for a simple response—*Okay, ill. See you soon.* He stopped walking a third time, turned to apologize to whoever had bumped into him from behind, and scanned for the button that would delete.

"What are you doing?" someone said.

Lincoln took a few more steps and then stopped.

"I said, *what are you doing*?" It was the yelling voice of a woman.

Lincoln gave up and was about to send the message without correcting it.

"Are you taking pictures?"

From the right a young white woman, no older than thirty, entered his field of vision. Her lipless mouth was pressed tight, a hard little line stabbed into her face. She grabbed a loose section of her hair and tucked it violently behind her ear.

"Are you taking pictures of the girls?" She was talking to him.

Lincoln panicked. "What girls? No."

"But I *saw* you. I saw you doing it," the woman said, her voice louder now. She meant the girls around them, the Goldfinch girls. He stared at the shock of prematurely silver hair at her temple to avoid looking in her eyes.

"Me?"

"I was watching you the whole time!"

"You think *I* was taking pictures?"

"Of the girls!"

The eyes of other women, white mothers gathered in a group as well as caretakers, fixed on them. A pigeon glided by, cutting a fine arc just above their heads. The keening of the girls hadn't stopped but it was quieter now; some of them watched the altercation as well.

Lincoln found himself blurting out, "Miss, my daughter was a student here. I work here."

"I've never seen you before."

"I mean, I work at the school down the street."

"Which school?"

"*Tilden.*"

"Why were you taking pictures of the girls?" the woman insisted.

"But I wasn't—"

"Show me your phone."

"You're crazy."

"You heard what I said. Give it to me!"

Lincoln found himself shouting then. "Who the hell do you think you are? What gives you the damn right to—?"

"I'm protecting little girls from creeps like you."

"You don't know a thing about me."

"I don't want to know you," she said, and he took a few steps away from her. "Pervert!"

When she took out her own phone, Lincoln walked away more quickly, bumping into several people before turning the corner onto Broadway.

For almost a mile he kept looking behind him. Though he knew after a block or two that the white woman could no longer see him at all, if she had ever seen him, the distance between the two of them seemed no greater. Her voice still rang in his ears. It wasn't that she was right about him. What she had said about him was completely wrong, the accusation wild and coarse, her words just hacking away. But he also knew that he carried guilt in him that was large, for something impossible to defend.

Lincoln walked without purpose. He took random turns but generally made his way south along the city's grid. *A creep*, the white woman had called him. *A pervert.* Under the awnings of storefronts, on the steps of churches, against the papered-up windows of failed restaurants, he would stop and delete a picture from his phone. He was willing to do now what had been unthinkable just earlier today, though doing it wasn't really about his will.

When Alexis had discovered the pictures, there'd been about thirty of them. It wasn't clear how long she had known, but judging from the change in her demeanor it had been at least a few days. She would get home about an hour and a half after he did, as usual, look at him and not say a word. She'd bring takeout Chinese or Thai food for dinner and leave some for him in the kitchen, eating her portion in the bedroom with the door closed, alone. During those evenings, she would run long baths even though she showered every morning. After a few anxious days of this, he came home to find a letter from her on Schomburg stationery. Even with what poured out in the letter, her handwriting had the constancy of a font—the upward flourishes at the end of each word, the fullness of the counters. She told him she would be staying at Donna's, but the letter never explicitly mentioned his pictures. *If you ever want to talk to me, to try to explain yourself, I might be willing to listen.* Each time he stopped on the street to delete an image from his phone, Lincoln took a long look at it, as if the thing that would fortify him for the talk with his wife might be there, as if he would discover what, until now, he had overlooked.

The news about her trip to Virginia came in a phone call. Lincoln noticed when she called that day, both times, but was afraid to answer. Finally, in the evening, Donna left a message that Alexis was going to stay with her mother, and that Tameka knew she was going but not why. "She's already gone but you know how to reach her," Donna said, and hung up without saying good-bye. Lincoln lay in bed that night staring into the glow of his phone, the pictures up to about sixty by then. In the dark he practiced explaining himself to several of the women's faces before giving up. He didn't feel lonely, not yet. Alexis hadn't completely given up on him, so he knew he still had time.

Somewhere west of the theater district, Lincoln spoke to the screen of his phone. "I just want to say . . . ," he murmured, and then deleted a more recent image. The light from the cloudless sky felt harsh on his cheeks and prickled his skin under his sleeves. He pulled his shirttails out of his pants and, making careful folds, exposed his arms past the elbows like a working man. He walked south through Chelsea and Greenwich Village, then into SoHo and along Canal Street, where he eventually faced the entrance to the Manhattan Bridge. Only two of the pictures remained on his phone now, the two from this morning. He deleted the one that had come out blurry. All that was left was the final one: the precision of the young woman's glare, her disappointed mouth, the bolts of heat bright along her face. Her eyes were worse than those of the white woman in front of the school. Eyes worse still, ones he only imagined for now, would remain with him.

Lincoln was sweaty and tired. The steel of the bridge's towers appeared ugly to him in the late afternoon light. He could have taken a cool subway the rest of the way, but he decided to go ahead and walk across to Brooklyn in the hot sun.

He stopped once, high over the water, to delete the young woman from his phone. After it was gone, he realized with some surprise that he hadn't taken any other pictures, not even a single one of his wife. He shut off the phone and stared at its dark screen until he felt it was time to go home.

It took a while, so Tameka was already there when he arrived. He hadn't seen her since the winter holiday. Her hair was different, twisted and dyed brown at the edges. She reminded him even more of her mother. She gave him a hug, pressing herself tightly against him. "Where were you?" she asked. She had waited for him at Port Authority, and had called him more than once. When he didn't answer her question, she stood apart from him and said, "Daddy? Look at me. What's the matter?"

At first Lincoln said it was nothing, nothing at all, but she continued to ask. She kept demanding to know what was wrong. Finally, he met his daughter's gaze and told her. He described every humiliating detail of what had happened to him in front of her old school. He told her what he could. He told her a lie.

Infinite Happiness

The new waitress came by that morning to refresh my coffee and give
Micah more hot water for tea. She had light brown skin and twists of
lovely russet hair. When she wasn't biting her lip, her nervous smiling
mouth reminded me of a cut strawberry's inner flesh. Micah watched
her walk back toward the bar, mumbling to himself as though casting a spell. Whether the spell was on himself or on her retreating hips
I couldn't tell.

"It's time," he declared, as he forked and held aloft a flap of potato
pancake. "It's time for me to put the booty-goggles back into storage."

I laughed, but only with my mouth.

"Besides, she likes *you*, blood. You see the way she was looking at
you?"

Micah steeped the tea, his own pungent blend of crushed black
and green leaves, which he carried around in a pouch. He guffawed,
as though late at getting his own joke, and his body shook within his
loose colorful dashiki. The crow's-feet etched at the corners of his eyes
were the only visible clues that he was on the cusp of middle age. He
kept his face and head cleanly shaven, so you never saw a speck of gray
on him. An excess of joy seemed to be Micah's burden in life. You
could see the effort of laughter taxing him like labored breath.

His girlfriend, Cody—A Black Girl Named Cody he sometimes called her, as if she were a myth, an impossibility—was returning sometime that evening from her family's annual trip to see the old maternal relatives in Ghana. Usually she would have been there at Saturday brunch with us. I often tagged along on their outings. Cody didn't mind, so whenever Micah invited me, I'd be there. For a long time, I'd been the camera verifying their love.

According to my watch, which I kept a few minutes fast, it was almost noon. I asked when Cody was getting in. She hadn't responded to any of the emails I'd sent in the past few weeks. Micah took a sip of his tea, smiled, and said her flight arrived around seven thirty. He knew this and I didn't. This may seem like an obvious thing to say, a stupid declaration, but sometimes the most mundane facts get imbued with deep feeling. The tiniest splinters of information can strike with hard weight when they're finally given to you.

With Cody gone those four weeks, Micah had been a creature uncaged in Brooklyn's simmering streets, chasing women as though their shorts and skirts were those little flags pulled from body to air during field games. Before brunch that day, while we walked to the restaurant, Micah stopped and asked me to smell his face. He closed his eyes and pouted a little. Somehow, these unsettling gestures softened the crassness of his request. I could do anything at all to him—spit on his chin, strike his brow with my palm—but all I did, stupidly, was stick with the script. I sniffed at his cheek and then told him he'd forgotten to wash.

"I didn't forget," he said, and grinned.

Ever since I was a boy, men like Micah have captivated me. They dress in ways that should be funny—hats wide or tall, shirts with collars like condor wings, fingers winking with jewelry, pants and shoes in outrageous colors—but no one ridicules them, because they are also always enmeshed in the rogue limbs of women. Some part of me wanted to be like those men we called, casually, "pimps." Despite whatever else I may have felt about them, I'd declared to my uncle that I wanted to be a pimp, as we walked with ice cream one afternoon on Eastern Parkway. Uncle Max made a face I couldn't read and told me, not for the first time, that black men used to be kings. Then he shifted his Good Humor bar to his left hand, and slapped me. Sometimes the pop of his ring still burns on my mouth.

Back at the apartment that day, Aunt Leigh asked my uncle what had happened to my face. He said he'd be back later, after a few rounds with the fellas, and slammed the door on his way out. When she asked me, I said I had fallen and left it at that. I didn't want to tell her anything. Her concern for me, for us, always came too late; reacting was all she seemed capable of doing. In that way, she resembled my mother—her sister-in-law. I felt sorry for her, that she was so feeble, just as I felt sorry for my mother, who had been dying long before doctors informed her she was. My father was, as they say, a rolling stone, and he had rolled right over her before he skipped town. That collision may have started her dying—I don't know. All I can say is that he left and she died, and so I ended up living with my aunt and uncle in Brooklyn. They had no children of their own.

Micah's studio apartment was two blocks from the restaurant. It still smelled of sex. I sat on his small couch as he pulled sheets from the bed, shut off the air conditioner he'd kept running, opened the windows. Cody's old copy of *Love in the Time of Cholera* sat on an arm of the couch, its torn cover and a few ragged pages fluttering in the rush of warm air. Micah's cat, Pawtrice Lumumba, watched the book for a while before leaping onto the nearest windowsill. He rubbed his face against the screen as a tumble of street noise spilled from Flatbush Avenue into the apartment. Micah dropped the sheets in a pile by the front door, then lit several sticks of a kind of incense I despised, which purpled the air with its thick, stony smoke. He stuck the wooden ends of the incense into various holes in the walls of the apartment. Though Micah hardly ever brought other women home since he'd started seeing Cody, there was something cool and mechanical about the way he moved around now. The last few weeks had been enough time for him to remember his old routine.

He cleaned in denim shorts and a pair of flip-flops, now shirtless, but he still wore his large yellow fedora tilted sideways on his head. The hat gleamed softly against his dark skin. For a moment he looked sad and oblivious—as if there were something he had forgotten or didn't know. His appearance dropped the cold, heavy glass clutched at my chest right into my gut. In his brief wistfulness and ignorance, he looked like a boy who had just been crowned.

He suggested we listen to some roots music, his cure-all, and played his favorite mix of Bunny Wailer, Burning Spear, and the Abyssinians. Everyone in Brooklyn had probably heard this mix. Reggae was a big part of the way Micah announced the syncopated cluck of his heart to the world. All of the lyrics were about Emperor Haile Selassie, spirituality, and a life of resistance to racism and government oppression. I listened for different songs, ones about betrayal and faithlessness. Life's smaller, inglorious oppressions.

"So what's up, stranger?" he said. "How's the writing going?" We hadn't seen each other much during Cody's trip.

"It's not."

"What's the problem?"

"Just can't find the words," I said.

"Brutal. You need inspiration, that's all. Yo, why didn't you go to the party last night?"

I almost snapped back and asked why he *did* go, but I just shrugged. I knew why. He went because he could and because he always had a good time, even though most people who went were probably my age, a decade younger than he was, if not more. The party was one of a series of fundraising events for a political prisoner. Flyers for such parties were always all over the place, on the internet, and in the windows of local stores and restaurants. FREE CHAKRA GIBBONS. This particular event was where Micah had met last night's girl. He had told me about her as we ate, in the usual way he had of talking about his women, first emphasizing the raw physicality of the initial encounter—how her body in that dress nearly snapped his neck, how her hips loosely swayed as she walked, how fragrant and soft she was as they danced. For him there was obvious purpose, a clarity of desire, in her every gesture. No smile was ever a curtain politely drawn. No laugh fretted with irony, no glance clouded with ambiguity. But then the story itself became cloudy as matters escalated and he got her to go home with him. The pace of his telling picked up, the language became more ornate. He and the woman were no longer attractive physical beings. They were something greater, deities of a kind, anointing and sanctifying each other behind a curtain he closed even to me, his audience.

And now all that was left of her, so soon, was a thinning perfume smothered by incense and soiled sheets heaped on the floor. In his fingers, a woman's panties were the strings of a rosary, but only for the few slow seconds that he creeped them from her waist and hips, from her sloped thighs, her ankles and tensed toes. Thereafter, flung on the floor, drained of the mysteries of his attention, they were nothing but strips of rag, the leavings of an act. Quickly the woman from the party, so fleshy and sensual in her dress, would also become the leavings of an act, among the stuff to be covered up or swept away.

I knew the ceremony of his bedrooms, or imagined I did, because he talked and talked to me. I hung on every one of his inflated words, felt for their edges, peered around them in search of patterns, clues: what it meant when he disclosed a bit more, used this or that adjective; what it meant when he withheld. He never said a word about his sex life with Cody though, even during the early stages when they were casually dating. That curtain stayed closed, completely.

Micah stopped cleaning and turned up the dial on the good cheer.

I must have been looking glum. He told me the words *Free Chakra Gibbons* never failed him in the booty department. Micah had a high number of tactics that supposedly never failed, and he'd offer these to me as if they had the power of currency.

"I approach women in the street," he said, laugh lines deepening, "honeys I've never even *seen* before, and say, 'Peace, sister, didn't I meet you at the Free Chakra Gibbons party last month?' Meet, see. It doesn't matter. Last month, last night, last year. Doesn't matter. Works every time."

"You must say it real sweet," I said. "Agave nectar pouring out of your mouth and everything."

"It's the ancient science, blood. Check it. If she knows who Chakra Gibbons is, you're golden, as the conscious brother. If not, it's the science. The words, the secret signs."

"Initiate me."

"*Free* is the American word. Free sample. Free consultation. Free shipping. Free your mind. Free the slaves. We love that shit. From the best to the worst, all of us. But then there's *Chakra*. Tantra. Yoga, you feel me? And Shaka Zulu. Freaky revolutionary vibisms, man. And then *Gibbons*. With that they hear *give, give*. Give thyself wholly to him. It's like speaking the ancestral tongue, on the lower frequencies, on some ill subliminalisms. *Free Chakra Gibbons* never fails to get the digits. And if you work it right: the honeypot."

"But what if they left their secret decoder rings at home that day?"

Micah laughed like the supervillain in a movie. "You underestimate your power, A.J.," he said. "You block your blessings." He plucked Pawtrice Lumumba from the sill and cradled him like an infant, rubbed the soft of his belly until he purred. "When's the last time you got blessed, yo? Weeks? Months? A year? Don't say a year."

"About a month," I said, a possible start to my truth-telling about Cody. But the woman I went on to describe wasn't her, and the encounter I sketched belonged to another month of another year, an entirely different lifetime. On top of that basic act of lying, of hauling in an alternative and irrelevant truth, came embellished details about that long-ago night of desperate, fumbled lovemaking. Micah placed his cat back on the sill and stood over me, beaming. He drilled the knuckle of his middle finger into my shoulder as he enjoyed my story. "She couldn't get enough of me," I found myself saying. "Kept calling and texting after that, you know. It was too much. I had to cut her off."

"Damn, blood, you gotta be careful. Can't go activating the pathways with every honey you bring home." To illustrate the pathways he traced parallel lines from his groin to his heart. "They're always looking for a reason to fall in love."

Micah used words like *blood* and *brethren* and phrases like *peace and love* and *don't block your blessings*, language so earnest and sappy the poet in me found it embarrassing. He had volleyed an entire glossary of it at me when we first met, three years earlier. It was the morning after he'd first slept with Cody, who was then my roommate. She and I had lived in a walk-through two-bedroom apartment on the edge of Clinton Hill. A friend of Cody's whom I knew from graduate school had vouched for me, saying I was a good guy, safe, reasonably clean, responsible. Boring, in other words, but a suitable replacement for the girl who was moving out. The apartment was affordable because one of the rooms, mine, was just a glorified closet. It was at the extreme end of the place and opened directly into hers. So it was like this: I'd have to knock on my door before coming out—to watch TV, to grab a bowl of cereal, even to take a damn leak—to make sure she was, as they say, decent. What does it say about me, about my situation of mind and nerve, that I never failed, not even once, to give those precautionary knocks?

The afternoon I first went over to meet Cody, it took a long time for her to open the apartment door. There were three locks, one of which she had had installed, and a security chain to undo. This struck me as odd. The neighborhood wasn't dangerous and the door itself was weightless, made of the flimsiest wood. The feeble thing swung open and Cody stood on the other side of the doorway, in a tank top and no bra. She was anything but decent. She touched the head of a foot-tall porcelain unicorn that stood on a little table, its crooked horn pointed at me.

After a quick tour of the apartment, which had lots of art in thick frames on the walls, we grabbed a couple of beers and chatted in the living room. She was a few years out of college, she explained, and now worked as a publicist for a fashion company. As she spoke I decided, perhaps because I thought I had to, that she wasn't my type. During the tour, I'd sized her up: kind of lank, with only a dollop of ass, and her legs rose to meet her hips farther out than you'd expect. I would discover in time that she herself made fun of these features, as well as of her light skin, blaming her white Englishman father and his side of the family. But Cody didn't lack confidence. She knew she was attractive. She had full, distracting breasts and large, dark areolae that I could see through her tank top. I worked so hard not to look that I lost track of our conversation. She was giving me an expectant look, her lashes and lips both floating from her face in the same way, following the same gentle circuits.

"I love the place," I said. "It's really a great place." I complimented everything there, everything but her. I even complimented her porcelain unicorn.

"Oh, it's not a unicorn," she said, looking at it. "It's an *abada*. Congolese." Striations, which gave the statue the appearance of whitened wood, indicated the hair of its mane and the lines of its muscles. Cody told me the creature was supposed to have two horns, which could cure the effects of poison, but one of them had broken off and was lost.

When I moved in, I was a graduate student, mastering poetry by degrees. I lived on a stipend and loans. Despite my best efforts, I started to look at her, and look at her. At those eyes and lips. At her hair, incredible no matter what she did with it: close-cropped, faux hawk, grown long, poofed out with whorls wide enough to put your hand through. It all took me for a ride. I started to notice other things, like her devotion to small collections of books and albums. She constantly reread books from her high school English classes, and invited folks over to listen to the same old Miles and Billie records. These made up the entire soundtrack of her existence. I always recommended volumes of poetry and novels, offering to let her borrow my own copies, but she always refused. "I'm fine with these," she said once, pointing down at her modest bookcase. "Just these. I'm happy getting to know them better." She told me libraries made her nervous in college. "Huge buildings with all those books, all those writers and their opinions and worlds. I used to think I'd be wasting my opportunity if I didn't try to read as many of those books as I could, but it's too much, too hard to wrap your heart around. They look so graceful lined up on the shelves, not messing with each other, so neat. It's nicer that way."

Cody and I lived together for two years and it wasn't long before I began to think that somehow, in a moment of weakness or realization, we would share her bed. Hers, not mine. Her bed was larger, better for the things I wanted to do to her and the things I imagined she would do to me. When tipsy with wine, feeling a little flirtatious, she had hinted at such things, at what she would do if only the world were a different place. Who knew what she meant by this? It was probably easier than saying *If only you were a different man.*

Given the terrible layout of our place, Cody had been kind enough not to bring any of her smutties around. After about a year of rooming together, though, Micah became the first and only exception.

I can't blame her. When she brought Micah over, she didn't know I was home. On hot nights I sometimes stayed with Aunt Leigh, now living alone in an air-conditioned place south of Prospect Park, but that night I had fallen into a heavy torpor. I was naked in my room with the lights out, completely still on my futon mattress, surrounded by books. Under these, the corners of printouts of poems by Auden and Lowell flapped in the air blowing from my box fan. I'd been trying to compose a long poem, an elegy for Uncle Max, but the writing wasn't going well. It was summer, the season of my anguished vanishing, my annual retreat indoors, and it felt as though the capacity for true language was being burned out of me. I never wrote that poem. I never could find the words.

When it gets hot, especially in New York, most people happily remove their clothing, favoring the merest layers between their vivid selves and the sticky flesh of the city. I'm different. I feel most like myself in dark jeans and heavy shoes, long sleeves, sweaters, and thick jackets. In shorts and T-shirts I'm just the ghost haunting them, billowing the fabrics and rattling my awkward lengths of bone. I can't hide how scrawny I am—the thinness of my wrists and ankles, my shins like blades—and I experience it acutely, my lack of substance. Even when I'm alone, nudity sometimes embarrasses me, and in my waking dreams I see myself being blasted away by a strong wind.

I was still awake when they came in laughing, well before midnight. I found myself taking more shallow breaths as Cody called my name to see if I was home. She sounded drunk. She called a few more times, but I said nothing, didn't move. After a few moments, I was hardly breathing at all. I moved in weightless slow motion, pulled on underwear, turned off the fan, pretended to sleep in case she came in, pretended to disappear. As I lay in that hot airless room, my body seemed unbearably loud—my stomach, the sound of my blinking. When I had to pee, I held it as long as I could. Finally, moving with agonizing slowness, I sat up and relieved myself into an empty beer bottle.

I listened all night, and deepened the vividness of my imaginings until they became grotesque. They had sex twice and once again in the morning, each time prefaced by his teasing and her joking protestations. It was as though, beneath him (on top of him? gathered like a leggy insect before him?), she herself melted from one rhythm and shape in order to be remolded by his flung hands and organ into another.

It was close to noon before I heard them leave. I came out of my room to slip away from the apartment, but Micah was there. He sat on our shabby living room couch, looking like the black Hatter. He beamed at me, showing the creases in his face, not concerned in the least about my sudden appearance.

He told me Cody had gone around the corner to grab pastries and soy chai lattes. After a moment, he added, "You must be Anthony." Cody called me Anthony even though I went by A.J.

He nodded cheerfully when I corrected him. Then came the Micah words and the Micah phrases. I felt grateful, in a way, despite his refusal to give much of a damn about the fact of my presence, as if it didn't matter one bit that I'd been there the entire time. He gave me his full attention now though. He seemed genuinely curious about me. Meanwhile I kept thinking, This guy? From certain angles he looked almost old enough to be her father. But he allied himself with me when Cody came back. He played along, nodding and grinning as I lied to her about having just gotten home from a wild night.

After that, through his oddly persistent efforts, we became tight. He showed me how to work a camera and operate a boom. I worked on the crew for some of his local film projects, mostly shorts, and when I was strapped for cash he hooked me up with work on other people's productions. He was always dragging me out, so I began to meet people around the city. These were people whose lives seemed beyond my reach, who showed up en masse during summer's cultural fairs and bazaars, filling the streets with color and music and rare sensuality before vanishing for the rest of the year. I could hardly believe they lived in the same city I did, but Micah knew where they went when it wasn't summer and he brought me to those places too. He was good to me. He was kinder to me than any man I've known.

As his favorite music played and summoned our racial glory, Micah and I drove through Crown Heights and Bed-Stuy, the parts that hadn't yet been touched by gentrification. I'd been avoiding him for the past few weeks but agreed to tag along on a few errands he wanted to run before picking Cody up at the airport. I intended to tell him what had happened between me and her. Again and again, I'd gone over the possibilities of how it could play out. On what ground could his anger stand? How could he, of all people, accuse me? I would tell him the truth, that I'd slept with her, and then the harder truth, that I was in love with her. This is a good time, I kept thinking, right now, just lower the music and face the man and speak. Instead I stared at the passenger-side window as he sang stray, discordant phrases of song. We dropped off his laundry first, then, from Nostrand Avenue, with its roti shops and gated supermarkets, we made our way to Fulton Street, where people poured out of the subway station on the corner and a man hawked DVDs in front of a chicken joint.

I noticed Micah had been silent for a while, and I could feel his eyes on me.

"What's up?" he asked.

We drove alongside a park I didn't recognize. Medallions of light twinkled through the gaps in the trees onto a stretch of patchy browned grass, and beyond the chain-link fence the backs of boys playing basketball gleamed like dark, wet stones. Above them a slim crescent moon persisted in the afternoon sky.

"You seem deep in it," he said. "Inner visions."

In response, I pointed up at the moon.

"Irie," he said. He was so excited that his voice rose again in song. When he parked the car, I turned to him with the first words I'd settled upon ready at my lips, but found his face close to mine as he leaned to look at the moon. There was something sweet and childlike about the gesture, his unembarrassed physical closeness.

The sky, he said, held a good omen. "The constancy of the moon on the day my moon returns." Sometimes he called Cody his "moon," sometimes his "earth." He, however, was always the shining sun. A smile played at the corner of his mouth while he looked up into the sky and absorbed all that the universe was confirming for him. "Synchronicity!" he exclaimed, and bounded out of the car.

We entered a bookstore without a sign out front. I had never even known the place existed, and had I known, I wouldn't have gone in anyway. The selection was limited, the shelves dusted with the sadness of another time. It immediately revealed itself to be a temple devoted to black hero worship and the erotic mysteries of the East. A few symbols and images predominated on the walls. Bared skin of the plummiest, oiliest darkness. Cowries. Ankhs. On a calendar, various figures—impossibly voluptuous women, muscled babies, regal-headed men—were fitted into the precise shape of the Motherland. Here one was as likely to invoke the name of Imhotep as I was to call upon Whitman or Stevens. My body stiffened in response to the place. I felt exposed as some kind of a sellout, scrutinized by the very walls.

The woman minding the store was almost as tall as Micah, and her hair was wrapped in a bright blue cloth. She came out from behind the register to give him a hug. She wore leggings that showed everything, smoothed everything, nudged all that flesh skyward just the right bit. Her body bruised my lonely, lusting heart. With its high arrogant jut, her ass seemed like its own organism, separate from the rest of her. She looked older, probably around Micah's age, but she was very attractive. I couldn't stand his easy way with her.

"Look at you, queen!" He liked to call black women "queens." I obsessed over this and constantly shouted complaints in my mind. In our attempts to love them, why did our women have to be queens? If we were kings and queens, then who were our subjects? It was impossible for every one of us to be royalty.

But the woman in the store clearly liked being a queen. With arms raised, she spun herself before Micah like a loosened feather. I considered bowing my head or genuflecting to claim a place in the ritual, if only to justify my presence.

"Gotta drink all your meals, baby," she said. "Health is wealth."

"A blessing!" Micah exclaimed.

"Hey now, so where you been?" the woman said. "You could call a sister. You could come around more than once a year."

She wasn't kidding. Micah's absence had really made her upset. In that moment, he nodded in my direction and introduced me. That timing of his. She glanced over with dulled eyes and then fixed on me, suddenly intrigued.

"This is what you do, Micah? I gave you that shirt."

The T-shirt I was wearing had the words MORE JUJU across the chest, declaring on behalf of its wearer powers that were African, magical, and sexual. Below this, two huge reddish spark plugs glowed. I was wearing it only because I needed to wash my clothes, but now I felt as though I'd been walking around all day making fraudulent claims.

"I can't believe this. That was a gift, for you. It's my design." She spoke as though the cloth were pulled from the fibers of her womb. But it was hard to tell if she was more upset with him or me.

"You know I don't rock no tight-ass smedium shirts. Too small. Only mess with them kingly robes."

He spoke in the Jamaican accent he sometimes affected. The rhyme or reason of its use was impossible to figure out, but somehow the accent and the words it bent earned him her instant forgiveness. She said she would get him another shirt, one in the right size. I imagined a version of my shirt that came down to Micah's ankles. They made up with another long hug, murmuring to each other, two liars locked in an embrace. I figured he was promising her two visits in the next year, two Nubian orgasms perhaps, twice as many reverent anointings of her ass, speaking the whole time in his half-baked accent. I wanted to remind him that he was from Cleveland, but they both seemed far away from me.

The woman held his face in her hands, but the look she gave him was maternal, not sexual. She left a kiss on the top of his head after he removed his hat and bent to receive it. Then she came over and pulled me into a hug too. She stood apart and studied me for a moment. With a honed sincerity she said how good it was to meet me. "You're always welcome here, son," she said. "Hope to see you again soon." The warmth of her skin, the sweetness of her breath, and the steady lights of her eyes extinguished the bitterness in me. It seemed suddenly and powerfully true: I really *was* welcome; she really *did* hope to see me again, even though I had done nothing at all to deserve her kindness. As I stood there, the business of this errand was finally conducted. Micah paid for a book he'd ordered through the store. He avoided the big chain bookstores and online retailers. According to him they were part of Babylon, against what was righteous and true.

The book was called *The Manual of Taoist Sexology: Infinite Wisdom and Methods*. In the car he told me to take a look. It was a thick volume, over three hundred pages. Clearly its wisdom and methods were for Cody, starting tonight. The introduction included this passage: "Correct sex circulates happiness among individuals and societies. Happiness is a form of healing, and correct sex conjures forth healing and infinite happiness. Incorrect sex—sex used as a weapon to be inflicted upon others—conjures forth decay and infinite pain." The book was more for him than for her. Or if it was for her, a genuine gift, then there was nothing of an apology in it. His intention in giving it wasn't at all to make amends for what he had done. His notion of correction wasn't concerned with morality; it was simultaneously physical, metaphysical, and cosmic. It struck me that telling Micah about what had happened, about my incorrect sex with Cody, wasn't about apology either. I hadn't been thinking of it that way at all. I wanted to shift Cody's position between us, and to shift his position too. My desire, like his, was to reorder the universe so it revolved around me.

Sometimes, because of the way he looked at me—the way he glanced and grinned now as I held the book—it seemed he already may have known my secret, that he suspected it or that Cody had already confessed. It would have been exactly like him to suspect or even know and, out of confidence or even arrogance, perhaps some mythic notion of ancient brotherhood, not to care very much. His concern, if he had one, wasn't me; it was the Ghanaians across the Atlantic, men of mind and flesh and throbbing blood who weren't mythical or ancient, men who were very much alive. But his logic of correspondences interpreted the daytime moon as a confirmation of her fidelity while abroad, and he saw no reason to worry about what she might have done here. As soon as I thought this, however, I told myself it couldn't be true. Micah had told me his relationship with Cody was the longest he'd ever had with a woman. He would care what she did, even if it was with me. He cheated on her constantly, yes, but he did love her. Both these things must have warred within him, but his body could—with apparent ease—contain such conflicts.

While waiting for a traffic light to turn green, Micah turned to me with a funny look on his face. I couldn't pinpoint the meaning of his expression.

"So, homegirl at the store," I said, just to say something. "She's a real trip."

"A queen," he said.

"One of your old pieces?"

Micah looked at me like I was deranged. "What? She's an elder, blood. She's got kids my age. Keeps herself looking right, but that woman's gotta be sixty years old."

Even her body lies, I thought. But it didn't feel like a lie, or not merely that, and this new feeling colored the way I had seen them hugging earlier. To so wholly throw yourself into fabrication, into falseness, stretching yourself into a different shape. People like that must have a constant need to be held.

We spent a good deal of time tracking down the herbalist Micah liked, so he could buy some bundles of dried sage. A few hours remained before Cody got in. Micah said our next task, which for some reason he also referred to as an "errand," was to participate in the weekly meditation for people of color. It took place, when the weather was nice, in Fort Greene Park. I've never been one to meditate. And *people of color* was to me an unsatisfying, even problematic phrase. It called to mind crayons or Magic Markers. But Micah promised that honeys would be there, explained on the way that these particular honeys would appreciate my "cerebral vibisms." He liked to add *ism* to certain words. He was a chief constructor of arcane theories and doctrines that only he, if anyone, understood. When you boiled it down, his language had just a handful of words, and few of them made any sense. They evaporated as soon as they left his mouth. He was so confident when he said them, even though his entire store of knowledge and wisdom was suspect. It didn't matter in the end, because of the way he made you feel. So few words, as if he had pared them down to get closer to the crucial beginnings of language itself, to notions so large and surprisingly simple they had to be shared.

Micah dangled the promise of women so I would go to the meditation with him. It was hard to understand—maybe I was only his foil—but he really seemed to want my companionship. There was no way he knew what had happened, I realized. No man with the barest degree of sanity would cling this way to another man, a friend, who had slept with his woman. So the burden of telling was still mine.

We walked through the park and passed children at play. The air was hot but not humid. We made our way past scattered oaks and elms, and then up the hillock in the middle of the park, emerging finally from a dappled tunnel made by a cluster of ginkgos. The sky, a huge blue sparkle, framed the thin, yellowed smile of the persisting moon. The group, made up mostly of women, had started to gather near the Prison Ship Martyrs Monument. At least three different languages drifted from them into the breeze. The monument's thick Doric column rose above the group like a phallic idol. Micah was right; many of the women were extremely attractive, but Cody was the person I wanted. The effect of the array was striking, however—one gorgeous collective personality—and no one looked at me as though I didn't belong. For a few solid moments—the first I'd had in a long time—the phrase *people of color* made complete and unassailable sense.

Micah wanted to introduce me to some women right away, but I resisted.

"Come on," he urged. "Blood, this is it. It doesn't get better. Open thy hand wide," he said, exposing the skin of his palms.

"Maybe after."

He smiled, but disappointment creased his face. "Don't make me do everything," he said, pointing a finger at my nose. "Because I will, damn you." We clapped hands and he pulled me into his chest, holding me there for a while. He really wasn't afraid to show affection for anyone, man or woman. "We'll find you your queen yet," he said.

Black love was one of his crucial notions, a heterosexual paradise in which a desirable woman existed for every desiring man, a queen for every king. When he called me "king," he believed it—more than Uncle Max had. Micah believed more fully in me. He seemed genuinely baffled, even concerned, that I didn't have someone.

Micah moved fluidly through the crowd. As always, he made each interaction tactile, kissing each woman on both cheeks, grasping their hands, touching their naked shoulders. He flirted and laughed easily, his eyes wide and receptive, and it became difficult to tell which people he already knew and which he was meeting for the first time. I walked a few feet across the coarse grass and sat at the base of the monument. Even through jeans the granite warmed the backs of my thighs. Warmth spread all over my body, making me feel vaguely feverish. Uncle Max used to take me to this monument when I was a boy. He used to tell me the monument was for our people, black people, built to commemorate those who had died on slave ships, those floating prisons. He didn't always narrate the monument that way, but I didn't mind. Sometimes he would tell me it honored blacks who had fought in the Revolutionary War, people who thought of liberty not as an abstraction but as a felt thing. Once, he gripped my shoulder and asked if I could imagine the ease of limbs freed from shackles, the beauty.

My uncle was a handsome man, with a serious face that could become severe. He worked as a copy editor for a tabloid newspaper and kept a photograph of Kwame Ture on his desk. His thumbs were often smudged with ink. Uncle Max wanted to write articles himself, but all his attempts failed. As he got more and more frustrated, he began to spend more time away from home, and when he wasn't fleeing from our apartment, he stretched its air taut with his bile. The quality of his writing was unknown to me, but he was a gifted storyteller, which is why I accepted his contradictory tales. He had a particular talent for conjuring motive, character, and blame right on the spot. In the story he made of his life, he blamed everyone—his bosses for being racist, my aunt for not loving and supporting him enough. He blamed my father for being, in his words, a "bum," and blamed his dead sister for loving a man who was no damn good. He blamed me simply for being my mother and father's child. For a long time, Aunt Leigh and I were both pricked by the edges of his well-honed fantasies, even after he became nothing more than a jagged rock in the world, even after he died. Only in his lowest moods, in the middle of the night during those last years, would he admit to himself that some of his failings might be his own; he thought these moments of slurred confession at the kitchen table were private, but sometimes I'd sneak into the living room, where I could hear him. His words terrified me. They let in everything a man's sense of self-preservation should keep at bay, and he was alone, I realized, so alone. I listened because I couldn't stop myself, but my listening did him no good.

As a high-school senior I felt exposed to my uncle's distinctive pierce again while walking through Fort Greene Park. It was five years to the day since his passing, and I hadn't been there since he was alive. After a while I came across an informational plaque and read about the monument's history, its true history. And there was my uncle, near me again, a kind of threat, as if his bones lay among those hardening in the crypt below.

The sound of Micah's laughter carried across our brief expanse of open sky. A woman with a nimbus of dark glistening hair approached the group he was standing in. On her brown arm she carried a basket that was beautifully woven, with triangular patterns of pale red, orange, and lilac. When the woman joined the group she reached into the basket and pulled out two spheres of bright yellow fruit. Micah and the others peeked into the basket, dipped their hands in, but didn't take anything, and the woman set the basket down in the grass. Other women, and two or three men, joined the circle, and Micah stood at the center of it.

For most people there is a gap, for some a chasm, between the way they dream themselves and the way they are seen by others. That gap might be the truest measure of one's loneliness. But seeing Micah as I often did, from across that gap, I was the one made to feel lonely. Everyone else seemed to be with him on the other side, always. At times, I couldn't understand this. He had hurt people, deceived people, among them perhaps some of the women he was now surrounded by. He had deceived Cody. Yet, knowing his reputation, or sensing it, people still clung to him. I had clung to him, as if this proximity could make me more like him. The thing was this: he seemed to be one of the few for whom there isn't a gap at all.

Disgusted, I had the urge to stand on the base of the monument and shout my secret at Micah, to make my confession to him into public testimony. It would hurt more, but which of us would suffer the deeper wound? Amid that crowd of beautiful, happy people, my testimony would get lost in the collective song of their laughter. Or so I told myself. The truth was I was afraid. It felt impossible to predict what the words would do. They caught in my throat and I could taste them on the back of my tongue.

How many of them, the meditative, the seekers, knew the simple fact that there were ruins of prisoners lying beneath us? I wasn't meditating, only pretending, looking around through squinted eyes. My jeans pulled against my knees as I struggled to sit cross-legged. Spears of grass pricked my feet. The squeals of children leapt from the distance. Above us, a passing flock loosed its bird-chatter. The air smelled of skin creams and hair oils. It was almost five-thirty; Cody would arrive in two hours. No matter what I did, my mind refused to be still. The woman in front of me was the one who had brought the basket. I lost myself in her flawless storm cloud of hair.

I closed my eyes and took a few meditative breaths, but what was the point of this pursuit? My eyes spotted with envy even when they were shut, even when I deeply inhaled what Micah called the "miracle of oxygen." I tried to clear my mind, to embrace a vision of nothingness, but instead came that miserable little room in the apartment I'd shared with Cody, Cody's lips pursed to sip wine or to kiss him, Cody's face in distress, Cody's face.

The day before she left for Ghana, I invited her out for a drink. Micah was away in New Orleans helping a friend on a film shoot. Micah did much of his dirt when he was away. Cody was sad he wouldn't be around to see her off, so I had an opportunity to comfort her. When I arrived, she was already at the bar with a glass of red wine. Cody was always early. She didn't have on anything special, just a white tank top and jeans, but she looked incredible. I searched for the lean of a stray bra strap toward the curve of her shoulder, but there was no bra. I tried not to stare as I approached. During our friendly embrace, her cheek shocked the heavy heat of the evening from my lips.

As always, she asked about the babies, by which she meant the seven- and eight-year-olds I worked with as a part-time teaching artist. I recited some funny lines from the kids' poems, and her insane laughter disturbed the other patrons. After a few glasses of wine, Cody allowed her hand to linger on my knee. She kept asking me if I was okay, which was strange. I was so happy.

After a couple more glasses she brought up Micah. She asked if it was true what they said—her girlfriends and her rivals. All of Brooklyn, it seemed. But I knew she was asking because she felt it in her gut. "Is he a player?" she said, almost whispering. "Is Micah fucking around on me?"

The way she looked as she let the question slip through her teeth suggested that she wanted some kind of false reassurance. Maybe not an outright lie, maybe just an evasion, a drunken sidestep that would leave the matter with her, with the two of them. But she knew I knew the truth—why else would she ask? I was happy she'd asked. Her hand wasn't on my knee anymore, and I longed for it to be there again. So I did what felt right to me. I told her the truth. She turned and faced the lines of bottles behind the bar. I considered saying sorry, but for what? I wasn't sorry at all. I ordered one more round and we drank in silence. She didn't cry or ask questions or rail against Micah, and for this I felt grateful. I didn't want to defend him, or condemn him any more than I already had.

As I walked her home, my mind raced. What was next? When should I tell her the rest of what I had to say, the way I felt about her? Would she accept this confession now? Why didn't I just say it? I had to take long strides to keep up with her brisk pace. Her shoes ticked against the pavement and her hair changed color as we moved in and out of blue and gray shadows. She unlocked the door to her building and held it open, then unlocked her apartment door and invited me in. I'd been there before, several times since we had roomed together, but the place felt strange to me now. Traces of the Egyptian Musk body oil Micah liked to wear lingered. Two suitcases stood by the door. What if he had come back early to surprise her? Throughout the night I would keep seeing him.

Cody went into her kitchen, flipped on the meager light, and stood at the sink. She ran water from the tap into a marbling glass. I stood behind her, and then against her. I slid my palms down her arms and my thumbs skimmed circles around the fine knobs of her wrists. Holding the glass, Cody's hands shook as much as mine did under the running faucet. She set her water down and twisted around to face me. Her wet fingers, on my neck, pulled my face down to hers. The kiss she gave me, ungentle, pulled air from my mouth, and her hands dampened my shirt at the shoulders and chest. With a quick lift of her arms, her shirt was gone, and I stood back so that her deep navel and her breasts and sinewy shoulders were finally exposed to me. She had to know how the dim kitchen light brassed her skin, and so, I felt, she must have been presenting herself to me in this way as a reward for my patience, for all the time I'd spent helplessly imagining her precise nudity. I understand now though, all these years later, that her actions weren't about me or my desperate longing at all.

Some of what happened after that eludes me, despite my attempts to retain every second in memory. I wanted to reach out and hold the weight of those breasts long in my hands. I wanted, despite our drunkenness, to say serious things to her that she would comprehend and happily accept. In those next moments, though, I touched her but hardly held her. We fumbled at each other and stripped each other. I tried to draw her into my arms and kiss her, but something fought within our embrace. It seemed like she was shoving me toward her bedroom.

Once there, she kissed me briefly, urged me onto the bed, and began rummaging through her nightstand and then her closet. She seemed frustrated. She was looking for condoms, I realized, and didn't know where they were. She and Micah probably didn't even use them anymore.

She found one on the floor of her closet and came back to the bed. With her eyes squeezed closed, she kissed me, again without tenderness, and slipped the condom into my hand. It was wrapped in paper instead of plastic or foil, and the paper felt worn, soft, the corners bent and dulled. Cody maintained control of the act throughout, and when I attempted to take hold as she moved on top of me, her writhing kept her from my grasp. There was no way it happened like this with him.

The sex ended quickly, too quickly. I started to apologize but was scared I wouldn't be able to control the words. They might spill out into a larger acknowledgment of everything that was wrong. Instead, finally, I held her. We both lay on our sides, my arm around her waist, claiming her, her cool buttocks tucked into my groin. I saw, as if through other eyes, a vision that made me smile, but I still couldn't tell her how I felt. Nothing I considered saying seemed right, so I stayed quiet. After a while I started to drowse against her, but then I felt her shaking. She twisted herself away from me, out of the warm pocket I had made for her with my body. I realized she was crying.

"What's wrong? What did I do?" I regretted the second question immediately.

"I just want you to go," she said, and then folded her underlip into her mouth.

I drifted through those next few minutes in confusion, standing from the bed, leaving the room, bending to pick up my clothes. In the dark I also groped at objects that weren't actually there, reaching for nothing but shadows. Dressed, and standing outside the apartment now, I turned to face her. She wouldn't look at me. Her hair was flattened against her head and she was wearing one of Micah's large, colorful T-shirts.

"Are you sure?" I asked, and extended my hand out to her.

"I have to finish packing for my flight," she said, and my hand dropped.

"Cody, I don't understand—"

"You're no kind of friend," she said, and then she closed the door.

The meditation ended up going well for me. Sinking into it felt like escaping the harsh midday brights of August and entering the darkened cool of the movies. Emerging from it, I found things milder, like a mellowing extension of a movie theater itself. Everything was at a fuzzy distance, and I felt a chest-calm. Smiling, the women unfolded themselves, and some of them gathered around the basket of fruit resting in the grass. A few began to discuss the details of a rally against police brutality happening the next weekend. Micah approached me, eyebrows raised. I thought I understood something about him then. His appeal wasn't about him as much as it was about the happy story he made of the past. He fully believed in that story, and he believed that its glories were still with us. Why wouldn't he? I thought. Why wouldn't any of us want to believe it? It's a generous story in which the universe has a definite shape and its movements throb with personal significance. Everything—even life's routine tragedies, even death—is a sign, and every sign can be understood, and language never seethes against you. Of course Cody still wanted him. She wanted a role in that story, and I did too. What could I offer her, what could I offer to myself, that would ever compare? All I had was a mess of sadness, with no language to clear the way.

Micah grabbed my shoulders and shook me playfully. "Righteous, right?" he said.

"Actually, yeah," I said. "I feel pretty good."

He looked at me in a serious way, and the lines disappeared from his face. "Meditation, man, it carries you to the truth." He exhaled loudly and nodded with conviction. "I gotta come correct. I gotta do better." He smiled again, and for a moment he looked wise. "The party can't go on forever. She's a queen."

I knew before Micah said this that I would never tell him about me and Cody. I knew another true thing—that I would go with him to LaGuardia and the three of us would go get dinner, together again, restored. What I didn't know was that on the way to the airport, in the car, it would be difficult for me to tell which of us was more nervous. I didn't know Micah could get nervous. I didn't know how surprised Cody would be that I was there, how awkward and terrible it would be at the airport, how her gaze would keep shifting from him to me. I didn't know how awful it would feel to receive a half smile from her, or the insubstantial pressure of her lips on my cheek. I didn't know that there would be nothing there, absolutely nothing.

I didn't know, hadn't noticed at all, how comparatively little I'd thought about Cody that day. I hadn't thought about the possibility of us being alone together at the restaurant. I hadn't thought about what would actually happen. Enough time has passed that I now face my own middle years, and I finally understand why I hadn't thought much about Cody: it was hardly about her.

At dinner Micah would excuse himself from the table to take a call outside. Cody would draw her eyes up from the scraps of injera left on our communal plate and look at me cruelly, as if to ask, *Why are you even here?* With a nod, she'd acknowledge the pact of silence we had tacitly made, but it would be a pathetic gesture, meaningless for having to be made at all.

I didn't know it as I stood in the park with Micah grinning at me, but that dinner would be the last meal any of us would ever share with one another. All I truly knew then, in my heart, was how open I felt, how full.

"Hey," Micah said, "what did I say about the honeys?"

I laughed. "Yeah, you were right."

He gave a sideways jerk of his head. "Over there, check it out. Yeah, those two. They look like twins, right, but they're not. I've already been blessed by the one on the right. Ridiculous, blood, both of them. Tiny little waists but then . . ." With one hand he drew an exaggerated curve in the air. "Horn of Africa!" he cried. "It hurts so good."

What he said about them was true. They were stunning, and their bodies were incredible.

"I gotta behave myself," he said. "New life, reincarnation. But I'll go say peace to homegirl so you can see what's up with her sister." He drilled one of his knuckles into my arm. "I can hook it up for you. Come on, king. She's so honey."

He was right, she was. Still, I wasn't interested at all. I agreed to meet her though, just for the hell of it, just for the beauty.

As we walked over to the sisters, Micah asked if I wanted to tag along for one last errand, to go with him to the airport. He said we could pick up A Black Girl Named Cody and go have dinner together at that Ethiopian spot we hadn't been to in a while. I said yes. He said it would be like old times.

Wolf and Rhonda

The reunion happened in the party room of the Tavern on Bruckner, which wasn't actually located on Bruckner. Purple and white balloons floated free to the low ceiling, just above the heads of St. Paul's Class of 1991. The elderly priest sat in a corner, nodding helplessly at his lap, lifting his wan head whenever someone came by to greet him. Old rap songs and declarations of love, music from twenty years ago, when they were in high school, played at a low volume from the wall-mounted speakers. The cake, frosted white and garnished with roses cut from gumdrops, would have stripes of rich pineapple filling between its layers. Wolf knew this. It was always this way at their reunions. Maritza Lopez, the organizer, was again wearing her formal, brightly colored dress. She had planned these gatherings from the start, and treated them like re-enactments of her quinceañera. Wolf admired her consistency, the sheer force of her determination.

The Tavern on Bruckner was in Mott Haven, near St. Paul's School and Church. Years ago, if Wolf and his friends had hung around long enough after dismissal, playing at the arcade or lingering in the magazine shop, they'd often see some of the faculty. These teachers would pass the church, turn the corner, and walk the long block to the bar for afternoon drinks. It had been funny for the boys to think of the teachers being driven to alcohol, funny to imagine them losing themselves, flirting, cursing, and shouting, breaking rules they enforced so strictly during the school day. Wolf found it less funny now.

Like many Catholic schools, St. Paul's was closing. In June it would recognize its final graduates. Other members of the Class of 1991 gave a few token acknowledgments of this fact and wondered aloud if today would be the last time they all gathered together. Although Wolf wasn't close to anyone from St. Paul's, he resented the school's closure but felt convinced the reunions should continue until they were all in their graves.

In the brightly lit room, he stood with a quartet of high school friends who still lived in the Bronx. They had all made something of themselves. Maritza co-owned a beauty salon, Lizzie Barnes was in line to manage a small office, Chucho Hernandez and Duncan Wardell were climbing the ladder at the same local company. At the reunions, they never got tired of discussing how pleased their parents were with them, and they even competed to show whose parents were most proud. Wolf, an advertising man, had done better than any of them, but his father never seemed happy with his achievements.

While they drank now, his childhood friends gabbed about the reports in the news, accusations that priests had molested children. Wolf hated when people treated disturbing matters with mere curiosity, gossiping like old gods high up on their mountain. It was as if achieving modest success meant they had never felt molested by life, as if making contact with the air never gave them the sensation of a cold, ash-white hand touching them.

"Jesus," he said to them, nearly shouting. "And what the fuck is it to you?"

They all stared at him. Their expressions changed from total confusion to wide-eyed alarm. A couple of them glanced over at the priest, Father Grancher.

Wolf vigorously shook his head. "No, no," he said. "Hell no.

Nothing like that." The old man had never done anything to him. He wasn't like that. If only the problem were that simple. Wolf took another tack: "Hey, what about Sterling? I just can't stop thinking about it." Sterling was a professional football player, an outspoken star who had died in a crash last month while racing his car. Controversy had followed him throughout his career.

"It's terrible."

"Awful."

"A tragedy."

The sentiments went on, but Wolf could tell they were just making conversation. He was obsessed with the man, who had become his father's favorite athlete. Wolf felt pangs of identification with Sterling, with his fearless way of talking and his uncontrollable urge for speed and risk. Earlier, at his father's apartment, he had tried to convey this connection. The big man grunted in response and shook his head. "That man could've been the next Ali," he said, and then took a sip of the beer he hadn't offered to share. "You? You don't understand a damn thing about him."

Wolf's old friends continued with all their bullshit, confirming the unstated idea that drove all of his meetings at work: most people in this country were stupid. He distracted himself by staring at Maritza Lopez. Back in high school her silhouette had been the shape taken by the boys' thoughts of sex. Pretty and curvaceous and, it appeared, ripening by the week, she had promised a future of endless pleasure. As recently as the last reunion, when Wolf was drunk enough, he could still envision Maritza as she had once been, pulsating with youth and vitality. But now she looked absurd in the frills of her purple dress. Squeezed into it, the odd lumps of her figure bulged like the scutes of a turtle's shell. Though only thirty-seven, she had the unnerving face of a witch. More alarming to Wolf, and maybe what caused the rest of it, was the spiritual malaise he saw overtaking her. The effect over time resembled the gradual darkening of a lamp. He didn't enjoy seeing her decline every five years, but he respected it. He understood it. It didn't hide the fact of her ordinary human suffering. If Maritza were more honest about life, if she chose to flaunt her soul the same way she did her body all those years ago, she might have been his ally.

"Don't look at me like that, Wolf." She raised her martini glass to cover the flirtatious smile forming on her thickly glossed mouth.

"Old habits. . . . ," he mumbled. But he wasn't sure how he was looking at her, had no idea what his face was doing. He used to know how he looked at women, long ago, maybe back when they were only girls.

What he felt sure of was the fact that he still loved being called Wolf. In Winter Garden, down in Florida, where he lived now, childless and unmarried, he was plain old Wilfred Jones. People there addressed him as Will, a solid name for a solid, prosperous man. He'd been popular as a boy because of his brashness, the unpredictable ways he performed being black and male, but that was before things changed between him and his father. His transformation became more pronounced when he went off to college, and then again when he moved to Florida. As he surrounded himself with increasing numbers of white people, people unlike those he'd grown up with in Mott Haven, his performance was by turns more timid and more exaggerated. He began to emphasize a more blatantly sexual approach to women, a consciously narrowed intelligence, and an inclination to keep any unpopular opinions to himself. He was conspicuous but never threatening, and for this he'd been rewarded. Wolf typically had been less cognizant of his acting than of being rewarded, and as the benefits became more substantial—more sex, more powerful connections, increasingly better jobs followed by the assurance of a fairly lucrative career—his practiced ignorance won out. Soon he was barely aware that he was acting at all. What he perceived instead was an irritation just beneath the skin, one he could claw at but never relieve.

The old nickname helped. It was a large part of the pleasure of flying up to New York and going back to the South Bronx: watching the word form on the lips of people who seemed to really know him. Hearing it. It came from early teasing about the sharpness of his baby teeth and, later, from his wildness as a youth. To his great relief, it caught on and stuck as he progressed through the grades at St. Paul's. His father had given him the nickname, but he no longer used it.

Wolf still had an instinctive response to it, a raw physical reaction, his head perking up and the muscles tightening around his ears in recognition of his truest name. More than this, though, it reminded him of what it felt like to be not accomplished but perfected, filled to completion with energy and pride. Wolf knew that people joked and laughed about those who were said to have peaked too soon in life. He laughed too, though it pained him to do so. The pain articulated what otherwise stayed submerged, his knowledge that most of these people joking and laughing had yet to peak, and most of them never would. All they had were the undiminished measures of their longing. While they looked ahead and hoped for themselves in vain, he had already lived as the best incarnation of himself. He'd had that feeling and he would also have an abundance of time left on the earth to recall it. The reunions corroborated his memories; every five years, they helped him recall the feeling most clearly, in his body, and savor it as an irrefutable fact.

He usually flew into the city early so he could spend time with his father, but no matter what, whether he'd gotten another raise or promotion, the big man was never happy to see him. As a remedy for these inevitable disappointments, he would go stand across the street from St. Paul's at dismissal time. Waiting there, watching, he would find duplicates of Maritza and Chucho and Duncan and other people in their class, but never another Wolf. He felt relieved. He was Wolf, the only one. Wolf was who he truly was.

Maritza, Lizzie, and the guys began to touch on the expansion of the Sahara, their tone making the topic dull and distant, as though nothing were actually wrong. These were his friends, supposedly. They referred to one another this way, and he was as close to them as he was to anyone in Winter Garden, which meant he was hardly close to them at all. While coming to the reunions gave him a taste of conviviality, none of his old classmates were people whose lives he was interested in, people he trusted. Wolf didn't have anyone like that.

He turned his back on them and immersed himself in the din of the party. He two-stepped with the music until the laziness of his movements made him feel old. He appraised the bodies of the women who danced and shook the hands of men as they walked by, greeting them as he would have twenty years ago so they could greet him in kind. But soon he was just standing there, alone in the crowd, swinging his head from the bartender's table to the cake. He pulled a balloon down by its string and batted it with all of his strength. The balloon rebounded about a foot away from him and then floated with perverse slowness back to the ceiling. As he searched for someone else to talk to, he was stunned to see Fat Rhonda struggling her way through the narrow, festooned door.

She wore a white belt over a tight dress that accented her broad curves. Twirling a couple of times as if to show off her outfit, she was like a pale green apple rolling in the sun. She smoothed her hair, done in a bob and streaked with copper, and glanced impassively around.

She had never shown up at any of the reunions before. Wolf could tell from everybody's faces, the way their mouths warped into ovals of hilarity and disbelief, that no one had ever expected her to come today. They didn't hate Fat Rhonda. It was just that their collective withdrawal from her had made a kind of community back in high school. The same was true now. The sixty or so people gathered in the oblong room reorganized their bodies and nudged each other into place, seeking out the old laws of gravity. Wolf felt a kind of shifting within himself too. He stared in her direction, while everyone shuffled away and opened a path for her, trying to anticipate her movements as she swaggered over to the bartender. His initial impression had been right: Fat Rhonda was even fatter now. He thought back to the day he had walked behind her in the church, when they were alone together between the pews.

That day, twenty years ago, had not begun well for Rhonda. She hadn't slept, had been up worrying about her mother, about meeting with the principal, about the massive question of her own life, worrying and tossing in bed. The fabric of her nightshirt felt stiff, prickly on her skin, and with a sick feeling she had watched the sun lighten the sky. She stared outside at 325, which was identical to 315, her own building, where she lived with her mother on the ninth floor. The windows of 325 emerged across the basketball court like hundreds of eyeballs opening at dawn to pry. They were so numerous in the solid wall of brick that Rhonda had the sensation of being menaced by their collective gaze. She pulled the sheet over her head.

"It's so unfair," she said to herself, as though voicing it rather than thinking it would function as a genuine appeal, with the force of prayer. She wasn't Catholic, but for three years she'd been praying in St. Paul's Church. Father Grancher had told her she could pray there. He told her why prayer was important, what it meant when you said *Amen*. She would go to her favorite spot, always the same spot, at the end of the pew beneath the red and white stained glass image of Christ. There she would lower herself onto the kneeler so she rested below the Good Shepherd's heavy-lidded gaze. She whispered the Apostles' Creed and then her favorite, the Act of Faith. At first her prayers had been about her body, that she could be thin and light-skinned. She wanted the other students to stop teasing or ignoring her. She wanted boys like Wilfred Jones to pay attention to her. But last year her mother's speech had begun to change; her words slurred and oozed from her lips. She spent more and more time in the bathroom, at times her vision fogged, and her steps got less steady as she walked. She was like a drunk, someone whose troubles rose as a stink from her flesh. Rhonda started saying prayers about her mother, but initially they were requests to God and His Son that the woman stop being so embarrassing. Maybe these had worked against the later appeals, the ones for her mother's health. Maybe all of her earlier prayers had been judged and she was being punished now for her selfishness.

"It's just not fair," Rhonda said, more loudly now. Her voice, the ferocity and volume of it, startled her, so she crossed herself and muttered the Act of Faith against it: *Oh my God, I firmly believe that you are one God in three divine Persons . . . I believe that your divine Son became man and died for our sins . . . I believe these and all the truths which the holy Catholic Church teaches, because you have revealed them, who can neither deceive nor be deceived. Amen.*

She got up and walked quietly toward the shower, but her mother called from her bed.

Rhonda came into the room but stayed close to the door. Wrapped around her mother's hand was the leather bracelet that had been worn by Rhonda's father. She rubbed it habitually between her fingers, softening its tough braid. He had been a good man, but why would her mother further infect herself with this memento of the dead?

"You gonna have to feed me," her mother said. "You gonna have to clean my teeth. You gonna have to bathe me." It was a continuation of what she had been saying yesterday as they sat with their dinner plates, as if no time had passed at all. Here were more additions to the responsibilities Rhonda would have, now that her dreams—of going away to school and starting a new life, her actual life—were deferred, if not entirely over. The litany continued: "When I fall, you gonna have to pick me up. When I can't talk no more, you gonna have to be my mouth."

Her mother spoke slowly, fighting to get some of the words out. She lay on several pillows, her head elevated almost forty-five degrees, as the doctor had instructed. Though it was only May, not yet summer, a small fan blew air through its dust-rimmed grille into her slackened face.

"Now that I got my trophy," she said, "I need you to help me."

Her mother wasn't ignorant—she knew good and well that the word describing her condition was *atrophy*—but her sense of humor had always been grim.

"Ma, I need to go. I'm gonna be late."

"I'ma need to know I can count on you, Rhonda."

"I already said so, yesterday."

"It wasn't supposed to be like this. I'm sorry," her mother said. "But I need to know those words were meant."

Rhonda retreated a step. "You always saying how you gave me this life," she said, "so you might as well take it back."

Though Fat Rhonda had packed on more weight, her body was firmer, no longer the nebulous mass it had been before. Wolf hadn't seen her since senior year. In those days she wore the uniform St. Paul's required of its girls, including a pleated plaid skirt. Near the end of senior year, after things had started to shift with his father, Wolf started calling her skirt a circus tent because it was so large. He'd joke about spotlights trained on the expanse of her rear end, acrobats tumbling, clowns doing pratfalls, foul-smelling elephants marching in line. There would be snacks in there too, he told his friends, peanuts and popcorn kernels trapped in the dimples of her thighs. Wolf no longer limited himself to talking back to teachers. He began to break more school rules and had started doing everything he could think of with girls. To further his reputation, he began to tell anyone who would listen that he was going to stick his head under Fat Rhonda's tent and have a look around. He ended up doing much more.

"I can't believe it," Maritza said. "I can't believe she's here." There was a blend of disgust and glee in her voice. "And that outfit!"

Wolf narrowed his eyes and tried to see Maritza's soul. No one else knew, but he wanted to believe in the soul.

"What? I mean it. She looks like shit."

"*You* look like shit," Wolf said. "We all look like shit."

Maritza and Lizzie acted offended, but Chucho and Duncan took it in stride. Lizzie's mouth kept trembling, in search of a response.

Wolf wasn't sorry. He felt he could make a presentation about them right now, similar to the ones he gave for clients at work. If he had his laser pointer, the one he used to dissect and dumb down every ad in progress, he would drag its red light from one of his high school friends to another, specifying each of their acquired flaws: the paunch, the stale fried hair, and so on. But unlike what happened at the office, where things came easy for him, where he could simulate mastery, here he wouldn't be able to show them what he really meant. If he had a laser pointer big enough, a light wide enough, he would step toward it with his eyes fully open, until he was lost entirely in the beam.

To cut the tension, Duncan spoke up and changed the subject. "Yo, Wolf," he said. "Remember when you did Fat Rhonda on the stairwell?"

"Get it right, man," Chucho said. "He did her in the damn church. Everybody knows that."

As Duncan held up his drink in reply, Wolf looked over at Fat Rhonda again. She stood on the other side of the room, near the cake. She had a pink cocktail in each hand and swayed to the music as she drank. People either ignored her or took sidelong glances as they talked about her. Back to the old routine.

Chucho had it right, and for Wolf, hearing this truth said out loud was like hearing his preferred name. He felt reignited. Having sex in the church, with Fat Rhonda of all girls, had served as the final augmentation of a fire soon to be extinguished. While her already poor reputation suffered as a result, his rose to its peak. The boy who would do anything had done just that, but Wolf hadn't ever said a word about it. He had planned to tell everyone, but afterward he'd changed his mind. He couldn't communicate what he had actually experienced and he couldn't tolerate lying about it. Fat Rhonda had been the one to spread the story.

"You know what you should do?" Duncan said. He choked on his own laughter. "You know what you should do?"

"Oh, I dare you," Chucho said, grinning. "I double-dog dare you."

Wolf drank deeply from his beer. He understood what they meant. It didn't even need to be said. Without realizing it, they had found the seed of the idea sprouting right there inside of him.

"Why else would she be here?" Dunk said. "It's like fated, man."

The two women smirked and shook their heads in disapproval.

"It can be just like it was," Chucho said. "You can do it the way it happened back then."

After showering and dressing that morning, years ago, Rhonda had prepared breakfast and lunch for her mother, simple tasks compared to what was coming: making sure she had enough salt and fiber in her diet, managing medications and appointments, keeping the rooms cool. Getting up in the middle of the night to check her breathing and the stuttering of her heart. Learning her language as it eroded and struggled to leave her throat. Becoming not only her mouth, but her eyes too. And for what? The doctor said her mother would be dead and gone in four years, five or six at most. Anger and despair clashed inside of Rhonda. She kept telling herself this wasn't the proper reaction, but it didn't matter. She felt it was her own life that was truly over. She'd done everything she was supposed to. She got excellent grades and no longer fought with the kids who teased her as she had in middle school. She'd been admitted to colleges upstate and in Maryland and Georgia. She'd gotten on her knees in church day after day, but the Good Shepherd looked down at her with something like scorn, deaf to her mumbled prayers.

No, she couldn't think this way. She was just being tested. Today she would have to explain to the principal why her family had fallen months behind on tuition payments, why they hadn't paid her grad-uation fees. She would need the firmness of her faith this morning, faith unbroken and, if anything, tempered by her troubles.

On the walk to St. Paul's, she passed, as always, the squat building that contained the management office. The white sign out front read WELCOME TO PATTERSON HOUSES, A WONDERFUL COMMUNITY, and below that, in smaller green letters, NEW YORK CITY HOUSING AUTHORITY. An image of the high-rises appeared among the words, an eerie green silhouette that reminded her of the way things looked through military binoculars in the movies. Rhonda hated this sign, the way it mocked the community with a lie. She felt it mocking her. She especially hated the word *authority*. When kneeling at the church, she tried to believe in what Father Grancher called "the highest authority." She tried to rid her deepest imaginings of the green silhouette that stood behind them, throwing down its shadow.

You are one God in many authorities, come to judge the living and the dead . . . Rhonda thought this but then silenced her mind. She stalled this sinful turning away and told herself it was good to be in God's eyes, and in the eyes of His divine Son become man.

On the corner, Kitty Towns slouched against a pole, having her breakfast of cigarettes. Kitty was in her forties, younger than Rhonda's mother, but she was always bent, looking over the edge of her own precipice. Rhonda had the impression she might, at any moment, disappear. Kitty lived in the apartment next door with her surviving children, four boys and two girls. Rhonda liked the kids. They were friendly and well behaved, loved fiercely by their mother, but for years, when she was drunk or mean with heartache, Kitty could be heard through the walls yelling at them: "You not better than me! You ain't shit and ain't never gonna be shit, you hear me?" Before Rhonda crossed the street, Kitty's eyes twitched up and she waved hello. Rhonda held her breath against the odor of menthol and hoped that Kitty wouldn't ask her for a dollar.

If he had known Kitty, Father Grancher would have given her the same message about the power of prayer. He would have told her that she should get down on her knees, that she was low, yes, but not low enough. As Rhonda passed the shuttered storefront of the botanica and the lean tabby licking itself in the doorway of Benny's bodega, she thought about Father Grancher's lined forehead and feathery eyebrows, his pointy nose and yellow lipless mouth. With his robe and his frosted laurel of hair, he used to remind her of depictions of ancient Greeks, as if he were an old philosopher or some other white man of great wisdom and influence. Now, in her weaker moments, she felt he simply had the face of a liar. He'd said Rhonda's prayers would still matter, even though she hadn't been baptized, even though her family was AME and she attended St. Paul's only to avoid the local public schools. When she'd told him months ago that her mother was behind on the tuition, he smiled and said she could pray about that too. He said the only real cost of being a Christian was giving up the habits and desires that did not align with the will of God. Well then, did God want Rhonda to remain in the ever-deepening shadow she'd been in all her life? Did God want her mother to die?

The facade of the church, its gray brick and stone, looked cold enough to burn her hand. It stood impervious to the springtime rays of the sun. Rhonda felt sick to her stomach again as she passed it. The red high-school building was next door. Students, mostly boys, lingered outside, standing at the foot the stairs that led to the entrance or sitting on the chipped metal handrails. Wilfred Jones and Ignacio Hernandez were reaching for the hem of Liz Barnes's skirt, as if it hadn't been rolled up at the waist enough already. Wilfred, who had become awful lately, blocked Rhonda's path as she attempted to sidle by. His lips pulled into a smile, revealing teeth starkly white against his dark brown face.

"And what do *you* have under there, huh?" he said. Ignacio and Duncan Wardell laughed like this was the funniest thing they had ever heard. "You know I'm okay with a big girl," Wilfred said. "I'm okay with a big nasty girl."

Rhonda sidestepped and walked up the stairs. She still felt his presence though, and when she turned she saw him following her, his head close, level with her upper thighs. He sniffed at her and said, "Smells like pork and beans. I woke up hungry for some pork and beans."

He said other disgusting things, but Rhonda didn't respond. Even now, as she thought about her mother and this meeting she was walking into, she hated that his attention, repulsive as it was, also thrilled her. Wilfred was the best-looking boy in their class, tall, with a wide, sculpted face. He already had muscles that pressed against his uniform. Best of all, he didn't accept any nonsense from the teachers—or at least this used to be true. Recently, he'd been acting out in boring, typical ways. Still, Rhonda felt worked up by him. Though she had this in common with many of the other girls, it didn't unite her with them.

Wilfred stayed close until she got to the doors, and though he didn't follow her inside, the agitation she felt from his words did. As she approached the principal's office, she prayed under her breath. She prayed against the inexplicable feeling that this beautiful, audacious boy aroused in her. But she also kept thinking about her modified prayer, about the possibility that Father Grancher was a liar, about the possibility of God and His son as no different from the housing authority sign, no different from Kitty drunk and yelling at her children.

Wolf told Chucho and Duncan to stop laughing like a pair of idiots. He drank the rest of his beer and handed off the finished pint. When he took a step toward Fat Rhonda, a hand clasped his shoulder.

"Hey, man," Chucho told him. "We were kidding."

"Get off me," Wolf said.

"It was just a joke, right?" Chucho said to Duncan.

"Yeah, just shits and giggles."

Wolf shrugged out of Chucho's grip and straightened his blazer, giving them all, even Maritza and Lizzie, a cold look. They didn't understand. This wasn't a joke at all.

As he approached Fat Rhonda, the shriek of a microphone tore through the room. Everyone looked up, shaking their heads and mumbling complaints as they used to at morning assembly. When Wolf slid closer to Fat Rhonda, he could see that Father Grancher, standing with the assistance of a current teacher, was about to address them. Using his familiar slow, deadpan sentences, Grancher delivered a monologue that described the establishment of the church. Early parishioners had referred to it as the "Cathedral of the Bronx." He detailed the reconstruction of the rectory and tower in the 1890s, and the subsequent building of what was then a primary school. As Grancher droned on about the history of St. Paul's, Wolf glanced at Fat Rhonda, but she ignored him. He inhaled the cloying spice of her perfume, and though the room was chilly from too much air-conditioning, the heat of her body warmed him. Grancher ended his speech by saying, "Never forget the power of prayer." He asked everyone to bow their heads, but faltered then, unable to recall what they should be praying for. This made it all the more obvious that his mind and health were in rapid decline. As people kept their eyes closed or gazed at the floor, Fat Rhonda sipped from one and then the other of her cocktails.

"I'm in from out of town," Wolf said to her. "You remember me." He made sure it wasn't a question. Sterling, he imagined, would have done the same.

"I do?" The bits of citrus pulp floated and slowly swirled in her drinks. She stared at them, rapt, as if each glass contained its own galaxy.

Drunk, he thought. Or ashamed now, after all this time, even though she had been the one to spread the rumor. A girl's shame was a scab Wolf knew how to pick.

"Twenty goddamn years ago," he said, "but sometimes it seems like last week. Not even. More like yesterday."

Fat Rhonda's head snapped up and she met his gaze. Her round face was touched lightly with makeup and, underneath, her pores weren't visible at all. Her skin, as deeply brown as his own, had a dewy appearance. "I don't know what kind of life *you* been living," she said.

Wolf wagged his finger at her in playful accusation. "What are you doing here?" he said. "It's a hell of a surprise."

With a sudden motion she guzzled one of her drinks and placed the empty glass on the cake table. She extended her arm straight out and made a gun with her free hand, aiming it at targets in the room. "Shot by a cop," she said. "Bang!" She jerked her hand and flexed her thumb, an imaginary shot she kept repeating with different targets: "Strangled by a boyfriend. Bang! Stabbed by a cousin. Bang! Blown up at war. Bang! Hypertension. Heart disease. Cancer. Bang! Plane crash. Car crash. Broken neck. Broken heart." Satisfied with her pretend kills, she blew on the tip of her finger and then opened her hand to make the gun vanish, all but saying *Presto*. "You know what's a surprise? That there's so many here," she said. "The Class of nineteen hundred and whatever: luckiest group of little hoodrats in the mystery of the country."

Wolf chuckled. "Realest talk I've heard all day," he said. "Realest talk in a long time."

"Makes you think. Probably they'll bomb this whole place to smithereens like they did—where was that? Philadelphia? Everywhere?"

Wolf pointed up. "A bull's-eye right there on the roof."

"That's right."

"Could happen any damn second now."

"We better get out of here then," she said. "Go somewhere safe." Her face lit up pleasantly for the first time.

Wolf grinned. So she wasn't ashamed. She was still the person who had spilled about being with him. He wanted to know who that person was. "You serious?" he said. "Just like that?"

She tilted her head back and drank the rest of her other cocktail in slow voluptuous swallows. "I'm not serious at all," she said with a laugh. "Nowhere's safe. But we should go there anyway."

So it would be this easy. Wolf enclosed both of his hands over hers, took the empty glass, and set it aside. As they went past his old friends, he acknowledged them by flipping the bird. The room got quieter as the two left.

Wolf chuckled. "They're watching us."

"Us?" Fat Rhonda said. "They're watching *me*. I'm the belle of the ball."

He walked behind her as they made their way through the main room of the bar, watching the jumps and undulations of her ass in the green dress. He'd developed a fascination in recent years for larger women, he realized, but he also recognized that none of them had ever satisfied him.

It was strange, but what Fat Rhonda had said was true. She *was* the belle of the ball, the center of attention. Wolf had another thought: whenever he had watched the St. Paul's dismissal from across the street, in the wake of another disappointment with his father, he had never seen another Fat Rhonda either.

Evening greeted them outside. The air was moist, the sky oddly green. They were near Willis Avenue, where a dentist's drab sign hung unconvincingly on the corner. Down the long block, toward Alexander Avenue, was a series of dusty businesses, all different from the ones that had been there before: a pharmacy, a Mexican restaurant, a 99-cent store, a pizza shop, a grocery with a half-lit logo. A couple of children scooted by with restless expressions on their faces. Wolf wondered where they were going. Behind the bus stop, where the arcade used to be, was a store that sold mobile phones. It was closed and appeared to have been that way for a long time.

"So where to?" Fat Rhonda said.

Wolf played along. "Not your place, I guess."

"I go from place to place," she said. "Dodging those bombs."

He smirked and rubbed his jaw.

"I can find us a place. Won't be much to look at though."

"Forget that. Tell you what, I got an idea."

"Honey, too many of those will wear you out."

"Not too many," he said. "Just one. And it's not a bad one. It's good."

"Sometimes," she said, "I'll have myself a weak moment and pretend I still know the difference."

"My idea's good."

She looked him up and down, admiring the quality of his suit. "Let me guess. You already have a place, and a key. To a room in a nice Manhattan hotel."

"I'm not talking about that," he said. "When's the last time you went to church?"

"Oh." She picked at her dress, suddenly occupied by the act of grooming herself. In the street a car sped past with its windows down, playing bachata.

"Well, what do you think?" With his chin he pointed toward Alexander Avenue, where St. Paul's Church loomed on the corner.

She blinked slowly at the building before she spoke. "You think *that's* a safe place?"

Wolf took a deep breath. He was getting annoyed by this back-and-forth. "Cut the shit," he said. "What, you just playing games with me?"

After a long moment, Fat Rhonda started toward the church, walking without saying a word. Wolf eagerly followed, but he had a sense she might go anywhere.

The school day hadn't ended yet, but Rhonda wasn't in class. She had decided to skip history. The green marble pillars of the church appeared garish and unfamiliar, and the many panels and flourishes of gold leaped out at her. Above the main entrance, in the gallery, the organ pipes flanking the illumined windows looked intensely gold as well. Even the uniform rows of wooden pews glowed a fiery red.

Rhonda had never noticed how tacky the place was. It was as if gauze had been peeled from every surface of the interior and now, when no one was supposed to be there, she was seeing it as it truly was.

Other than the occasional noise, something like a clumsy footfall or a hard object being dropped, the place was silent. She was standing at the front, where Father Grancher stood as he placed communion wafers in people's hands or on their tongues. Not being Catholic, Rhonda had to shift her thick legs to the side to let other students pass from the pew to the central aisle to receive the Eucharist during school Mass. They often stared or huffed at her, complaining that they still didn't have enough room to go by. School Mass had always been frustrating and mysterious to her. Urged or sometimes forced to be present, she was simultaneously held outside the circle of its mysteries. She liked when Father Grancher swung the censer from its chains and spread the fragrant smoke out over the pews. She could smell faint traces of the incense now, slightly sweetening the air, but knew she was inhaling something she didn't understand at all. The idea of the sacraments had also appealed to her, but she wasn't permitted to pursue them.

The meeting with the principal hadn't gone well. Without payment of tuition and fees, Rhonda wouldn't be able to graduate. All morning during classes she had been apportioning the blame for what was happening. Her mother's dormant faith, which couldn't be called "faith" at all. Her insistence that Rhonda, effectively, live without faith too. Father Grancher's lies, which made her believe her prayers were anything more than useless kneeling and begging. The school itself: the principal telling her its charity had already reduced the amount of money her family had to pay, telling her nothing more could be done. Now even the dignity of graduating would be deferred, if not denied. Rhonda wouldn't even get the pleasure of the ceremony. She blamed them all, and she blamed herself for accepting the nobody role they had cast her in: a non-Catholic in a Catholic school, praying in a Catholic church to a Catholic God about people and matters of absolutely no interest to Him.

Another noise, the fourth or fifth one since she'd been there, startled her. When she looked to her left, Wilfred was standing in the same doorway she'd come through. A passageway through the rectory connected the school and the church. Wilfred walked right up to her, grinning. He glanced back at the tabernacle and then up at the painting of the Last Supper. He rubbed a section of the altar cloth between his fingers and then placed his large hand on top of the communion table, patted it a few times.

"We should do it right here," he said.

Wilfred would also sit idly in the pews during Mass while others got up to accept the Eucharist. He wasn't Catholic either. For some reason this similarity had mattered to Rhonda. It had been a factor in making her listen rather than walk away when he'd come up to her in the library and said more disgusting things, whispering in her ear what he wanted to do to her in the back stairwell or the boys' bathroom on the third floor. It had influenced her when she'd called him Wolf, which she'd never done before, and told him to meet her here instead.

"No, I know where," she told him now.

Strong light poured in through all the stained glass windows, as if the sun were a fiery ring surrounding them. They made their way down the central aisle.

"Don't worry about anyone coming in," Wilfred said. His friend Juan, an altar boy, had assured him.

"I'm not worried," Rhonda said. She turned and maneuvered her body along the pew that led to the window of the Good Shepherd. Like the other features of the church, it was brightly lit in a grotesque way.

"Here?" Wilfred chuckled. He was standing behind her, close.

She turned for a moment and saw him looking up at the stained glass. In her mind, she repeated the line from her invented prayer: *You are one God in many authorities, come to judge the living and the dead . . .*

"You want me to kiss you or something?" he said.

The folds in the Shepherd's red and white robe were dense black lines, and his left arm, holding the staff, emerged out of pure darkness. In his other arm, the lamb was small and starkly white, with the elongated face of a pouting child.

"I know you don't want to do that," she said.

As Wilfred's hands undid the buttons of her shirt and hastily pulled her breasts from the cups of her bra, she was captivated by the background, which she hadn't taken notice of before. *I believed these and all the lies . . .* The landscape and sky were both rendered in wavelike sections. It was hard to tell where the land ended and the sky began, and the variety of colors—orchid, brass, royal blue, rose, crimson, and aquamarine—made Rhonda think of a terrible, unpredictable storm.

Wilfred's hands grabbed and slid across the folds of her stomach while she studied the disk of light around the Shepherd's head. He touched her back and she leaned toward the window, resting her elbows on the tops of the pews. She saw that tiny pearls described the entire curve of the Shepherd's nimbus. His skin was white, almost as white as the lamb's wool, but it was the eyes she was most interested in. As Wilfred's hands fumbled under her skirt, Rhonda thought of her mother and Father Grancher. *Your authority deceives and must be deceived . . .* She leaned even closer and tried to find the Shepherd's eyes underneath his lids, hoping to feel something real and blatant and sharp, much more than she'd managed to feel or convey with her old prayers, something the Shepherd's downcast eyes couldn't ignore.

Before Wolf reached for the wrought iron handles he knew the doors would be locked. He'd had a glimmer of hope because the gate was open, but as he'd suspected, the church was inaccessible.

He shook the doors by their handles to no effect and then looked up at the gray bell tower. The sky still appeared green, an illusion probably: there was no trace of rain in the air. He cursed under his breath. Of course it would be like this. Of course, when his mind had already committed itself entirely to repeating the act they had engaged in.

"Are you cold, baby?" Fat Rhonda said in a lazy voice.

A slight breeze had picked up, rearranging the garbage on the street, but it wasn't chilly. He sagged to the ground and sat there with his legs straight out in front of him, his shoulders heavy against the doors of the church. He wanted to fall backward into the lake of old feelings and be immersed in them. But whatever he genuinely wanted seemed barred from him, as emphatically closed off as his father's disappointed face.

"I'm fine," he said, and after a moment he patted the ground next to him, inviting her to sit too. She lowered herself and adjusted her clothes. Wolf put his hand on her right knee. He began to slide it up to her thigh, and then underneath the skirt of her dress, but Fat Rhonda wouldn't let him. She flung his hand away so it landed in his lap.

Wolf looked at his hands, tightened them into fists, and released them. He'd always had powerful hands, which he had used to break and tear things, to take what he wanted and go where he wanted, to make other people feel small. He had intended to humiliate Fat Rhonda in the church all those years ago, to reduce her to just a tiny thing, a bit of dirty wax he could roll between his thumb and forefinger and then flick away.

But Wolf had enjoyed being with her. It had been much more than sexual pleasure, much more than the risk of getting caught. Yes, he'd liked the sensation of gripping her in the light of the stained glass, but had been surprised by how much joy he took in the impression that there was always more of her—actively extending, thickening, deepening—more than he could ever possibly reach. He couldn't have explained what he was doing, making such meaning of her body. He was too absorbed in the experience. It made him feel as though there were more of him too.

In ways that Wolf wasn't fully aware of, this feeling reminded him of slapboxing with his father, when things were still good between them. The last time they'd played in this way was earlier his senior year, after he had gotten in trouble at school again. He had cursed at Ms. Pritchett during a history lesson about slavery and told her she was teaching lies. A single parent, his father had gone to school and sat beside him in a meeting with Ms. Pritchett and the principal. As usual, he didn't apologize for Wolf's behavior, but he said what was necessary to make sure there would be no expulsion. Later that afternoon at home in their living room, he and his father laughed, as they often did after such meetings. "You keep giving them hell, boy," the big man said. "Keep on giving these white people hell. The devil is a liar." His father gave white people hell too, which was why he had trouble keeping jobs and often had conflicts with police. "You ain't nobody's brainwashed monkey," his father said. "You're my Wolf." He'd had his arm over the boy's shoulders and then, growling, pulled him into an embrace. They held each other for a moment. When his arms were around his father, Wolf liked that his fingers barely touched.

They started to slapbox then, Wolf's favorite thing in the world. After a few minutes of roughhousing on the couch, they began to grapple and eventually rolled onto the rug. The big man was stronger, but Wolf was quick and he drew energy from the odor of his father's skin and sweat and warm, sour breath. Their limbs rubbed and slid as they fought for leverage and escaped each other's attempts at a decisive grasp. Their grappling was going on longer than it ever had, and Wolf began to think it was possible that he would finally win. He made an unorthodox movement with his knee, stunning the big man, and then plunged his hand in an attempt to grab an unguarded wrist. He touched his father in a place he shouldn't have, an accident. The big body flinched, and for a moment their eyes met before his father wedged his forearm between them and flung him off with more force than he had ever felt. Wolf landed hard on his tailbone but he stopped himself from crying out or shedding tears. Standing, his father watched his face for a while. "What's wrong, Daddy?" Wolf asked. "What's wrong?" His father didn't reply to this. He took his time straightening his clothes and then said, "You go on and get cleaned up. I'm gonna get this dinner on the stove."

This was when Wolf started getting into much more trouble, and not just for talking back to teachers who were unfair or taught lies. He broke so many school rules, he almost didn't graduate. His father had to come in for meetings more frequently, but they no longer laughed together at home about them afterward. When Wolf tried to slap-box or grapple with his father again, the big man told him he wasn't a kid anymore. Smiling warmly, he said, "You're too old to play those games."

"We were meant to be here," Wolf said to Fat Rhonda now. "It has to be here."

"What does?"

He hadn't told anyone what they did the first time, but if they did it again, tonight, he would tell everyone. Maybe even his father. "I can feel it," he said. "You and me, we're connected. We're supposed to get inside."

She didn't say anything. She turned her head to watch a man ride slowly past on his bicycle, a phantom slipping idly by.

He and his father could get drunk on beer together and laugh about it. "We can try to get in through the school."

She shook her head.

"We can break one of the damn windows," he told her. And he could tell his father about that too.

"It's just not interesting," she said.

"There's gotta be another way to get back in. Don't you remember a way?"

"Lots of things," she said, "I try not to remember."

The man beside her slumped farther down against the door of the church. Rhonda listened to him, but not really. She had changed her mind. He seemed too sad. Nothing would happen between them tonight.

"I didn't even say anything," he said. "Not a word. I was going to, but I didn't tell a soul."

She listened with half an ear, even less, as he talked about a day years past that had meant something to him. She had long ago decided it wasn't worth it to pay much attention. The world was too awful. What you loved—family, friends, notions of yourself—you would lose. And what caused you pain would hurt all the more if you gave it any space in your mind. Her mother had lived much longer than the doctors said she would, years longer, but each day that went past the sentence they had given was only a further withholding of mercy. Whenever Rhonda thought of her mother, she scolded herself. Her goal, though she knew better than to chase it with too much passion, was to forget as much as she could.

"But you did," the man beside her said. "You told."

She looked up at the sky. It was terrifying to hear about things she might have done. Terrifying, though she felt resigned to being coldly observed, to think she was still, always, under judgment. When her mother finally died, ten years ago yesterday, Rhonda began to wander, like people did in the ancient stories she'd once committed to memory. She went south through several cities—Philadelphia, Baltimore, Washington, Richmond, Charlotte, Atlanta—and then west, taking jobs and men as she could find them, in the same thoughtfully uncommitted way. She had the idea that she roamed where nothing could see her—an illusion probably, but one that made her feel free.

"You told," the man repeated. She wondered how and why he'd gotten stuck on such an insignificant thing.

Something had made her come back to this place, where she'd been born and raised and had suffered, something more than just the simple fact that it was the anniversary of her mother's death. Whatever it was felt out of her control, as though some bird-instinct, the pull of mineral bits in her skull, had guided her here and told her this was the time to return. The mystery of this caused some familiar stirrings of conviction in her now, which she usually knew better than to pursue. Authority was beyond mystery, she believed, so there was no reason to dwell on either one. There was no reason to hold on to anything: to hope, to love, to faith. But why had she come back? She couldn't help wondering about it now. It may have been this: you never knew if something had lost its power over you if all you did was keep running away.

It had been a fine test to go back to Patterson Houses, to go back into building 315, ride the elevator up, and stand outside the door of her old home. A test, yes, to go to her old school, to see the notices about the reunion and not feel a thing. It had also been a test to go into that barroom with its gaudy decorations. She hadn't expected to see so many people there—still alive, not yet subdued—people who still cared about their yesterdays. But she felt relieved to find that none of their faces held a scrap of significance for her. Not one. The priest's deathly face, his inarticulate call for prayer—these didn't mean anything to her at all.

"You wanted it that way," the man beside her said.

This was the last year of the school's existence. Maybe I'll come back here again, Rhonda told herself. Maybe I'll come back on the morning they open these church doors for the school's final graduates.

"You wanted everybody to know," the man said. An odd suggestion of cheer had risen in his voice, but it didn't match the expression on his face. He looked up at the sky again and remarked on it, as if he had never seen it this way before.

In some ways, men like him were familiar to her. Many of them existed, well-dressed, successful men who were nonetheless unhappy and often alone. She thought he would be just another one of these men, someone she could spend a pleasurable night with and never think about again. But this man, he had the heaviness of desperation. She couldn't help but notice the particular burden he carried. She glanced at the man and thought, Maybe what tonight means is I shouldn't come back at all.

"Tell me why. Answer me, please." He was still looking up. "Don't treat me like some nobody. I'm here. Why did you tell them?"

His voice had changed. Now, as he alone furthered the conversation, he sounded angry, disgusted. A tone she recognized in the voices of men vibrated from his throat. Along with the tone, his body was growing tense.

"What we did was between us," the man said. He looked down and smashed a fist into the palm of his other hand, a lonesome gesture. "It was *our* thing. Why the hell did you tell *them*?"

When Rhonda didn't reply, he cursed at her and said she was a bitch. She wondered why she didn't feel threatened. She waited, examining the texture of the ensuing silence. What he'd said, she decided, was only juvenile name-calling, a helpless tantrum.

The man sitting next to her had been a boy she once knew. If she tried she could remember that boy, but she didn't, she wouldn't. She refused to. When it became clear that she wouldn't answer him or respond to his insult, he looked at the sky again and resumed his talking, repeating himself endlessly, repeating his frustrated pleas. She stared across the street, at the line of parked cars, and then raised her face to the breeze. The air tasted like rain, far away but approaching. She raised her head higher, and higher still, until its angle was the same as his. He kept going on about his memories, laying them out like an arrangement of stones. His words piled on themselves in a strange rhythm. They formed walls that he could take shelter in. So be it, she thought. So be it. She opened herself, just for a while, to the man who had been a boy she refused to remember, listening as he went on and on about some distant day, a weightless speck of time. Then, thinking of where to go next, she reached through a gap that had yet to be closed off by the past. For a few moments, she interlocked her fingers with his.

Clifton's Place

The sign outside the bar had appeared only recently. It announced the bar's name and hours of operation, clear indications that this was not just another townhouse basement. Still, despite the listed business hours, no one got in before the sun went down, even in summer, even if you stood right outside the locked gate, peered in, and waved. The ones who stood waving by the sign—twilit, ignored—were the newest of the new, the people whose need for signs and schedules and business cards and happy hours was most acute.

Only when night fell did the gate to this other world open. An old man in his eighties, Julius, checked IDs from his chair by the door. Julius saw himself as he had been decades earlier, a tough and wiry young man, still every bit a bouncer. Once they got past him, the newest of the new sat where everyone unaccustomed to the place sat, at the tables lining the paneled wall across from the bar. Rarely did newcomers of any kind come alone; mostly they arrived in pairs or in larger groups. They commented on the Christmas lights strung wildly across the low ceiling and nodded to the music playing faintly from the old, hulking jukebox. These people amused themselves by pointing at the outdated appliances massed in the corner near the kitchen: an enormous microwave oven, a rusted hot plate, a few coils detached from an electric stove, a clock whose remaining hand twitched at the number 9, things many of them couldn't even name. Until they learned better, they sat as if they would be waited on, as if they would be handed menus. At Clifton's Place there were no menus.

Neighborhood people who had been coming there for years—regulars, or "the folks," as they called themselves—knew that no one named Clifton had ever been formally associated with the bar. They knew that the owner, Sadie, had fallen for a man named Clifton back when she still turned heads on the streets of Bedford-Stuyvesant. Their love affair didn't last. They fought for weeks until Sadie, known for her reckless tongue, told him she never wanted to see him again. So he left her and then, they said, he left the city too. But Sadie came to realize she had made a mistake, and the name she gave the bar when she opened it was her way of letting Clifton know he could come back to her. The folks knew that Sadie's friends chided her and said he would never return, that she would feel like a fool owning Clifton's Place after her feelings for him had gone cold. Her friends had predicted the humiliation of the days when she would have to fill out the forms to change the name. "Good thing for you there's no sign to replace," Julius had said. Forty years later, however, there was a sign and the bar was still called Clifton's. Sadie appeared there any night she felt up to it, wearing heels and one of her many colorful dresses. But she didn't feel up to it as much as she used to.

Ellis was one of the folks. One summer evening, at his usual place near the door, on the stool where the bar counter curved and met the wall, Ellis tapped his fingertip against the sharp point of his pencil and held the eraser in his mouth, the ferrule giving easily between his teeth. As he often did in those days, he wondered about Sadie. It seemed true, as folks said more and more often, that her mind was no longer right.

Her nephew Sharod, who had become the bartender, heaved himself into motion and settled his bulk on the slabs of his forearms, directly in front of Ellis, covering his stack of drawing paper. "You stay sucking on that thing like it's your favorite titty," Sharod said.

The pencil had been taken fresh from the box before Ellis left his tiny apartment, turned in the sharpener until the graphite peeked out just the way he liked. The eraser, out of his mouth now and as yet unused, gleamed in the bar's irregular lights, the solid pink nub slick with his spit.

"Don't look all confused," Sharod said. "A man likes what he likes on a woman. Even though what's best about those things is that she got two of 'em." He held out his hands, cupped to suggest breasts. Ellis noticed how often men used their hands to suggest the bodies of women. "Just last week," Sharod continued, "I got yelled at 'cause *my* crazy ass don't know how to spread the love. Then *her* crazy ass up and decide she got jealous parts and kicked me to the curb. How you gonna be jealous of your own self?"

Ellis wasn't sure if he was supposed to answer this question.

"And how's a man gonna play favorites with what a woman got?"

"I don't know," Ellis said, but he could imagine it. He heard what men said to women out on the streets. He sometimes felt he should say something to the women too, something nice to correct what the men said, but he never did.

"Well, I'll tell you," Sharod said. "All of a woman is too much woman to love."

Ellis blinked at him. "There's gotta be hope for us, right?"

"Ah, you useless piece of shit," Sharod said, standing upright now. He stared hard at Ellis for a moment before allowing a big smile. But the smile wasn't comforting at all. Sharod's mood, particularly bad tonight, sat like a weight on his face, deforming the curve of his lips.

When Sadie came into the bar, she brought the smell of burned hair with her. Julius ignored it and said, "May I see your ID, young lady?" As usual she laughed at their joke and said, "Thank you, young man." When Sharod asked about the burned smell, she said she'd just had a little accident with the curling iron, but it looked much worse than that. Ellis saw that a section of it was gone nearly to the scalp.

Sadie went behind the bar. As she began to make her usual, a Golden Cadillac, the tall bottle of Galliano slipped out of her hand and shattered. Sharod raised his voice at her. He had grown impatient with her mistakes and confusions. As he yelled, Ellis's hand began idly drawing the shape of smoke. Without moving or speaking, Sadie stared straight ahead with eyes as wet and broken as the glass at her feet. Ellis set down his pencil and hurried to her. He brought her around to sit next to him on a stool.

Sadie gazed at Ellis's drawing. "Well, isn't that pretty," she said. "Is that for me?"

Ellis hid the drawing underneath the rest of his pages, afraid she'd come to think the drawing was an insult to her. When their eyes met, she smiled and then said, in a low voice, almost flirtatiously, "Well, baby, it's late. Maybe we should get on home now." He stood, ready to help her on her way, but then Julius butted in. He gripped Ellis's shoulder and used surprising strength to sit him back down.

"Let a real man take care of this," he said. "Things have changed around here, but there's still trouble to be found out in these streets."

He left with Sadie, and Sharod cleaned the mess behind the bar. Ellis stayed quiet in his seat. He could still smell Sadie's scorched hair, as strong as it had been when she was there.

He wasn't much of a talker. He preferred to pass his time at the bar sipping blended Irish whiskey and sketching whichever people or objects caught his eye. Like most of the other solitary regulars, Ellis dressed elegantly. Tonight his yellow necktie made a pleasing streak of heat against the faded blue field of his shirt. In those days he often wore a flashy tie, and he'd recently become aware of his tendency to run the full length of it through his hand, as if to remind himself, or others, of his vitality. One of the youngest of those who frequented Clifton's— he'd turned forty last December—he was among the few who stayed cleanly shaven and didn't wear a hat. There was a time when he'd worn a fedora, mostly because his receding hairline and premature patches of gray, contradicting the boyish appearance of his face, used to embarrass him. Now he understood that none of the clothing worn by regulars at Clifton's was meant to hide anything. They tended to be honest about themselves and the things that ailed them, and he tried to be honest too.

Among the other folks there was an attractive old woman, Yolanda, said by some to be Julius's lover. The unintelligible looks that passed between the two of them convinced Ellis the rumor had to be true. Old Mr. Edmonds used to sit across the bar, but he no longer came by. He said that things just weren't the same at Clifton's anymore. Ellis had acquired the habit of flashy neckties from him, and wore them now in his honor. When the man's attention wasn't fixed on the silent television mounted above the array of liquor bottles, Ellis used to have an impression of being scrutinized by him. Of course it had been ridiculous to believe that Mr. Edmonds, or anyone else, would give him that much attention. Impossible, Ellis told himself now, just a flaring up of his old self-consciousness, or a touch of ego as he sought a tiny measure of comfort with the dullness of his life. He missed Mr. Edmonds.

Dyson, another regular, was a skinny, arthritic man who enjoyed drinks flavored with licorice. The bar stocked Fernet just for him, because it was said to soothe the stomach, the place in the body where many neighborhood people believed insanity resided. Dyson had nonsensical, somewhat violent outbursts, a peculiarity that had started around the time Clifton's stopped being a bar only for the folks. Some nights, he ranted and tore his voice, but whenever the tables were empty, when the bar looked and felt the way it used to, he didn't utter a word. He began cursing under his breath now, however, a kind of low spastic muttering. Though it was a slow Monday night, two newcomers, a white couple, had stepped into Clifton's. They tried to make small talk with Julius, who had returned to the door. As usual with newcomers, he was rude as he checked their IDs.

Ellis watched as the couple ordered food and beer at the bar and then huddled together on one side of a table. When the food was ready, the woman ate her fried fish with her hands, breaking off small pieces with her long fingers and dipping them into the blot of ketchup on her plate. She encouraged the man to do the same, flirting with him, Ellis thought, and after some resistance, even a little annoyance, he began to eat with his hands too. They appeared to be enjoying the music, in a familiar way. They didn't yell, as some newcomers did, for the volume on the jukebox to be turned up. They didn't dance foolishly. The two enjoyed the music and mood of Clifton's Place just as they were, and the woman even mouthed the words to a blues. A rectangle of space several feet long separated the tables from the bar, but to Ellis it seemed as though he could extend his arm, place his whiskey glass on the red plastic cover of their table, and join his voice to the woman's in singing "Mean Old World."

He began to sketch the couple, on the same page he'd used to draw Sadie's smoke. The pencil moved easily and felt good in his hand. It wasn't long before the drawing took on the couple's likeness. The woman's fingers holding a piece of fish and her sad singing undefeated mouth. The man's admiring gaze. Though it was just a sketch, something felt alive in it, an affinity between the subject and the lines on the page that Ellis rarely saw in his work. He stood and approached the couple's table, grasping the sketch in both hands. They looked up at him, eyes puzzled and amused as he stood there, not saying a word.

Ellis smiled and gave them the sketch. "A little something for the lovebirds," he said.

The man's eyes changed before the woman's mouth did. His face tightened as he held the sketch. He glared at the woman and crushed the page into a tight ball. Rising, he pointed at Ellis and then shoved his shoulder. "You're a fucking perv," he said. "Sick son of a bitch." The man shoved him again, threw the crumpled paper so that it bounced off his chest. He seized the woman's hand and pulled her out of her seat. As he dragged her out, past Julius, and out the door, the woman looked back at Ellis, all the features of her face reduced to tiny points. Julius stood as if ready for a brawl, but by the time he got all the way up they had already gone.

For her, Ellis decided, the trouble of the night was just beginning. It had been clear as day that the man was no good.

But then Sharod picked up the crumpled page and flattened it out on the bar. As Ellis looked at it, the page revealed what he had actually drawn—the shading of her open mouth, how it seemed to suck lewdly on the fish in her fingers. The figure of the woman took up most of the page. Ellis hadn't taken the time to render the edges and folds of the dress against her skin, so she appeared to be naked. The man, rendered in fainter lines, was hardly there at all.

Sharod barked out a laugh. "A man likes what he likes on a woman," he said, and Julius joined in with some light teasing. Sharod ripped away the part with the ghostly man, made two dots on the woman's chest with Ellis's pencil. Still laughing, he walked around to the other side of the bar and taped up what was left of the wrinkled page there, displaying it like a cheap pinup.

"Take it down," Ellis begged, but Sharod refused.

"It's about time you drew something worth a damn," he said. "I think I'll just keep it there."

When Ellis's further attempts failed he grabbed his supplies and left as fast as he could, twice humiliated. He told himself he'd never return.

He thought it would be easy to stay away. With his regular hours at the art store and the discount he got there, he figured it would be no problem at all. He'd have more money to spend on supplies and more time to work on his drawings, but it was difficult for Ellis. He kept thinking, though he tried not to, of how destroyed he'd been when his parents, a beautiful couple, died within months of each other a few years ago, leaving him alone to wonder at his own weakness, to wonder how it was possible that other people routinely endured such losses. He looked at drawings he'd made of each of them in their sickbeds. The loneliness of his apartment choked him. He ached every time he was unable to introduce himself to a nice-looking woman at the store or on the bus. In a little over a week he was back at Clifton's, in his usual seat. He expected the smell of Sadie's burned hair to be there, but it was gone. His torn, wrinkled drawing still hung behind the bar.

That night a woman approached from a loud group of newcomers at the tables. Ellis watched as she leaned over one of the empty bar-stools. He could see she was very young, still a girl in some ways. She was short, likely paler in the winter months, and had an eager grin that climbed all over the features of her broad face. She had the pleasing density of an athlete, maybe a runner or a gymnast, and to Ellis she looked pretty in her form-fitting jeans. Sharod looked down at her and twisted his mouth into a hard little smile that said, *State your business.* She ordered three Mexican lagers.

"Nine dollars," Sharod said.

"Seriously?"

"Nine dollars."

Not satisfied with the good prices, and ignoring the sound of Sharod slamming the bottles down, the white girl tried to make small talk. "Hey, are you Clifton?" she asked.

Sharod, used to this question by now, gave her a once-over and wiped his always-watering eyes with a knuckle. "Naw," he said. "What's your name? Molly? Katie? Or they still call you Miss Anne?"

"Shit, I'm sorry," the girl said. "Didn't mean anything by it." She seemed sincere. Her smile was reined in now, measured, without a hint of the condescension Ellis had seen in other new patrons. She introduced herself as Allegra, but Sharod didn't respond.

Allegra left fifteen dollars on the bar and grabbed the three sweating bottles of beer by their long necks. She returned to her friends at the tables, sitting with her back at an angle to Ellis. The faces of the other white girls, just as youthful and free of blemish, glowed red and green and yellow in the blinking Christmas lights. Their voices could be heard over the low strains of "Yesterday," as sung live by Donny Hathaway back in 1971. Allegra marveled again at how cheap the drinks were, and another said, "Told you so." When they lifted the beer bottles, rings of moisture shimmered on the red plastic table cover. Ellis watched Allegra and her friends and the shadows their bodies made.

"Well, well," Sharod said. "Back on the scene, huh? Glad to see it. Can't have these ofays running us out of our own goddamn establishments."

"I guess not," Ellis said with a glance over at the taped-up drawing.

"*I guess not. I guess not,*" Sharod teased. "Backbone, motherfucker. I told you we can't have none of that soft-ass, bearing-gifts-for-massa, wannabe native informant bullshit. I see you eyeballing that white girl, but don't get it twisted. The gentry don't give a fuck about you."

Ellis made a few stray pencil marks on a page and listened to Julius cough behind him. Most of what Sharod had said was unnecessary, even cruel in its simplicity, but men were often rough in their affections.

Ellis peeked over at Allegra again. He'd never paid much attention to white girls before, but yes, she was pretty. One of her rounded hips jutted off the edge of the chair she sat in. She looked corn-fed to him, maybe raised in the Midwest, maybe even the South. He may have heard some accent in her voice earlier, but he wasn't sure.

The bar began to fill with more newcomers. At first just groups of two or three showed up, but then a raucous group of about fifteen people arrived all at once, filling the entire space. At the other end of the bar, Dyson's muttering became more audible. As he raised his voice, some of the people in the crowd laughed and gave him funny looks. One man, tall with a baseball cap backward on his head, nodded at Dyson as if they were having a conversation. He had an expression of mock seriousness on his face.

Other than the unavoidable interactions with Julius and Sharod, most of the newcomers remained oblivious to the folks, even to Dyson's intermittent shouts. Sharod was at his surly best, especially as he picked up the dollars left as tips. His kindness wouldn't be bought. He denied their requests for food, even for the baskets of potato chips and pretzels he usually set out, and he delighted in telling them the jukebox would never be any louder than it was. Many of the newcomers danced anyway, yelling out words even to songs they didn't know.

Dyson fell silent, though he kept moving his lips, and the man in the baseball cap lifted his beer in comic salute. Ellis saw why Dyson had stopped his rant. Amid the confusion of shouting and singing, and the spasms of dance and drink, Julius cleared out space near the open door with wide swings of his arm. His other arm was raised above his head, where he held a familiar, still-graceful hand. Sadie was back.

"And where is your ID, young lady?" Julius joked.

"Get out of my face," she said in a brassy voice. She snatched her hand away and looked around, somewhat disconcerted by the crowd. "We need some toys for all these babies."

"Miss Sadie," Julius said after a fit of coughing, "who brought you over?"

"Brought *myself* over, young man. Me."

Elegantly curved brown lines crossed her jade green dress, which extended just past her knees. Her arms moved freely in the loose, longish sleeves, silver bracelets sliding along her wrists. A varicolored necklace of wooden beads rested around the wrinkles of her neck, and her hair was stylishly cut, shorter, Ellis saw, than it had been last time. He couldn't discern the section that had been burned away. She grinned as she turned her head jerkily around, and bounced her purse against her hip. But something was wrong: Sadie limped as she walked, as though one of her legs had gone lame.

Ellis jumped from his seat. "Miss Sadie, do you wanna sit here?"

"Plenty of places to sit," she said, barely registering his presence. "But I ain't come here to sit. Anyway, I got all these babies to feed." She called for Sharod and began to make her way through the crowd toward the kitchen area, tottering like a damaged windup toy. On the back of her dress, just above the hem, a large black spot seemed to grow, as if an invisible hand pressed it with the tip of a leaking pen. Of course the spot couldn't be growing, Ellis told himself, but he knew as well as the other folks that something tragic had touched Miss Sadie, that the first prick of a spreading contagion had been made a good while ago.

The smell of hot cooking oil began to fill the air of Clifton's Place as Sadie prepared the food that Sharod had denied the crowd. In the atmosphere of her cooking, Dyson even stopped moving his lips. Sharod looked chastened as he leaned on his elbows and glared at the stiffly moving bodies between the bar and the tables. Four white men converged on Allegra and her friends, standing over their table. Whether the girls wanted them to or not—and Allegra seemed openly annoyed—the men lingered for a long time. Ellis wondered if Allegra was accustomed to handling herself here in the city. One of the men made his way to the bar to order several shots of vodka. Ellis, tucked in his corner, glanced up from time to time. He sketched abstractedly, the page a chaos of thick lines and dark calligraphic forms.

Someone bumped him, a white man standing behind him in the crowd, causing Ellis's hand to make a dark errant line across his page. The man turned with an indignant expression on his face. "Sorry," Ellis said. He started to erase the mark, but then studied the page and the other sketches he'd made tonight. They'd gotten worse, more formless, and somehow more forlorn.

The men at Allegra's table seemed to have made some progress.

They all tossed back more shots and joined the large cluster of dancers. It was difficult to maintain sight of Allegra in the crowd, but Ellis could tell from glimpses of her face that she wasn't enjoying herself, moving her body in a perfunctory way.

Before long, Sadie was dancing through the crowd with her fried delights, chicken wings and fillets of whiting. She invited the newcomers to pick them right from the tray, flicking her tongue across her lips all the while. She swayed as she went along, her head plunging to the left with every other step.

"Look at her go!" someone shouted.

"She's gonna break a hip."

"Tell her to bring that fish over this way."

"Look at her shoes," someone else said.

Ellis could see now that she was wearing mismatched heels. Behind the bar, Sharod turned to him and said, "This is fucking bullshit."

"The poor woman just isn't well."

"She's making a fool of herself. And us."

"Her shoes. It's awful," Ellis said and then immediately regretted it, feeling as though he'd betrayed Sadie in some small way. "I should take her home."

Sharod looked up from his clenched fists. "All she'll do is come back. She just keeps bringing her ass back. It would kill her not to. This here's the only damn thing she's got."

It can't be true, Ellis thought. He felt it just couldn't be that the thread sustaining a person's life could be that fine, that terribly frayed. But then he thought about the way his own life had been the past ten days. He looked at his drawing taped up behind the bar. Even humiliation couldn't keep him away for long.

"Hey, leave that alone!" Sharod yelled. But it was too late—the music began to blast out of the jukebox and the white man who had been tinkering with it raised his arms and nodded vigorously at his friends. The newcomers began jumping up and down and they told

Sadie to jump too. Ellis couldn't tell what she was doing. She was lost in the motion of the crowd. Dyson yelled, louder than he ever had, so his voice wasn't drowned out by the music. Near the kitchen a length of Christmas lighting, yanked loose by someone's swinging arms, dangled from the ceiling.

Sharod made his way from behind the bar and pushed toward her. Ellis stood and excused himself as he maneuvered around a few dancers. He passed Julius, whose head was in his hands, opened the door, and walked out. He intended to keep going, maybe all the way home, but outside, in the vast warm night, he found Allegra, her trembling hand holding a lit cigarette.

She looked at him. "You smoke?"

He told her no, feeling like he was answering more than one question.

"You obviously drink." She nudged her head toward the closed door behind them. "Bar," she added uselessly. "God, I don't even know why I come to these places. I'm so tired of them."

"But you're too young to talk that way," Ellis said.

"What do you know?" she said. "A girl gets tired in no time at all."

"Well," Ellis said, "your friends looked like they were having fun."

"You think?" The sarcasm made her seem very young, though up close she looked more like a woman than he'd first thought. Her odd complexion gave her the impression of being weathered, like a rock beaten smooth by hard rain. He could hear now that her accent wasn't Southern.

"Where are they—your friends?"

She took a deep pull on her cigarette and her next words came in little clouds. "Couldn't tell you. Gone. On their backs probably, legs open to the world."

"Well," Ellis said, "people should be allowed to enjoy their lives, right? Especially when they're young."

"I'm not judging," she said. Then she studied him for a moment, and he noticed the unsteadiness of her gaze. He felt himself reaching for the soft fabric of his tie. "I don't think you're old enough for the wise guru bit, mister."

The way she said "mister" canceled some of what he'd detected in the rest of her words. "Are you gonna go back in?" he asked. He'd had no intention of going back tonight, but realized this woman-child could change his mind.

"I'm going home, before I turn into a pumpkin."

"It's way past midnight," Ellis said, and then suggested a car service. He imagined hailing the cab for her, holding open the door as she got in.

"I don't live far. I'll just mosey on up the block." She dropped her cigarette and stepped on it.

"Well, like you said, it's late. This neighborhood used to be a little dangerous."

"And so it isn't anymore."

Ellis glanced back at the door. It seemed to vibrate from the music and motion inside, a portal to an entirely different place.

"Are you gonna go back in or walk me home?"

"You're okay with that?"

"The neighborhood's not dangerous," she said. "Are you?"

Ellis walked not quite beside her, but just behind. Her head barely reached the height of his chest and her thin sweater showed the shape and power of her shoulders. Her wavy brown hair, blown back at him by the breeze, had a slightly sour smell. He liked what it suggested, that she was casual, that she was okay with being just a little unclean.

"It's pretty interesting working at the art store," he was saying. "You realize how many people live these artistic lives in secret. You get to hear what they're working on, and sometimes you get to see."

Allegra looked back at him for a moment and gave a little hum.

"I get a discount there, which is nice. I dabble in drawing—well, more than dabble actually. I've been drawing since I was a kid. My parents put me in classes. Once, I got to show my work with other local artists, at a Laundromat. It was nice. Lots of people came, even a few who weren't there to wash their clothes."

"Hurry," she said, and jogged across the street against the light to avoid an approaching car. Ellis ended up stuck on the corner, and just watched her hips and legs as she went. After the car sped by, he caught up with her.

"Can't run, old man?" she said with a laugh.

Ellis couldn't think of a clever response so he just laughed too. He tried to pick up the thread of their conversation, the exhibit in the Laundromat, but he didn't know how to do that either.

They stopped at a corner grocery store because she wanted to grab some milk. Ellis had been in there before but the interior was different, cleaner, more brightly lit, with expensive organic products on the shelves. "Just a couple more blocks," Allegra said as they left, but then she fell silent again. Ellis forced himself to talk, telling her about the bar, how it was sort of a second home to him, telling her things about it that only the folks knew, about Dyson's strange outbursts, about Julius and Yolanda, about Sadie's Clifton lost in time. "Oh wow," she kept saying, changing the tone of the words to suit the subject. Finally, to hear her speak again, to pin down her voice, he asked about her.

"Well, I'm from a little town in Illinois, and my parents named me Allegra." It suggested her parents had certain expectations, she told him, expectations Ellis sensed she'd never met. "My name towers over me," she said, sounding like a perceptive child. The comment made Ellis think about how far he'd have to bend to kiss her, how awkwardly she'd have to reach up to put her hand on his cheek. No matter how awkward, however, he wouldn't make the same mistakes he'd made before, not being bold enough, being too timid to cross boundaries he'd been given license to cross. And it must be, he thought, that she was telling him to cross. She didn't seem very drunk. Maybe his words about enjoying life had struck her, or maybe she wanted to match her friends, or outdo them, by spending her night with him, an older man, a black man. Why else would she invite him to walk with her?

"I'll be twenty-five next year. Twenty-five and what do I have to show for it? Almost every dime I make goes to bills and rent. I'm broke enough to prove I live in New York, and I've kissed enough city boys to know what that's all about. God," she said, "what am I doing here?"

Ellis walked beside her now. From what she said and how she said it, and the way she avoided looking at him, he expected her to cry. Instead she pounded a fist into the palm of her left hand.

"Fuck," she said. "I'm sorry. I didn't mean to dump all that on you. I don't even know you."

They walked in silence for a while alongside a large building that Ellis knew as Kingsbury Hospital. Recently it had been turned into an apartment complex. He had heard the folks in Clifton's gossip about the renovation and complain about the high cost of rent, but this was his first time seeing it since the change. His mother had been born in Kingsbury. He saw, as they passed several entrances to the complex, that it was now called New City Gardens. They approached the end of the block and Allegra stopped at the last entrance, in front of two barred, heavy-looking glass doors. She turned to face him and smiled. "Well, thanks for walking me, mister," she said.

Ellis felt himself sweating, as if they had walked for miles. "You live *here*?" he asked.

"Welcome to my palace," she said sarcastically.

"This used to be a hospital."

"I know. It's so gross. Don't remind me."

Ellis wiped his forehead. He cut through the noise of his racing mind by telling himself he couldn't wait. He knew what waiting, especially in the presence of a woman, could do to him. He tilted his face to hers, let his mouth go slack.

She made a noise of disgust and turned her face, her cheek now curtained by her hair. "Hey, sorry," she said, "but it's not that kind of party, okay?"

"I thought—"

"I don't know *what* you were thinking," Allegra said. She took a step back from him. "God, I don't know what *I* was thinking."

He took a step forward and said, "I'm sorry, but I—"

"Are you going to make this difficult?" She glared and reached into her purse.

Ellis understood the threat and moved away from her. "Of course not," he said. "I'm not dangerous, remember?" He smiled weakly, ruefully.

She didn't respond. Her key turned in the lock and she shouldered her way in, her eyes on him the whole time. Before darting up the short staircase, she pressed a palm to the glass, quickening the door as it closed and clicked shut.

Ellis walked through the warm streets, wondering how the possibility had been lost, if he had said something about himself, about his life, that gave him away. Maybe she felt his job at the art store was pathetic. Maybe saying the bar was a second home made her think he was a drunk. Why had he gone on like that? He knew a woman didn't owe him anything, but there had been a possibility there, he was sure of it. Even if only for a night, one night of being open to the world.

Then he felt anger rising in him. It was unbelievable that people lived in the old hospital, that she lived there. It would have made me sick to go up there and make love to Allegra, he kept telling himself. It would have been wrong. An insult to his mother's name.

Several minutes passed before Ellis realized he was going back in the direction of the bar. He stopped a few blocks away, on Bedford Avenue, concerned for a moment about his pencils and sketches, but the work was poor, the pencils easily replaced. And the last thing he wanted was to hear what Sharod would have to say, to see that picture still taped up among the bottles. He thought about the terrible loudness of the place, that awful crowd, and changed direction, heading south toward his apartment.

"Can you help me?" The voice of a woman behind him, another woman in need. No need to worry, he thought, the neighborhood's safe. Just go home. You'll probably find a doctor there. He kept walking.

"Can you help me, please?"

Ellis wondered if this woman had her pepper spray ready too, in case the gentle-looking black man in the new and improved neighborhood ended up being dangerous after all. He could see it: One hand open, pleading for assistance or love, the other with its fingers wrapped around the canister.

"Please, young man. Can you help me, baby? Somehow I've lost my way."

It was "baby" that he heard first, and then it was "young man." He turned and found Sadie there, close enough to kiss. The old woman was tall, much taller than Allegra, nearly Ellis's height in heels.

"Miss Sadie? Is everything okay?"

"Wouldn't be asking you for help if *everything* was okay, baby. This ain't no April Fools."

"Does anyone know you're out here?"

"Yes," she said. "You."

"Where are you going?"

"My, but you do have some silly questions. I'm going home! What you think I am, a lady of the night?"

Ellis apologized. "Don't worry, I'll take you home."

"There you go. Wouldn't be no good to me if you didn't."

"You have your house keys, Miss Sadie?"

"No, baby, I figured you could slide me down the chimney like Santa Claus."

Arm in arm they walked toward Lafayette Avenue. All the folks knew where she lived. Because of her shoes, the heels of different heights, she shambled along, her body chopping the air to the left of her. She was fragrant with perfume and cooking oil, her hand and forearm dotted with cornmeal and flour.

"Miss Sadie," Ellis said, "where's your purse?"

"Oh, that? A nice white man a few blocks back said he'd hold it for me. I told you I didn't have no keys."

Ellis stopped walking, and she did too. Who knew how long she'd been wandering around alone? What man had she encountered? He should have taken her home from Clifton's. "Are you sure you're okay?" he asked.

"Right as rain now," she said, and he couldn't help but believe her. Her smile was so serene, her tilted head held effortlessly, poised as if on a pillow. Aside from the brier of her hair, she looked fine, otherwise untouched by whatever had happened to her.

"We're almost there, Miss Sadie," Ellis said, offering his arm again. "Let's go."

"Hang on, baby. Isn't it beautiful out? Just look at it."

She observed the sky, her gaze drifting across it, as if she weren't in the city and could see the galaxy, thumb-smeared along the dark glass of night. She was gowned in the glow of streetlights and, looking down at his shoes and creased pants, Ellis found himself oddly glossed as well. The nearest light hummed electric above them, a hard bright disk from which illumination was drawn to the two of them like tiny moths spiraling, helpless and particulate.

The feeling of Sadie's hands on his startled him, but he didn't resist her touch as she undid the buttons of one shirt cuff and then the other. Carefully, she folded up both sleeves.

"Gotta let yourself breathe," she said. "There, isn't that better?"

She linked arms with him again, and against his wrist her skin was warm, her bracelets cool.

To Ellis's relief and dismay, both the doors to her building and her apartment opened with a simple turn of the knob. "Miss Sadie," he said at her threshold, "you've gotta remember to lock your door."

"If I had done that, we wouldn't be able to get in," she said slowly, as if explaining to a fool. "Now don't just stand there. Come on in. I'll fix you some chamomile tea."

Ellis stepped inside and chuckled a little.

"Tell me the joke," Sadie said. "I wanna laugh too." She flopped onto her sofa. "You gonna have to give me a minute with that tea." She removed her shoes and held the pair in her hands. One was a black pump with a heel two inches higher than the other, a pink sandal. "Well, would you look at that," she said. "Is this what you were laughing at, baby?"

"No, of course not, Miss Sadie."

"My feet are killing me," she said. "Might have to soak 'em." She stretched her feet and rubbed their soles. Spider veins lined her calves and ankles, and her long toes were bunched together. "Well, what was it then?" she said. "The joke."

"Just men and women is all."

"Oh, that *does* seem like a joke, don't it?"

For a few moments, Ellis heard himself saying some of the things that might have crushed his possibilities with women over the years, the boasts about the art store, the illusions, the premature declarations of love. Or, more often, saying nothing at all. He saw himself as he'd been, as they had seen him, with the receding hairline and longing eyes, the fedora that didn't suit him, the neckties that were maybe a touch too garish.

"I'm not sure what else it could be, Miss Sadie."

"Not sure what else what could be?"

After spending that first night talking to her until dawn, Ellis began a regular habit of seeing Sadie at her apartment. At first it was two or three times a week, but then, with nowhere else he felt comfortable going except maybe the art store and his own home, he started seeing her every day. She often cooked for him, insisting on doing so, dazzling him with the many dishes she could make beyond the fried chicken and fish he knew from the bar. If she felt up to it, she would get dressed up to go there a little before midnight. Ellis made sure her shoes matched, that no spots of ink grew on her dresses. He walked her as close to Clifton's as he could bear and then went home. He did what he could to make sure folks looked after her.

More and more often, however, she didn't feel up to it. On those nights, when her mind was too confused, Ellis sat with her. He listened to her complain about Sharod and the other family and friends who helped keep an eye on her during the day. He listened to her talk about people she may not even have known.

"It's so sad about Julius," he said to her one evening.

"Who?"

"Your friend, Miss Sadie. Julius. He passed away. He'd dead."

"Some friend—why didn't he tell me?"

It had been several months since the night Ellis escorted her home. In the last twelve years, since he'd first started going there, he'd never spent so much time away from Clifton's. He didn't miss it as much now as he had during that week away. Mr. Edmonds may have been right—it just wasn't the same anymore. It may never have been what Ellis had wanted it to be.

"You should think about a facility," he said to her one day. "Where they'll look after you. A place for long-term care. I'd visit you. All the time."

After a few moments she said, "That's where you go when you don't want to be found, baby."

"That's where you go when you need help."

"Then *you* go," she said.

Things started to get so cluttered in Sadie's mind that she stopped leaving her apartment entirely. It seemed as if the mess there was so vast she could do little more than sit and stare at it. She refused to go to appointments with her doctor, and appeared not to care, or even notice, when she was told news about the bar. Some folks called it neglect, just letting her waste away like that. Others felt that the way she spent her final years was up to her. Any elder deserved to make that choice for herself, they said, even if she lost all good sense.

By this time, Ellis's hours at work had been reduced. A big chain had purchased the art store, and soon he would have to look for a second job. He spent one free Wednesday in his apartment, making a detailed drawing of Sadie. He used a pastel pad instead of regular copy paper and worked from memory, re-creating her image from the night he had helped her get home. With some details he hesitated, but he ultimately decided to render her exactly as she was. He took the drawing from the pad and put it in a nine-by-twelve-inch frame, giving it luster with a paper towel and a few sprays of furniture polish. When he was done, he got dressed, wrapped the drawing in tissue, and took an evening bus over to Sadie's apartment.

On the bus he recognized a woman who must have lived in or near his neighborhood. He'd seen her on this route before, and more than once he had longed to talk to her. She was about his age, maybe a bit younger, her long neck wrapped in a thin scarf. She looked pretty in her late-autumn clothes, her long skirt and boots, but Ellis had no desire to talk to her. He smiled to himself, thinking how strange it was to be out in the world and not feel it: his old everyday ache.

Sadie was in pajamas when he arrived, her hair frazzled and in need of a cut. A dress lay beside her on the sofa, even prettier than the one she'd worn all those months ago, prettier than the one in his drawing. It was cobalt blue with shorter sleeves, and the modest neckline had black and white lines shooting from it, the way the sun's rays are depicted by a child.

She looked up from her hands writhing in her lap and smiled. "You're here," she said.

"Hello, Miss Sadie."

"Oh, we going for the formalities now? All right, Mr. Man. I guess you *have* been away a long time. I should be furious with you. I know what I said—it was wrong—but how could you stay away?"

Ellis tried not to frown, but she was more confused than ever. "I haven't been away long at all. I was here just yesterday."

She smiled again. "Just a blink of an eye when it comes down to it."

"I have something for you." He held the framed drawing out to her. In the past few weeks certain objects—a photograph, an old book of stories, a skein of yarn—had helped to tidy her mind. He hoped he'd gotten the drawing right this time, that he'd seen her as she would want to be seen.

Her eyes went from suspicious to approving to something he couldn't quite discern. "Another gift?" she said. "Ain't you slick. You're always getting me gifts." Moving her fingers precisely, she peeled away the tape and slid the frame from the yellow tissue. "Such a pretty wrapping. Almost matches your tie."

She studied the drawing, tilting her head from side to side to assess it. "I love it," she said finally. "It's wonderful."

She stood and hugged him, then stepped back and gazed at him, shaking her head.

"What?" Ellis said.

"I'm just glad to see you, silly man." Her voice was low and flirtatious, as it had been the day she burned her hair.

Ellis was afraid of how she looked at him, her eyes dancing over his features in the girlish way he'd seen women look at other men. Something was happening that he didn't deserve, something he'd never had in his life. But he found himself unwilling to stop it from happening. Along with his fear came an awareness that both of them needed this to happen, whatever it was. Speaking the hard truth right now would break the spell and them along with it. I won't allow it to go too far, he thought, and so settled for a softer, more modest truth: "I'm glad to see you too. It's so good to see you."

"Better be more than good if you tryna get lucky tonight."

Ellis was hushed by this. He couldn't find a single word.

"Well, I have a gift for you too," Sadie said. "But it isn't here."

"Where is it?"

"We need to go to it. Just *wait* until you see it, just *wait*. Don't worry. It's not very far."

"When can we go?" Ellis said, despite himself. He knew he was getting carried away.

"It's a little early but we can go now, if you want." Her fingers were right there at his neck, adjusting the knot of his tie. She went to the window and opened the curtains. "There goes the sun," she said. "Going, going, soon gone."

Ellis peered out at the darkening sky.

"Do you want to go now?"

Yes, he thought, and for a moment all his fear was gone. Let's go.

"I can't wait to introduce you. Some people won't remember. And some won't . . ."

Her face slipped into confusion, almost anger. Ellis could see her looking at things newly spilled in her mind. "Some won't know anything at all," he said.

Her face softened. "That's right. They won't know a thing."

"Should we go?" he said.

"As soon as I get myself pretty." A sly smile formed on her trembling mouth. "Help me with my dress?"

"Oh. No, I'll just wait here while you get ready."

"You some kind of gentleman all of a sudden? Ain't nothing here you haven't seen before."

She unbuttoned her pajama top. Her stomach was smoother and flatter than he'd expected it to be, just a small paunch. Her bare breasts hung low and seemed to reach for her hips. Watching her body as she undressed reminded Ellis of seeing pictures of nude young women as a boy. The same excitement and panic overwhelmed him in the face of something he wasn't ready for but was certain would come. She eased into her clothes and gave him her back. As he helped her, his fingers grazed the skin along her spine. Zipping up her dress felt like the most intimate thing he'd ever done.

"Thanks, baby. Now for my shoes."

She sat and Ellis held each of her feet as he helped her with the shoes. The skin was hard on the soles but surprisingly soft on top. Her toenails had been painted the same shade of blue as her dress.

"Which reminds me," she said. "Sorry to say it to you, Clifton, but the ones in the picture are all wrong."

Ellis was relieved she had said the name. He'd already been envisioning the man, constructing his personality. Now that it had been said, he felt like he could breathe. "I'm the one who should be sorry," he said, the way he imagined it would be said. "For staying away."

"Am I still your fox?" she said.

"Of course you are. My beautiful fox."

Ellis knew the risks of what he was doing. He was aware of being stared at as he walked with Sadie, hand in hand like lovers, fingers interlocked. He was aware, as Sadie looked up at him—unshy and wondering, her stride steady and elegant—of the lie as it unfurled, and he knew what was likely to happen when they got to the bar. The thing he refused to break in Sadie's apartment would be broken anyway. But there would be people there who didn't know he wasn't Clifton, so there was a chance. There's a chance, he thought, that the folks would allow her this gift. Maybe they would think of it as a gift for him too. Just for tonight.

The sound of the jukebox could be heard from the far corner of the block, so loud that the music was muffled, impossible to identify.

"Listen," Sadie said. "Isn't it beautiful? We used to love this song. This was our groove."

"I remember. Can't be an accident that it's playing right now."

As they stood outside the bar, Sadie pointed at the sign and shook with laughter. "You see? It's for you. I knew you'd come back. Oh, I'm embarrassed. Do you think I'm a fool?"

"No, baby, of course not," Ellis said. Then he shut his eyes and held them closed for a while. None of us deserves to be loved, he thought, and so all of us should be. He opened his eyes, and said, "Let's go inside. I want to get me a Golden Cadillac."

"You're still drinking those too?"

"Not one thing about me has changed."

"Come on then," she said. "I want everyone to see you."

"I want everyone to see me with you."

He felt the door vibrate as he opened it for her. The song, heard more clearly now, happened to be one he enjoyed, but the loudness of it hurt his ears. Of course Julius wasn't there to greet them or playfully check IDs—no one was—and, as Ellis knew, Sharod no longer tended the bar. Mr. Edmonds was long gone, and Julius's lover, Yolanda, had vanished into grief. For a Wednesday the bar was pretty filled, but almost entirely with newcomers. So much more had changed in so little time. Ellis observed Sadie and what she seemed to recognize: the tiny kitchen in the back, the pile of junk in the corner, the Christmas lights wild on the ceiling. Dyson was there, shouting as usual. Sadie seemed to recognize something about him as well. He was the sole neighborhood person there, and only later, long after being introduced as Clifton, would Ellis regret how happy this made him. All of us should be loved, he thought again. No matter what, even if it's just for one night. He slid his arm around Sadie's waist, as Clifton would have, and she wrapped him in her arms. Together they watched Dyson, though it was unclear whether he had seen them. His voice got louder, and his mouth became a tense, widening oval. They watched him as if they could hear his words and understand them. As if he weren't yelling at all, but singing along to their music.

ACKNOWLEDGMENTS

For generous support during the writing of this book, thank you to the Iowa Writers' Workshop, the University of Iowa's Provost Postgraduate Visiting Writers program, the Wisconsin Institute for Creative Writing, and the Bread Loaf, *Tin House*, and Napa Valley conferences. I'd also like to thank Kimbilio Fiction, the *Callaloo* Creative Writing Workshop, the *Kenyon Review* Writers Workshop, the Key West Literary Seminar, and the Juniper Summer Writing Institute. Thank you to all the good people I met at these places.

Heartfelt thanks to my agent, Jin Auh, a real pro. She took me into the fold based on scanty evidence, gave me a nudge whenever I needed one, and guided me with brilliance as this book became a reality. Thank you, as well, to Jessica Friedman and Alexandra Christie.

I am so grateful to Fiona McCrae and Steve Woodward, my editors. They read my work, over and over again, with incredible care and acuity. Thank you to Katie Dublinski, Marisa Atkinson, Caroline Nitz, Casey O'Neil, Yana Makuwa, Karen Gu, and all the wonderful folks at Graywolf Press.

Thank you to the editors who took a chance on my work, especially Brigid Hughes. I can't say enough about how important Brigid and *A Public Space* have been for me and my writing.

I've been blessed with many amazing writing teachers, whose kindness, intelligence, good humor, and high standards continue to inspire me. Anyone who disparages the instruction of writing must not know that people like this exist: Mat Johnson, Nelly Rosario, Myung Joh Wesner, Nick Dybek, Lee K. Abbott, Margot Livesey, Jim Shepard, Helena María Viramontes, David Haynes, ZZ Packer, Ethan Canin, T. Geronimo Johnson, Kevin Brockmeier, Charles Baxter, and Marilynne Robinson.

Three teachers in particular, all geniuses, deserve special mention. Lan Samantha Chang literally changed my life, through her encouragement, her institutional leadership, and her example in the classroom. Yiyun Li demonstrates unwavering faith in my stories, never hesitates to let me know when the sentences just aren't good enough, always reminds me of the best questions a writer can ask, and lets me know when I need "more chill." Finally, no one has done more to make me a better reader and writer than Charles D'Ambrosio. His rigor, depth of insight, generosity, and friendship have been tremendous gifts for which I will always be grateful.

My thanks to Connie Brothers, Deb West, Jan Zenisek, and Kelly Smith, for all that they do at Iowa.

Thank you to more friends, readers, classmates, and fellow writers than can possibly be named, but particularly to these folks for any combination of conversation, comments, kindness, guidance, and good company: D. Wystan Owen, Garth Greenwell, Jennie Lin, Jake Andrews, Alex Madison, Sarah Frye, Noel Carver, Ellen Kamoe, Willa

Richards, Novuyo Rosa Tshuma, Nyuol Tong, Catherine Polityllo, Marcus Burke, Carmen Maria Machado, Chaney Kwak, Andrew Dainoff, Sam Ross, Margaret Ross, Kathryn Savage, Jessamine Chan, Phillip B. Williams, Solmaz Sharif, Jamey Hatley, Steven Kleinman, Keith Leonard, Alice Kim, Noah Stetzer, LaToya Watkins, Maud Streep, Kenyatta Rogers, Matt Kelsey, Derrick Austin, Natalie Eilbert, Sarah Fuchs, Marcela Fuentes, Jordan Jacks, Barrett Swanson, Roger Reeves, Brian Gilmore, William Fisher, Vernon Wilson, Marzia Severi Wilson, Nick Bentley, Kaori Miller, Shawn Sadjatumwadee, Tene Howard, Cindylisa Muñiz, Gabriel Louis, Lance Cleland, Julia Fierro, Megan Cummins, Tanya Diallo Welsh, Shivani Manghnani, Karin Davidson, Zahir Janmohamed, K.C. Sinclair, Ploi Pirapokin, Rachelle Newbold, Bryant Terry, Alexia Arthurs, Ayana Mathis, Danielle Evans, Amaud Johnson, Tayari Jones, Victor LaValle, and Kima Jones. Special thanks to Lakiesha Carr for convincing me to bring a story back from the dead.

Thank you to all my New York City people. Thank you to the legendary João Oliveira dos Santos, *meu mestre*, and to all my capoeira angola people, especially the 36 crew. Thank you to my friends, colleagues, and students at the Double Discovery Center, the Trinity School, the Sackett Street Writers' Workshop, and the Iowa Young Writers' Studio.

Warmest gratitude to Jean Ho, for everything.

Deepest thanks to my family.

ABOUT THE AUTHOR

Jamel Brinkley's writing has appeared in *The Best American Short Stories 2018*, *A Public Space*, *Tin House* and elsewhere. He was a finalist for the National Book Award and won the 2018 Ernest J. Gaines Award. A graduate of the Iowa Writers' Workshop, he is currently a Wallace Stegner Fellow in Fiction at Stanford University and lives in California. *A Lucky Man* is his first book.